THE NEPTUNE PROJECT

THE

NEPTUNE

PROJECT

POLLY HOLYOKE

SCHOLASTIC INC.

ISBN 978-0-545-69580-0

Copyright © 2013 by Polly Holyoke. All rights reserved. Published by Scholastic Inc., 557 Broadway, New York, NY 10012, by arrangement with Hyperion Books for Children, an imprint of Disney Book Group, LLC. SCHOLASTIC and associated logos are trademarks and/or registered trademarks of Scholastic Inc.

12 11 10 9 8 7 6 5 4 3 2 1   14 15 16 17 18 19/0

Printed in the U.S.A.   40

First Scholastic printing, January 2014

FOR MY DAUGHTERS, SARAH AND JESSIE,
WHO HAVE PATIENTLY LISTENED TO DOZENS
OF STORY PLOTS AND HELPED ME TO DEVELOP
A PLETHORA OF CHARACTERS OVER THE YEARS.
YOUR SUPPORT AND ENTHUSIASM FOR MY
WRITING HAVE MEANT SO MUCH TO ME.

THE

NEPTUNE

PROJECT

chapter one

I WAKE TO AN urgent tap at my window. My heart thudding, I sit bolt upright in bed. The night is hot and still. I push my sweaty hair away from my face and try to ignore the twist of fear in my gut. No one brings good news at this late hour. I slip from my bed and peer cautiously through my window.

Cam is standing outside, his dark eyes shadowed. "The Marine Guard just sank Jac's boat. We need the dolphins to look for survivors. Are you in?"

"Gillian will kill me if she finds out." My mother hates smugglers, but some of them are Cam's friends.

"Please? They might still be alive."

"Fine." I sigh. "Just a minute." I step into my boat shoes but don't bother to change out of my faded black shorts and my brother's old brown shirt. Dark clothes are good for tonight's work. I wiggle through the small window headfirst. When I get stuck, Cam pulls me the rest of the way.

"Thanks, Nere. I owe you one," Cam says as he steadies me on my feet. His hands are rough from hauling lines and nets on his father's fishing boat. The silver light from a slim crescent moon highlights his black curly hair and the strong planes of his face.

I want to tell him he doesn't owe me anything, but already he's turning away and jogging down the steep winding path that leads to the dolphin dock and fishing pier in the harbor below. I can feel the day's relentless heat radiating from the dirt and gravel beneath my feet.

"Let's take Gillian's zode," I tell Cam breathlessly as I hurry to catch up with him. He looks back at me like I'm crazy.

"There's no wind tonight," I explain. "It'll take forever to get there in your sailboat."

"Gillian will kill us if she finds out." Cam flashes me a grin.

"Well," I say, panting, "it's nice to know I'll have company when my mother murders me."

At the next turn in the path, my chest starts to tighten and burn. *Please, not now.* This is the worst possible moment for my useless lungs to fail me.

"I'm sorry. I need to go slower," I have to admit after three more steps.

Cam stops and looks at me searchingly. "Are you all right?"

"Yes." I grit my teeth. "I just have to walk this last stretch."

"I'll run ahead and get the zode ready."

"I need to call Mariah. Where did Jac's boat go down?"

"Just off Reynard Point." Then Cam's away, racing down the final switchback with a healthy speed that makes me jealous. I breathe slowly and carefully, trying to relax the muscles in my chest. I have an inhaler in my pocket that I can use if I have a full-scale lung attack, but I only have three doses of the precious lung med left.

I reach out with my mind to contact the dolphins. I hope they aren't too far away.

:Mariah, a boat just sank. The crew may need our help.:

Mariah's mind stirs at my touch. :we heard the explosions up the coast from us.:

:Their boat went down near the point where the bat rays like to feed.:

:we will meet you on the way there,: she promises me.

Walking as fast as my burning lungs will allow, I finally reach the dolphin dock. My heart pounds even faster as I study the harbor. I see no sign of movement on the fishing boats tied up at the pier. The stone cottages on the hillside above us are dark and still. The hardworking fisher folk of Goleta obey our government's curfew. Only smugglers—and desperate friends of smugglers—are reckless enough to defy it.

Stepping down into my mother's zode, I see Cam has already disconnected its electric motor from the solar panels on the dock. The batteries should give us plenty of juice to reach Reynard Point and get back safely—assuming we don't run into an armed Marine Guard vessel somewhere along the way.

Cam switches on the silent motor. Just as we pull away from the dock, a small shape hurtles through the air to land in the middle of the boat. The zode rocks from the weight of our new passenger.

Cam's little brother, Robry, grins at me, his teeth a flash of white in the moonlight. "Hi, Nere."

"Hi yourself," I say.

Cam points the boat back toward the dock. "Nuh-uh. This is not happening, squid-face. There's no way you're coming with us."

"I can handle the boat while you two look for survivors with the dolphins. You know you can use an extra hand, especially if someone's hurt."

Robry's right, and Cam knows it.

"All right," he agrees after a long moment. "But if we see any sign of the Marine Guard, you're going to jump overboard, head for shore, and hide until this is over."

"I promise," Robry says with uncustomary meekness, but he grins at me again as he crawls forward. He perches himself on the bow pontoon, his big feet just skimming the surface of the water. I settle myself on the middle pontoon, facing backward so I can talk to Cam.

I relax a little as we leave the harbor and surge ahead across the smooth sea. The only sound I hear is the slap of small waves against the side of the zode. I love being on the water. The burning in my lungs eases as I breathe in the damp sea air. Despite the light from the crescent moon, the stars shine like bits of precious ice in the clear black sky.

"Tell me exactly what happened to Jac," I say to Cam.

"He and his crew were coming in to unload their cargo at the sea cave just beyond the point," Cam replies, even as he keeps an eye out for other vessels. "The Marine Guard was waiting for them and blew their boat right out of the water. Jac barely had time to tell me their location before his radio went dead."

I can hear how worried he is about his friend. They haven't been as close since Jac fell in with smugglers, but Cam is one of the most loyal people I know.

"He's probably fine. Jac has more lives than a cat, and he knows this coast as well as anyone," I say, trying to comfort him.

"I think he's already used up most of those lives," Cam says shortly. "The Marine Guard almost caught him last month. I tried to tell Jac he would be headed for a prison camp if they arrested him, but he wouldn't listen."

I hear the gust of a dolphin breathing through its blowhole. The next moment, Sokya leaps out of the air beside the zode, the water cascading off her back in a shimmering silver arc. She lands a little ahead of us on her side, sending up a big splash that douses both Robry and me. The night is so hot, I relish the feel of the cool seawater on my skin.

"She's such a show-off." Robry grins and wipes the water out of his eyes.

Sokya circles around to swim beside us. :a shark came and we scared it away,: she informs me smugly. :I chased an octopus from the rocks, and it tasted delicious.:

Sokya is Mariah's youngest daughter. She's only five, which means she's still a dolphin teenager. Sometimes I think she's more like a demanding sister to me than a marine mammal I'm supposed to be training.

One by one the rest of the pod catches up with us until twelve Pacific white-sided dolphins are coursing through the sea beside the zode. They bombard my mind with happy images of what they've been doing since I swam with them this afternoon, but only Sokya, her brother Densil, and their mother, Mariah, seem to possess the ability to use human speech to communicate with me.

:Do you hear any boat engines?: I ask Mariah.

:the sea is quiet,: she reassures me.

Still, we stay close to shore, where we might be able to find a hiding place quickly if we stumble across the Marine Guard.

An hour later, Cam slows the zode as the dark mass of Reynard Point looms over us. I'm aware of a sudden dryness in my mouth.

"You're sure the Marine Guard isn't out here, waiting for someone to come and pick up survivors?"

"I can't be positive," Cam says with a shrug, "but Scarn said he and his men were going to lead the Marine Guard away from here so that we could try to help. Smugglers look after their own."

I hate that Cam's been talking to the head of the most daring smuggling gang along this coast. He's risked getting sent away to one of those awful inland work camps, but I don't have time right now to yell at him.

Seconds can make all the difference when a person is drowning.

Quickly, I reach out to Mariah again. :Please start looking for the crew.:

I've practiced this drill with the pod many times. Their ability to echolocate makes dolphins amazing searchers. "How many were on board?" I think to ask Cam as Mariah and the dolphins go streaking away from us.

"Scarn thought there should have been four."

"The Marine Guard already caught the two who were unloading cargo in the sea cave," Robry chimes in.

"Just how do you know that?" Cam frowns at Robry.

"I picked up a Marine Guard transmission on my short-wave after I heard you sneak out to get Nere."

Cam's face tightens, but he doesn't say anything more. He knows he's in no position to give his brilliant little brother a tough time about listening to his homemade illegal radio. What we are doing right now is ten times more illegal and a hundred times more dangerous.

"Tell Mariah she's looking for two men, then."

I relay his message to Mariah.

Shortly, she reports back to me. :we have found their boat. it is sitting upside down on the bottom below you, but we have not found the men yet.:

I glance at my mother's depth finder. Sure enough, I can see the outline of the sunken boat. It lies in forty feet of water right beneath us. I close my eyes and concentrate on the images the dolphins are relaying back to me.

"The dolphins have spread out all around Reynard's Point," I tell Cam. "But they can't find the last two smugglers anywhere."

"Maybe the Marine Guard caught them all," he says bleakly.

"Wait . . . I think maybe Densil's found a person," I say, sensing Densil's rising excitement. Densil is Sokya's older brother, but their personalities are totally different. Cool, calm, and dependable, Densil would only be feeling this excited if he'd actually found someone.

:there are two people inside the boat,: Densil reports to me, :and their hearts still beat.:

chapter TWO

I RELAY DENSIL'S MESSAGE that he's found two people alive in the boat. Cam looks at me, his face strained. "Can you use your telepathy to find out if one of them is Jac?" he asks.

I draw in a breath. Cam and Robry both know I can call the pod without using the sonar signal other dolphin trainers use, but we rarely talk about it. I inherited my telepathy from my mother. She was abandoned as a baby in the chaos following the Eugenics Wars, and we've always assumed one of her parents must have been a genetically engineered supersoldier. If anyone in the government ever found out my mother and I are telepaths, we'd both end up in a Western Collective work camp, or worse.

Cam clears his throat. "I mean, can you read his mind without his knowing?"

My parents have told me I'm never, ever supposed to use my telepathy with other humans. But Cam's been my best friend ever since I can remember.

I swallow hard. "I can try."

I close my eyes and extend my senses outward. I push past the emotional static from Cam's worry and Robry's excitement. Suddenly I can hear scared and angry thoughts coming from someplace close by.

"It's Jac, all right," I tell Cam. "And he's wondering why you're taking so long to find him. I think he's helping another smuggler who's injured. They're running out of air down there."

Cam pulls two compact aqua-breathers out of his pocket and starts peeling off his shirt. "Guess it's time for a swim. You coming?"

My cheeks burn. "I'd better not," I admit. "The last time I used an aqua-breather, I had a bad lung attack."

"I'll come," Robry offers eagerly.

"I think he's a better swimmer than I am, anyway," I tell Cam, trying to hide my embarrassment. Robry often helps me train the dolphins now that Cam has to work on the fishing boat with his father.

"All right, then." Cam nods to his little brother, and Robry is beside him in a flash.

"I'll keep the zode in position right here," I promise. "Mariah and Densil can pull you down to Jac's boat. I'll ask the rest of the pod to keep an eye out for sharks. Someone might be bleeding down there."

Cam and Robry pull on face masks and fins and place the breathers in their mouths. They slip over the side. Mariah and Densil are waiting for them, with Mariah's calf, Tisi, swimming in excited circles nearby. The dolphins let Cam and Robry take hold of their dorsal fins. Moments later, they all slip beneath the surface.

I keep the zode over Jac's sunken boat while I scan the sea for any sign of the Marine Guard. A few years ago I could have easily made a dive to forty feet with a breather, but my lungs seem to be getting worse and worse. With a shudder, I wonder what will happen after I use up my last lung meds. I know Gillian has been trying desperately to find me more, but meds are hard to come by in the Western Collective these days.

I'm startled when Jac suddenly surfaces next to the zode. I search the water all around, but there's no sign of Cam or Robry yet.

"They're on their way up with my crewmate," Jac reassures me. "That big dolphin is giving them a tow. Your pod is amazing. I knew they'd find us."

"Thanks." I put the ladder down off the stern so that Jac can climb aboard.

He holds out a hand, expecting me to help him, but I turn away, willing Cam and Robry to surface soon. Jac shoots me a cocky smile, oblivious to the fact that I don't like him. At least he didn't leave his injured crewmate to drown.

I let out a long breath when Densil, Robry, and Cam break the surface a minute later, towing an injured boy who has Cam's breather clamped between his teeth. With Jac helping me, we soon get the shaking, wounded smuggler on board. Slumped against the center pontoon, he bleeds from deep gashes on his forehead and leg. The boy is younger than Cam and so painfully thin that I wonder if he joined the smugglers just to get three real meals a day.

I peer over the side to check on Robry. "There's something else I need to fetch from down there," he takes his breather out of his mouth long enough to tell me. "I'll be back in a minute."

Before I can protest, Robry dives beneath the surface, quick as a dartling.

:Mariah, please keep an eye on Robry, will you?: I ask her. I'm still worried about sharks.

:we always do,: Mariah says. :he and Tisi are too good at finding trouble.:

:We're going to be lucky if we don't all end up in trouble before this night's over,: I say.

I go forward and find the first-aid kit. I'm no medic, but my mother's made sure I know basic emergency care. I'm in the midst of bandaging the gash on the smuggler's forehead when Robry climbs into the zode, holding a large, angry lobster.

"I can't believe you're thinking about your breakfast at a time like this." Cam shakes his head while Robry tosses the lobster into the specimen tank that Gillian keeps strapped against the center pontoon.

"Actually, I was thinking if we ran into the Marine Guard, we could at least say we were out looking for food," Robry says as he struggles to pull the dive fins off his big feet.

"Good thinking," Jac tells Robry with a grin. "You'd make a fine smuggler."

"Over my dead body," Cam says grimly, and points the zode straight out to sea.

"Where're we headed?" I ask him.

"We're going to rendezvous with Scarn."

"The chief will probably take me across the border to hide out in the Southern Republic for a while," Jac boasts. "Unfortunately, the Marine Guard got a good look at my handsome mug."

I bite back a retort. I can't believe we're risking our lives to help this idiot. With Robry's help, I finish bandaging the young smuggler and cover him with a blanket. A half hour later, we rendezvous with a sleek, fast, dark boat.

"Try not to look at their faces," Cam warns me and Robry quietly, as the boat pulls up beside us. "You'll be safer if you can't recognize them."

We toss the crew mooring lines. Two smugglers step down into the zode and lift the boy. He thanks me weakly before they help him aboard their vessel. Jac climbs up after the others.

"That's a good-looking zode you have there," one of the men says in a deep, gravelly voice, and shivers skitter down my back. He can't take the zode from us! My mother needs it to conduct her research, and the fish we caught from it kept us alive during the last famine.

Despite Cam's warning, I glance up. I can't help staring at the smuggler's craggy face because it's pockmarked with tyrox scars. I gulp when I realize he must be one of the survivors of the tyrox outbreak that killed most of the population of LA forty years ago.

"It is a good zode, Scarn, and you are not going to steal it from the Hansons after what they did for you tonight," Cam tells him sternly.

Scarn chuckles. "Cam Cruz, you've got guts; I have to give you credit for that. You can have a job with me whenever you want."

"I'll stick to fishing. I might live longer."

Scarn nods to his crew and they toss the mooring lines back into the zode. Without another word, Cam powers up the motor and we head toward home.

We're quiet on the way back to Goleta. I carefully pack away our med kit while Robry washes down the zode thoroughly, making sure there are no telltale signs of blood. When we're finally finished, I sit beside Robry on the bow, the sea wind cool on my face. The dolphins keep pace beside us, leaping and playing in our bow wake. Laki and Mali show off by performing flips. Robry leans off the side of the zode and holds out his hand. We laugh when little Tisi tries to jump over it.

I wish we could keep the zode out all night. But every minute we stay on the water increases our chances of encountering a Marine Guard vessel.

Just before we reach the harbor entrance, Mariah contacts me.

:you are safe now?: she asks.

:We should be fine.:

:then we go to rest.:

:Thank you for your help tonight,: I say.

"Tell Mariah I'll save her any squid we take in the next few days," Cam promises. I relay his message to her. Mariah slaps a wave of water at Cam with her tail.

"I guess she likes that idea." I grin at Cam as he wipes the seawater from his eyes.

It's dark and quiet when we enter the harbor. I check my marine watch. It will be dawn in another two hours. Cam will have to hurry to be ready to head out fishing with his father before the sun rises.

Suddenly, Cam starts swearing under his breath.

I glance up and see that Hycault, the tall, lanky fishmaster, is waiting for us at the end of the dolphin dock. I bite my lip. Hycault is the most important government official in Goleta. We've broken his curfew and left the harbor without his permission.

Both offenses are serious enough to land us in a world of hurt.

chapter Three

MY NIGHT VISION is freakishly good, but right now I wish it wasn't. I can clearly see the gleeful expression on the fishmaster's face, and it makes my stomach churn.

"I've finally caught you," Hycault says to Cam. "I knew your friend Jac was a smuggler, but I wasn't sure about you until tonight."

"I'm no smuggler," Cam says bitterly as he brings the zode up beside the dock.

"The Marine Guard sank Jac's boat five miles north of here," Hycault continues, as if Cam hadn't spoken, "and I spotted you entering the harbor from the north. That can hardly be a coincidence."

"You have no proof I smuggled anything tonight."

"I don't need any proof except what my eyes tell me right now," Hycault says, growing more strident by the moment. "You took this boat out without my permission, and you broke the curfew—"

"Actually, Fishmaster"—my mother's cool voice interrupts him—"my daughter and her crew members don't need your permission if she's out on the water doing research for me or training our dolphins. I believe we've discussed this issue several times before."

I've never been so glad to see Gillian. She is standing beside Hycault now, her expression amazingly composed.

"Boys, you can tie up the zode and hurry home," she continues on. "Cam needs to eat a good breakfast before he heads out with the fleet. Thanks for helping Nere tonight."

"You're welcome, Dr. Hanson," Cam says as he and Robry tie up the zode. Cam sends me a quick grateful look, and then he and Robry slip away. I, in the meantime, stand in the middle of the zode, wishing I could just disappear.

"You've no right to send them out without consulting me first," Hycault says furiously.

"You can check with the Department of Fisheries. I have the right to send my boat out whenever I want to do research. The Western Collective needs more protein for its citizens, and the Department of Fisheries values the work I do," my mother replies.

"Just you wait," Hycault says with such menace, I tremble. "In a few days you'll be sorry for all the times you dared to challenge my authority here." With that, he stalks up the dock.

"I sincerely doubt it," Gillian says to his retreating back. She steps down into the zode and reconnects the boat batteries to the solar array. From her tight expression, I know I'm in deep trouble. Wordlessly, she retrieves the lobster from the specimen bin, kills it with a deft knock against a dock piling, and strides quickly toward home.

I follow her up the path toward our stone cottage. I stop

at the little spring where Cam rigged a pipe so that we have a shower we can use to rinse off seawater after a swim. I stay under the cold trickle for as long as I dare.

The instant I close our front door behind me, my mother asks, "What on earth were you thinking? You just risked your life and your freedom, all for some fool of a smuggler!"

"I thought the point of our dolphin program is to save human lives," I make myself say. I hate arguing with my mother. She's so brilliant, she always wins.

"I'd rather see our dolphins save worthwhile human lives. You may have saved Jac's life tonight, but that idiotic boy will be risking it again tomorrow for nothing more than a few dollarns and some thrills."

"You've said yourself if it weren't for smugglers who brought in meds from the Southern Republic, I'd have died long ago."

"Well, those were principled smugglers, not like Scarn and his gang, who just traffic in black-market luxuries. They're little more than scum." She pauses and seems to collect herself. "Do you have any idea how I felt when I saw that your bed was empty, and then that the zode was missing?"

I look at her set face, and I feel my eyes burn with tears. "I-I'm sorry. I didn't mean to frighten you."

Her tight expression eases. She crosses the room and gathers me into her arms. "I know you didn't mean to, sweetling," she says in a gentler tone, and smooths a lock of hair away from my face. "And I know Cam probably asked you to help. I'll have a talk with his mother. Alicia's probably going to be angrier about this than I am." She gives me a quick kiss on my forehead and steps away.

"What happened tonight will never happen again," she says, returning to her usual cool, brisk scientist mode. "Do I make myself clear?"

I nod quickly. Then I can't help yawning.

"Well, it's obvious you won't get much out of school today," she declares. "You might as well go back to bed. I'll figure out your punishment later. I think the dolphin dock pilings need scraping again."

After I close my bedroom door behind me, I make a face. Even though I hate scraping the dock pilings, I'm getting off pretty lightly. Shortly after I lie down on my bed, I fall fast asleep.

When I wake up, I'm surprised to hear voices. I check my watch. It's already two in the afternoon, and I'm starving. I open my door quietly and peer around it. Ben Reece, a dolphin trainer from down the coast, is sitting at our kitchen table talking with my mother. Their expressions are tense and serious.

"Rumor has it they're going to make a big announcement tomorrow," Ben is telling her. "The smuggling incident last night may be the last straw. This could be the crackdown we've all been dreading."

My mother glances up and notices me. I see her make an effort to smile. "Good afternoon, sweetling. I left a fish bar and some of Alicia's bread for you on the counter."

"Hi, Nere." Ben gives me a nod. "I saw you working with the pod last week. Your dolphins look sharp. Maybe your mother will let me borrow you to work with my pod one of these days."

I have a hunch that Ben would much rather borrow my mother. But the one time I was brave enough to ask Gillian about Ben, she only laughed and said she was a one-man woman, and her man was gone. What I saw in her eyes then has kept me from asking her that question again.

Pain twists inside me when I realize that my father has been dead for over two years now. He was washed overboard during a sudden wild storm, and even our dolphins couldn't find his body. Some nights before supper, I catch myself listening for his footsteps and his whistling as he hurries up our path from the harbor.

Although I want my mother to be happy, another part of me is relieved that she's not interested in Ben. But men like him will keep trying. Despite her years spent in the sun and on the sea, she is still beautiful.

Every day I wish I'd inherited more of her looks. I have her pale skin and blond hair, but they look weird on me. Some days I think my blue eyes are almost pretty, but barely anyone sees them because I have to wear huge, blocky, dark glasses to keep my weak eyes from tearing in bright sunlight. I'll never be curvy like the town girls because I spend so much time swimming with the dolphins.

No wonder I only have two friends. Robry and Cam don't seem to mind my freaky coloring or the fact that I'm as skinny and strong as most fisher boys. But I mind.

I linger in the main room and start in on my lunch, hoping to find out more about the big government announcement Ben had mentioned.

"Let's head down to your boat," Gillian says to Ben. "After you finish your lunch, Nere, please start on your lessons for this afternoon." She motions to my learning pad and a long list of articles she's left for me on the table.

As she leaves, I yank out a chair. Usually the lessons my mother teaches me about marine biology and oceanography are more interesting than those I have to learn at school about the rise of the Western Collective and the devastation created around the world by global warming. But over the past few months, her lessons have been getting longer and harder.

When she comes inside a short time later, I gesture to her list. "I don't see why I have to learn about giant squid and how to treat lionfish stings. I'm not going to run into a lionfish working as a coastal dolphin trainer."

"Your oceanography lessons are more important than ever." I'm surprised by the strain I hear in my mother's voice.

"What I teach you now might save your life someday."

I open my mouth to argue, but something in her face stops me. She's been looking haunted for months now— it's even worse than when my father died or when my big brother, James, disappeared last year. She stays up late, working and pacing the cottage long into the night. I've tried to ask what's bothering her, but Gillian has always had her secrets.

I bend my head and go back to reading while she chops vegetables and stirs the lobster stew we'll be eating later. When she's finished cooking, she quizzes me on my navigation skills and assigns one final article on ocean vents. I keep reading the article while we have an early dinner. A couple of times Gillian looks like she wants to say something, but then she doesn't. Even for my mother, she's acting strange.

When the silence gets too awkward, I decide to break it. "Has Ben heard anything about James?"

Her expression goes from distracted to closed. "No," she says.

I stare hard at my plate. One morning we woke up to find that James had disappeared with the sailboat he'd made by himself. I know he'd been in fights at school, and he'd had some awful arguments with my mother, but I still can't believe he just left us. The secret police came looking for him because James had cut out his locator chip, but we couldn't tell them where he'd gone.

He's always loved the Channel Islands, though, and I think he's hiding out there.

I look up from my plate. "Why can't we take the zode out to the islands and look for him?" I ask, even though I've already asked her this question a dozen times.

"Sweetling, I know you miss him. I miss him, too," she says with a catch in her voice. "I promise we'll both go look for him soon, but now is not the right time," she adds, with such finality I know there's no point in arguing with her.

I stand up and blink back my tears before she can see them. James can be grumpy and impatient sometimes, but still, he's my big brother, and I wonder all the time if he's okay. Now our cottage seems twice as empty and quiet, with both him and my father gone.

After dinner, I go down to the dolphin dock for a long swim with the pod. When I'm ready for sleep, Gillian comes to sit beside me on my bed.

"Ben really was impressed with the dolphins last week. You've done a wonderful job since you took over their training on your own."

"Thanks," is all I can think to say. I wish we weren't so awkward together. James made everything easier. He knew how to make her smile and laugh.

"Well, sweetling, you get some rest. Tomorrow's likely to be a hard day. I'm going to be up late tonight." She kisses me on the forehead and blows out my lamp.

I'm just starting to doze when I hear a sound I dread. She's dragging our table across the floor, and I swear to myself. Then I hear her roll our rug back and pull the trapdoor open. I know Gillian is about to climb down the wooden ladder that leads to her secret, forbidden lab full of secret, forbidden lab equipment and computers that we speak of even more rarely than we speak of James or my father.

I get out of bed and stalk to the top of the ladder.

"Knock when you want to come back up," is all I say. After she climbs down the ladder, I slam the trapdoor shut and roll the rug back into place. I drag the table over the rug, taking care to make sure it all looks normal. I even leave a dirty plate and mug on the table. The secret police can search a house at any time, looking for illegal technology like computers or radios. Gillian has all of those things and more in her lab.

I hate it that she takes these risks. I hate it that she does the kind of research that gets people arrested and taken away.

We're already a family of two now. What will happen to me if the Western Collective sends her to a work camp, and there's only me left?

chapter four

THE SECRET POLICE *have found out I'm a telepath. They chase me down the dusty yellow road from Santero. I pump my arms and run as fast as I can. My chest is burning. If I have a lung attack here, I know they will catch me. Suddenly, someone grabs my shoulder and yanks me to a stop. I turn. Hycault is there, a triumphant grin splitting his narrow face. . . .*

"Nere, wake up, sweetling; you're just having a bad dream."

I open my eyes. The light filling my little bedroom tells me it's early morning. I'm sweating and gasping for air. I realize my mother is sitting on the edge of my bed. She must have been shaking my shoulder just now.

"You'd better get up and dress in your best skirt. We're all being called in to Santero to hear an important government edict," she tells me as she strokes my damp hair.

"Do you have any idea what it's about?" I ask her between taking in deep breaths and trying to push the frightening dream from my mind.

"I'm not sure, but the entire fishing fleet is still at its moorings. Whatever the edict is, it's important enough to keep fifty men from the sea."

I get out of bed and stumble to my window. When I see she's right, a nasty, queasy feeling begins to build in the pit of my stomach. Government edicts never contain good news.

Gillian is quiet over breakfast, and she seems to have as little appetite as I do. There are dark circles under her eyes from working in her lab until four in the morning.

I want to ask her what she was doing, but a part of me doesn't want to know. That way if they ever do take her away, they can't torture me into admitting something about her work that could get us both killed. Instead, I resort to staring at her balefully, but she's so preoccupied, my stare isn't having much impact.

After breakfast, I change into my best skirt and brush out my hair. Right now I don't look too ugly, I think while I stare at my mirror. My nose is straight enough, and some days I think my mouth is pretty. But then I slip on my horrible big, dark glasses, and Freak Girl abruptly returns.

I sigh and turn away. "I'm going down to see the dolphins before we leave," I call to Gillian, who is still dressing in her own small room.

I head down to the harbor to be with the pod. When I reach the end of the dolphin dock, I'm not surprised to find that Robry's in the water. While I watch him being towed by Nika and Pani, two of our youngest and most playful dolphins, I can't help smiling.

:your breathing is good?: Mariah asks me as she lolls by the dock.

Sometimes I feel like I have two mothers.

:Yes, it is fine today. You had a peaceful night?:

:we are all safe.:

Distracted by Mariah, I don't notice Sokya stealing up behind me until it's too late. Suddenly, I'm drenched with cold seawater. Sokya and her mischievous cousin, Laki, have splashed me.

:Oh, no, Sokya, it matters what I look like today!:

:now you look wet—wet is good.:

I sigh. Dolphins don't care about appearances, nor do they know how to apologize. But they do have a wicked sense of humor, and I can feel Laki's and Sokya's joy over the prank they have played on me.

There's no time for me to go wash up and change. Now I face being salty and sticky throughout the long trip inland. At least I'll be cooler while I walk.

:No squid for you later,: I think at Sokya.

:we can find our own squid,: she replies, sounding very pleased with herself.

"We have to go now, Robry," I say. His mother, Alicia, is waiting for us at the end of the dolphin dock. She's always been surprisingly patient about Robry's fascination with the dolphins.

My mother joins us as we leave the dock and merge into the stream of people heading inland to hear this new edict from the Western Collective. Alicia walks along beside her. Neither Robry nor I speak much as we trudge along the dusty road. I'm sweating and my lungs feel hot and itchy by the time we reach the farmers' town. Santero consists of rows of flimsy government houses that are all beige, squat, and ugly. Beyond Santero, the empty fields stretch for dozens of miles, this year's corn crop already withered to dead stalks beneath the relentless sun.

I shiver, despite the heat, when I see the first of hundreds of soldiers standing along the road, wearing body armor and carrying solar rifles. Gillian and I exchange grim looks.

Cam leaves his friends and deliberately walks between Robry and me and the soldiers. Even though he's only fifteen, Cam looks formidable. I would feel safer, except that I can see the resentment burning in his dark eyes. I think he has too much sense to do something stupid, but what if he doesn't? My stomach twists tighter.

When we reach the center of the town, the adults and youths like Cam who no longer attend school continue on to the large community hall. My mother sends me a reassuring smile. I must look terrified, because Cam says, "It will be all right," even though we both know it may not be. "Wait for me afterward."

Then he goes on with Gillian. I force myself to follow Robry into our school. Inside, he and I are separated when they herd us straight into our classrooms.

At least today I don't have much time to think about how miserable I feel at school. I've always been too shy to talk to the town girls, and usually they ignore me just like the fisher girls do. Mostly I try to be invisible, and I've gotten good at it.

As I slip into my classroom, I can't help glancing around for Lena. I hear a trill of laughter, and then I see her. As usual, she's flirting with Thisen and Rom, the two most popular boys in our year.

"Rom, that's just such a horrible thing to say to me." Her laugh rings out again on a day few of us can find anything to laugh about.

She doesn't even look at me while I walk past her and quietly take a seat in the back. Being ignored by Lena still hurts. She used to be my only other friend besides Robry and Cam. Like me, Lena has parents who went to university. Like me, she's always had weak lungs and had to wear dark glasses. She used to come swim with the dolphins and me all the time, and then the summer we both turned ten, she suddenly just stopped being my friend.

I watch Lena toss her long, dark, curly hair and open her brown eyes wide as she gazes at Thisen. She hardly squints at all here in the brightly lit classroom. I wonder if she's wearing protective contact lenses. They are horribly expensive, but then again, her parents had the money to buy her a pair of dark glasses on the black market, which make her look like an old-time movie star.

At last our teacher, Mr. Casey, hurries in carrying a

clipboard. His face is shiny with sweat, and he looks worried. I feel sorry for him. Unlike many of the teachers at our school, he truly cares about his students. He loves literature more than anything, and he was thrilled that I liked the few novels he'd been allowed to assign us.

Mr. Casey clears his throat. That's all he has to do today to get thirty of us to quiet down and quickly find our seats.

"We are honored that Deputy Minister Torpel of the Department of Population Allocation for our southern sector is here today. He has come to personally deliver a special announcement that affects us all."

The classroom falls silent as the deputy minister enters our room and strides to the front. There, he turns to survey us. I tremble when I realize how cold and dead his eyes look. In the back of my mind, I try to figure out where I've seen eyes that cold before.

"The Department of Agriculture," the deputy minister says in a curt, crisp tone, "has determined that the crop yields here in Santero have been below average for five years now."

Someone dares to snicker at that. We all know that in this case, "below average" is "nonexistent" in government-speak. The deputy's expression tightens. "I'm surprised you young people find that amusing. I can assure you that your government does not." He stares at each of us so intently I sink lower in my chair.

"The Department of Border Defense is likewise concerned about the rampant smuggling that continues to flourish in this region," he continues at last, "despite the Marine Guard's dedicated efforts to eradicate it. Citizens of the Western Collective are to share their resources, not hoard them or use them to buy luxuries, especially during times of hardship. Smugglers cater to the selfish, privileged few, and we are determined to stop them once and for all."

Everyone in my classroom knows that members of the government *are* the privileged few most apt to buy goods from the smugglers, but no one dares to point out that fact to Deputy Minister Torpel.

"We believe the fisher folk of Goleta continue to aid and abet these smugglers. Therefore, the Ministers of Agriculture, Population Allocation, and Border Defense have decided it's time to move the people of Santero and Goleta to various communities farther inland, where their efforts will help boost food production for our entire nation."

I struggle to understand his government-speak, and then his meaning slams into me like a killer wave. Minister Torpel is here to make the fishermen abandon their boats and move inland. That means my mother and I are going to have to move away from the sea, and from our dolphins.

chapter Five

I DIG MY FINGERNAILS hard into my thighs, trying to hold back the cry of protest building in my throat. My classmates aren't so careful. Angry murmurs rise all around me.

The murmurs cease as the deputy minister raises his hand and coldly surveys us once again. Suddenly I realize where I've seen eyes like his before. The big sharks, like makos and great whites, have cold, dead eyes just like the minister's.

"We are giving your parents two days to pack and prepare to leave. I suggest that you young people do everything you can to help them." He goes on to talk in a more friendly tone about what wonderful places we may get to live, but his shark eyes are anything but friendly.

Several girls start crying noisily the moment he leaves our classroom. Mr. Casey dismisses us in a choked voice. He wishes us good luck as we file by him, but he tugs at my sleeve to halt me.

"Nere, I hope you keep up with your reading," he says urgently.

"I'll try," I mumble. As much as I've loved his books, reading about tormented people hundreds of years ago just doesn't seem that important to me right now. There's plenty of torment in my present.

Walking out of our school, I can't slow the torrent of questions rushing through my head: how can I possibly leave Mariah, Sokya, Densil, and Tisi? How can I live away from the sea? My lungs are always so much worse in the dry air inland. What if lung meds are as scarce there as they are here? This government plan could kill me.

Cam is waiting for me in the street, a pale Robry already at his side. Cam's face is cool and guarded, but I can tell he's furious. I want to cry on his shoulder, but I don't want to embarrass him.

"Your mother's already headed back," he tells me. "Wait here. I have to talk to someone."

I gaze after him, stunned that Gillian has already left. My whole life is falling apart, and she can't stay away from her work?

I feel even worse when I see Cam walk straight up to Lena. She brightens at his approach and starts to turn up her flirty act. But whatever he is saying quickly wipes the bright smile from her face. She looks over at me and scowls. He seems to be urging her to do something, but she shakes her head vehemently and dashes off.

His face tighter than ever, Cam doesn't even pause as he passes us. "Let's go," he says, and Robry and I hurry after him.

"What did you say to Lena?" I gasp as I run to catch up with him.

"You mother asked me to give Lena a message, but I can't tell you what it was."

So we're back to my mother and her secrets.

"Do you know why Gillian was in such a hurry to go home?" I ask.

"She didn't say, but I gather it was important. She wants you and Robry to hurry, and both of you are to go straight to your cottage."

Cam strides along so swiftly I can't keep up with him. "Cam," I say, hating the wheeze I hear in my voice, "I can't walk this fast."

Twice we have to step off the road into fields of dead cornstalks as convoys of armored troop carriers race by us heading toward Goleta. They must be sending more troops to make sure the fisher folk don't cause any trouble.

"How can they make all these people give up everything they care about and leave like this?" I wonder aloud.

Cam's eyes are hot and bitter. "Because we actually believe that our leaders helped us survive the famines and the tyrox outbreak before them. Because we're so grateful to be alive, we've become sheep and let them tell us what to do."

"You're not going to do anything stupid, are you?"

"I suppose it depends on how you define stupid."

"You're not g-going to fight them?"

"No. If it makes you feel any better, I'm planning to run away. My brothers and I have talked about this before. We'll slip away with the *Sandpiper* and become black-market fishermen."

"Maybe you could take me with you. With the dolphins' help, you could be the most successful black-market fisherman ever." I blurt the words, not really thinking about what I'm saying, but Cam stops dead in his tracks.

"Nere, if only I could take you." There is something in his eyes that I've just caught glimpses of before. He raises his hand and cups my cheek gently. "But your mother made it very clear to me years ago that she has other plans for you," he says, and he drops his hand and starts striding along again.

"What do you mean, she has other plans?"

"Ask her," he says. I'm shocked by the anger in his tone.

"What other plans? Cam, you can't keep this—"

"Something's burning!" Robry interrupts my protest.

"No!" The hoarse cry is torn from Cam, and then he's pounding up the rise to the headland above the harbor. Robry and I run after him as fast as we can.

When I reach the top and see what's happening in the harbor, I feel like the air's been knocked from my lungs. The first of the wooden fishing boats is engulfed in soaring yellow and orange flames. A sleek, deadly Marine Guard cutter blockades the entrance to Goleta Harbor. Soldiers, with their solar rifles at the ready, block the access to the pier to make sure the fisher folk don't try to save their beloved boats.

"Oh, Cam," I say, my voice breaking, "I'm so sorry." There will be no escaping on the *Sandpiper* for him now. Even as we watch, another fishing boat bursts into flames. The smoke from the burning vessels twines like a massive black snake into the sky.

"They tell us people are starving inland, and then they do this," Cam says, his hands clenched into fists.

My eyes flood with tears. I can't believe Cam's going to lose his boat and I'm about to lose my dolphins. What if Cam and I don't get sent inland to the same community? I couldn't bear to lose him, too.

I reach out for Mariah.

:Are you all safe?:

:yes. the big boat with motors came, and we swam beneath it. we hunt now down the coast. you are safe?:

:I am.: I don't want to explain to her now about our having to leave. Surely there will be time for that later tonight.

:your mother told us to stay near. be careful.:

Gillian again. :I'll do my best.:

Cam takes my arm. He's staring down at the soldiers guarding the pier. "Come on, we've got to get you home," he says, and almost drags me toward my cottage.

"But what about the *Sandpiper*?" I protest even as I dash away my tears.

"I don't want to watch them burn her," he says, his voice rough.

No one stops us from reaching the cottage. My mother meets us at the door.

"Robry, Nere, thank heavens you're here." She starts dragging back the table the instant I close the door behind us. Is she really going to let Robry and Cam find out about the lab?

"We don't have much time," she continues as she tugs the rug back. "You both need to head down to the lab right now. Cam, cover up this trapdoor with the rug and the table once we're down the ladder. Keep an eye out for Lena and her family. Show them the way down to the lab if she comes, and tell her parents to hide the door. The soldiers will find the lab eventually, but I need to buy us all the time I can."

"I want to say good-bye to Nere before she goes," Cam says. "You owe me that."

My mother pauses and meets Cam's gaze before she starts down the ladder. "Very well," she says after a long moment. "It's going to be dangerous for everyone, but you can meet us at Tyler's Cove an hour before sunrise tomorrow. Make sure no one else comes with you."

"All right." Cam nods slowly.

"What is going on?" I'm almost screaming in frustration.

"Come to the lab, and I'll explain everything," my mother says curtly, and then she disappears through the trapdoor.

Robry, his expression anxious, follows her. I pause at the top of the ladder, feeling somehow that this is the start of a separation I'm not sure I can survive.

"Cam?" I can't keep the fear from my voice.

"I promise I'll see you tomorrow," he says, his face grim. "I'm so sorry about the *Sandpiper*."

"I know, but your staying alive is a hundred times more important to me than any boat. Now go."

I climb down the ladder. My gaze clings to his. As the heavy trapdoor swings downward, it cuts off my view of Cam and drops closed with an ominous thud.

chapter six

"I WANT THE TRUTH, and I want it now. I'm sick of your secrets!" I shout at my mother the second I reach the bottom of the ladder.

"You'll get the truth, but we don't have time for dramatics. Roll up your sleeve. I need to give you a shot. Robry, you're about to get one, too."

"Why do I need a shot?" I ask.

"To keep you alive where you're both going." She grabs my sleeve and rolls it up to my elbow.

"Aren't there better hospitals inland?"

"You're not going inland. You're going to meet your father."

"What? Are you crazy?" I snatch my arm away, wondering what, exactly, is in the syringe I see next to her on the counter.

"No, I'm not crazy," she says brusquely. "But I will get angry if you don't give me your arm back. Your father is very much alive and living up north in the Broughton Archipelago. Or at least he was six months ago, which is the last time he managed to get word to me."

I stare at her in disbelief. I hardly notice the coolness where she's swabbing my arm with alcohol.

"Now I know you're crazy. Dad died two years ago."

"No, we faked his death during that storm so that the secret police would believe he was dead."

"Dad's alive?" At first I can't believe her, but I see the truth in her eyes. I feel like screaming for joy. My father is alive! And then I want to hit her.

"You lied to me. You know I cried for months. How could you do this to me?"

"Because we both felt that the work he was doing was too vital and too dangerous. We couldn't risk you telling anyone that he was still alive, nor could we take a chance that the secret police might someday torture that information out of you."

The level, matter-of-fact way she speaks gives me chills. She takes advantage of my momentary shock and confusion to plunge the needle deep into my arm.

"Ow, that stings!"

"Sorry, sweetling." I see a flicker of humor in her eyes as she kisses my forehead. "I'd give you a candy, but I don't have any."

She turns to Robry, who already has his sleeve rolled up. "All right, my brave boy, it's your turn now."

"This is going to change us all the way, isn't it?" he asks her quietly.

My mother looks startled. Then she searches his face carefully. "How long have you known?"

"Since we studied the Eugenics Wars in school, and I came home and took a long look at my feet. I'm glad, though, truly. I'm ready to go."

"What do you mean this is going to change us all the way? Where are you ready to go?" I can't help yelling again.

"Into the ocean, for always," Robry says calmly as my mother gives him his shot. "I think your parents altered our genes before we were born to create a new species of human that can survive under the waves."

I stare at Robry, trying to sort through his impossible words. Suddenly, I hear a scraping sound overhead. Someone is moving the table back from the trapdoor.

We freeze. Have the soldiers found us? My heart gallops in my chest. Gillian calmly takes a lethal-looking solar pistol out of a drawer, powers it up, and points it toward the trapdoor. My mother owns a solar pistol? I can't believe that she has one, or that she looks so comfortable handling it.

My mouth goes dry as the trapdoor swings open.

"It's all right, Gillian, it's me," I hear Mr. McFadden, Lena's father, call down the ladder to us.

"I don't want to go down there," I hear Lena whine.

Lena's here? I'm trapped in a nightmare where nothing makes sense. I hear raised voices upstairs, and seconds later a red-faced Lena comes stomping down the ladder. The trapdoor shuts, and I hear the rug and table getting moved back into position.

Lena's eye makeup is smeared from crying, and her long hair is in a wild tangle.

"What is she doing here?" I ask Gillian while Lena crosses her arms and glares at us.

"Her parents brought her because they know she'll die, just like you will, if the Western Collective moves her inland."

"So whatever you did to us, you did to her, too?" Now I'm furious for Lena's sake. "What Robry said is true?"

My mother nods and tries to speak, but I cut her off.

"So you're the reason why I'm a freak!" I shout at her. "We're all experiments. How could you do this to us?"

"Because we thought this was your only chance—humankind's only chance—to survive. The earth's atmosphere is continuing to heat up at an alarming rate."

"You're wrong. The climate scientists keep saying the earth is finally cooling again."

"They're all lying. So far, none of the carbon dioxide removal programs have made any difference. Severe droughts and blistering temperatures mean more famines lie ahead; famines on a scale that will lead to even more catastrophic wars. Our own government will only grow more repressive and cruel. That's why we agreed to join the Neptune Project. Your father and I wanted you to have a chance to live free of the Western Collective."

"You think we can actually live in the sea? You know how dangerous it is down there. We'll probably get eaten in the first twenty-four hours."

"No, you won't, because the dolphins will protect you. You can defend yourself with your spearguns. Your father and I have been preparing you for this moment all your life."

The idea that my father has been a part of this is like a slug in my gut. My mother turns to Lena.

"Lena, I have to give you your shot now. The soldiers could find us anytime, and it takes several hours for the virus to trigger the final changes in your lungs that will allow you to breathe water."

"I'd rather die than become some kind of fish mutate," Lena says defiantly.

"Are you very sure about that?" my mother asks her in a level tone. "Because that's exactly what will happen. The next time you have a lung attack, the doctors inland will take a sample of your blood, and then they'll realize just how different you are from most humans. I expect they'll put you in some sort of prison, and without the right meds, you will eventually die, gasping for air, and they'll let you."

Lena pales. After a long moment she jerks up the sleeve on her shirt.

"I will never forgive my father, my mother, or you, for doing this to me," she says coldly.

For the first time in a long time, Lena and I see eye to eye.

chapter seven

AFTER LENA GETS HER SHOT, my mother moves us out of the lab and down the passageway that leads to the sea caves beneath our cottage. The air here is damp with mist thrown up by the waves smashing against the black rock walls below us. It's dark, too, with just a little daylight filtering in from outside.

My mother stops in a small chamber above the first of the caves. She switches on an electric lantern and opens up the seapacks. Over the echoing rush of the waves, she explains the equipment she's put together for us. I'm still too shocked to concentrate as she points out the navigational tools and charts, spearguns and knives, food, hammocks, and some small gold discn coins she says we'll need.

Robry, though, listens carefully to everything she says. Lena huddles off to the side with her arms wrapped around her knees, not even pretending to listen. I might feel sorrier for her if I weren't so busy fighting my own fear.

I stare at the black waves plunging and frothing against the glistening sides of the cave below our chamber. I love the sea, but the idea of living in it terrifies me. My mother was right about one thing: she and my father have packed my brain full of information about the ocean. The world beneath the waves can be beautiful, but it's also a dangerous place, where larger predators constantly devour smaller ones.

I don't want to be devoured. I don't want Robry to be devoured, either. I wouldn't even wish that on Lena.

I look at Robry's determined face as he listens to Gillian's equipment lecture, and anger burns through me again. "I can't believe you did this to Robry. How could Alicia have let you mess with his genes?"

My mother stops talking and sighs. "Let me? Nere, she begged me. One day I was careless and she found her way down into the lab. She'd read enough about the Project on a computer to grasp what we were trying to do. That night Alicia told me she believed the Western Collective would take her sons from her one day, and she desperately wanted at least one of her children to have a chance to be free." Gillian's gaze turns distant and sad. "Alicia is my only friend here. In the end, I had to do what she asked."

Robry reaches a hand out and touches her arm. "It's all right," he says simply. "I don't want to move inland. Somehow I've always known I was going to live in the sea."

"Well, I've never known anything like that," I fling at her. I draw in a breath to deliver another retort, but I can't get enough air. I cough and wheeze helplessly, but this is different from a lung attack. This feels like my lungs are stiffening inside my chest.

"What's happening to me?" I manage to gasp.

My mother is by my side in a flash. "Your gill filaments are starting to swell. We have to get you on oxygen."

Quickly, she places a mask over my mouth and nose and dials up the flow from a nearby oxygen tank. Then she holds my hands and anxiously watches my face.

I suck in three deep breaths. When I don't feel like I'm suffocating anymore, my panic eases a little. I let go of her hands and snatch the mask off long enough to ask, "What do you mean, my gill filaments are starting to swell?"

"Your lungs are full of dormant gill filaments. That's why you've always had problems breathing when you exert yourself."

"You mean, we're already half fish?" Lena looks revolted.

"I mean we gave you the same respiratory tissues fish have so that someday you could breathe underwater."

I stare at my mother in disbelief. "Are we really about to breathe water? Have you ever done this to someone before?"

"This transformation has been completed successfully hundreds of times," she says, avoiding my eyes.

There's something she's not telling me, and then I get it. I jerk the mask off. "You mean *you've* never done it!"

"You're not helping Robry or Lena here," she says sternly. "You've got to be the brave one."

No one asked me if I wanted to be brave. No one asked me if I wanted any of this.

My gaze falls on Robry. He's starting to look frightened. I can tell from the way his chest is rising and falling that he's having problems breathing, too. As I put my mask back on, I decide I can try to be brave, for his sake.

My mother hurries around, slipping oxygen masks over Robry's and Lena's faces and turning on their tanks. Then she places clips over our fingers that are linked to monitors.

"I'm reading the oxygen levels in your bloodstream," she explains to us. "Even with this rich oxygen, that level is going to start falling eventually. When it gets low enough, we'll know it's time."

I take the mask off for a second. "Time for what?"

"Time for you to jump into the water and start breathing it instead," she says coolly.

My mother is trying to make it sound like it's no big deal, but I almost drowned once, and taking water into your lungs is not something your body wants to do. Ever.

A shudder goes through me, and then I realize something else. My skin is starting to prickle with heat. That doesn't make any sense, because the caves are always cool. I kick off my shoes and roll up my shirt sleeves. I glance across the chamber and see Lena is doing the same thing.

"Your metabolism is changing, too," Gillian explains to us in her detached, scientist voice. "The three of you have never liked hot weather because your bodies are designed to conserve heat in the colder waters of the sea. Right now your sweat glands are shutting down permanently. Your vision is changing, too. You will be more comfortable if you put your dark glasses back on. We altered your eyes so that you could see better in an underwater environment, where much of the surface light is lost."

Stop talking about how you designed and altered us. You're making me feel like an experiment, I want to shout at her.

Suddenly, my mother's voice is in my mind. :Of course you are more than an experiment to me, sweetling.:

I look at her in astonishment. My parents have always forbidden me to use my telepathy to communicate with people. They told me again and again that the secret police would take me away if they found out I was telepathic.

:Telepathy between humans is no longer forbidden for you, Nere,: she assures me. :In fact, all of you should start exploring your telepathy because you are going to use it to communicate in the water. The virus should have switched on Lena's and Robry's latent telepathic capabilities by now.:

Robry and Lena exchange startled glances.

:I think you'll find you can send or broadcast thoughts you want to communicate as easily as talking. If you want to talk privately with a single person, you will direct your thoughts to that individual only. Instinctively, your mind will shield itself from 'hearing' the surface thoughts of others and keep from broadcasting your own private thoughts. All three of you should have path ratings of five or higher, which means you should have no problems understanding one another, even across two or three miles of ocean.:

Lena and I look at each other. Without using telepathy, I know we're thinking the same thing. Of course Lena and I will have problems understanding each other.

Robry, on the other hand, has always understood me and my moods almost as well as Cam does, without using any telepathy.

:Robry?: I reach out carefully with my mind.

:I can 'hear' you fine,: he replies quickly.

Robry's mental voice is cheerful and sweet, but I can feel the fear he's trying to hide.

:Lena?: I reach out to her.

:Stay out of my brain, Fish Girl!:

:You're one to talk. Your lungs are changing just as fast as mine.:

:I'm not talking, if you haven't noticed, thanks to the highly illegal gene splicing your parents must have performed on me before I was even born, and I haven't spent most of my life swimming around with a bunch of dolphins.:

:No, but you used to swim with them all the time. Mariah still misses you.:

I feel Lena's sudden confusion and sadness, and instinctively she closes her mind to me. I sense I could push deeper into her thoughts, but I don't really want to know what Lena's thinking right now.

:Very good, Nere.: My mother breaks in on my thoughts. :You're right. You could reach deeper into Lena's mind. You were born such a strong telepath, you can push past others' natural shields the way I just did with your own. But you must never invade another person's privacy unless you absolutely have to. It's wrong, and trust me, you'll be happier if you don't know too much about what the people around you are thinking.:

:So, what happens next?: I ask. As strange as it feels to talk to her with my mind, I decide to keep using telepathy. I need that oxygen flowing through my mask.

:We wait for your oxygen levels to drop, and then we send you into the water.:

:I mean, if this crazy experiment of yours actually works and we start breathing water, what happens to us after that?:

:We head out to the Channel Islands. You'll swim there with the dolphins, and I'll come by boat when I can. There I'll help you with your transition to your new life in the sea, and then you'll travel north to join your father. He's been building an undersea colony for you called Safety Harbor in the Queen Charlotte Strait.:

She doesn't say that she's going to come as well, but I'm too furious with her right now to ask what she's planning to do.

Then her words sink in. He's building a colony? :You

mean there are others of us?:

:She did say that hundreds had gone through this transformation before us,: Robry points out.

My mother sits where she can read our monitors. I notice the solar pistol is never far from her hands.

:Twenty years ago, as our planet continued to heat, and people fought devastating wars over scarce resources like water and food, a group of geneticists devised the Neptune Project. All life came from the sea. In our darkest hour, they hoped the sea would save our species. So they set about altering their own unborn children in an effort to create humans who could survive in the ocean.:

I look into my mother's eyes and I see a light in them that frightens me. I realize this has been her dream all along.

:So I'm just a specimen you grew and operated on in a petri dish to make your dream come true.:

:That isn't true.: Her mental tone sounds much more like a mother suddenly, and her eyes soften. :I never knew how much I'd grow to love you and James. Your father and I risked everything to give you both a better life.:

:James! You altered his genes, too?:

I can tell she's choosing carefully which thoughts to send me next.

:We made a mistake with some of the genes we altered in James's case.:

:What do you mean, you made a mistake?:

:That's between James, your father, and me.: Her mental voice is tinged with a deep sadness.

I wonder if she'll feel that sad if she finds out she's made a mistake with me, too—like maybe those gill filaments in my lungs aren't going to work underwater and I'm going to drown in a few hours.

She gets to her feet and brings me a cup full of dark blue fluid. When I hesitate to take it, she says aloud, "There's no turning back now."

I snatch the cup from her, take off my oxygen mask, and drink it down. It tastes bitter and sour—nastier than any medicine she's ever given me before. Then she takes cups to the others.

"To our dear, darling parents, who stole our future before we were ever born," Lena says, her eyes glittering as she raises her cup in an angry toast. Then she downs its contents.

I wish I'd thought up that toast.

Almost right away, I start yawning. :What exactly did you give us?: I ask my mother.

:A chemical to hasten your transformation and a med that will make you sleep. The next phase is painful. It's better if you sleep through it.:

Normally I'm in favor of avoiding pain, but the trust factor is now at an all-time low between us. I fight to keep my eyes open.

What if the soldiers come, and Lena, Robry, and I are

unconscious? They'll probably kill us as soon as they realize what mutates we are. My mother's drug feels like cold
seawater creeping through my veins. My muscles relax, and
I slump over on the stone bench.

:If we all die from what you've done to us, I hope you
feel guilty for the rest of your life,: Lena says to Gillian, and
sends her a venomous glance.

My mother looks stricken by her words. As my heavy
eyelids sink shut, I can't help wondering if I'll ever wake up
again.

chapter eight

THE SECRET POLICE are chasing me down the dusty road to Santero. I can't run fast enough because my lungs are burning—I can't suck enough air into them. Suddenly, I'm in my school classroom, and everyone is laughing as I gasp and flop around on the floor because I have no legs. I've become a monster that is half fish, half human.

Somehow I have legs and feet again, and I run from school and dive into the sea. I see the Sandpiper in the distance. I wave desperately. Cam is at the helm. He raises a hand and steers the Sandpiper my way. When the boat comes near, he smiles and reaches down to help me aboard. He grabs my wrist, and finally I'm safe. But then his eyes fill with horror at what I've become, and he lets go of my hand. I fall back into the cold water, and Cam sails away, leaving me to cry my tears into the empty sea.

The dream changes again. I'm four and I hate the life vest my parents make me wear whenever we go out on the zode. I wiggle out of the vest while they aren't watching. I see a pretty orange fish deep beneath us. I reach for it and fall over the side.

I sink quickly through the cold, dark water. I open my mouth to cry, and the burning seawater comes rushing into my mouth and throat.

I sit up, instantly wide awake. This part of the dream is true. I'm drowning now, trying to breathe air! Gasping and panting, I rip off the oxygen mask. This is worse than my worst lung attack.

Dimly, I realize I'm sitting right next to the water, and the larger waves are actually slapping and pushing at me.

"Nere, it's time for you; you must go into the water and breathe!" my mother shouts.

I don't have enough air left in my chest to speak.

:I'm too scared!: I cry mentally instead. :I don't want to drown. You almost let me drown before.:

"I know, sweetling, but you have no choice now."

She kneels and smiles at me tenderly, and the next moment she shoves me into the water. I scrabble at the slippery rock, trying to find a handhold, trying to climb out. I have to get my face out of the black water. I have to breathe oxygen *now*!

Her relentless hands grab my head and force it under the water. I hit at her with all my strength, but she's too strong for me. I try to rear back and swim away, but somehow she tied me to the rock while I was unconscious.

:You'll be all right, sweetling.: I hear my mother's words in my mind. :I promise you. Just relax and breathe in.:

My lungs are pure fire now. I have to breathe. I have no strength left to fight her.

I open my mouth and the water rushes in, and I'm dying.

Black spots dance across my eyelids. Then I cough and choke, and I'm not dying anymore. I can breathe. I inhale and exhale, trying to get used to the incredible sensation of cold water rushing in and out of my chest.

I open my eyes underwater. Instantly, I realize my vision is different, too. I can see a carpet of purple and gray anemones growing on the rock floor far below me, small crabs scuttling about between them. Dozens of fish dart above the anemones, and clusters of starfish grow like strange orange flowers along the sides of the cave. I can see in the dark waters here better than I could before, even with a bright dive torch.

:Nere, are you all right?: my mother asks me urgently.

:I-I think so.:

I'm aware that Lena is in the water nearby me, and she's thrashing and flailing about. Gillian is kneeling right above her, trying to hold her head in the water. While I watch, Lena lands a punch on my mother's cheek.

:Just relax and breathe in—you can breathe water,: I call to Lena.

She lashes out at me so violently that I give up and leave her to her terror. Instead, I pop my head out of the water and look for Robry. He's on the other side of me, still sitting on the rock ledge, gasping for breath, his eyes dilated with fear.

:Robry, don't be afraid. I can breathe water fine now. You'll be all right.:

I strain against the harness holding me to the rock, and I reach out to him. I don't want his transition to be as terrifying as mine was.

:Take my hand, dartling.:

He grabs it and slides down into the water beside me.

:Just put your face in the water and breathe. It's easy as anything.: I try to keep my mental tone light, even though a part of me still can't believe I'm breathing seawater.

Because he trusts me, it's easier for him. He puts his face in the water, and with incredible self-control, he breathes in. He chokes the first time, just as I did, but then he gets the hang of it.

:This is *so* amazing,: he says.

:It gets more amazing. Open your eyes and look down.:

:I can see everything!:

I turn away from Robry to check on Lena. She is floating very still in the water next to me, her arms braced against the rock, her face in the sea.

:Are you all right?: I ask her tentatively.

Lena turns her head and glares at me. :Yeah, no thanks to your homicidal mother. She held my head under the water!:

:She did that to me, too. At least you punched her a good one.:

It occurs to me then to check on my mother. She sits slumped all alone on the ledge, her face deathly pale. That's when I realize just how scared she was for us. Even as I watch, she drags her sleeve across her eyes and seems to gather herself. She stands and walks up the tunnel toward our lab, the solar pistol back in her hand.

chapter nine

AFTER MY MOTHER CHECKS to make sure the secret police aren't coming down the tunnel in the next few minutes, she helps us out of the harnesses that kept us anchored by the rock ledge. After we all put on dive fins, Robry darts back and forth, exuberant as a young dolphin in the water.

:Why can't we go out there right now?: he says, looking toward the open sea.

:Because,: my mother tells us firmly, :first you need to realize that on land you were the top of the food chain, but in the sea, there are plenty of creatures capable of hurting and eating you.:

:I know there are plenty of dangerous predators in the ocean,: I say, interrupting her lecture. :That's why I still can't believe you've done this to us.:

:It's good that you're aware of the dangers, Nere,: Gillian replies, back in her scientist mode. :That awareness can help you stay alive. You must never forget how vulnerable you are, and you must never go anywhere in open water without the dolphins and a speargun.:

She tosses a weighted buoy into the water. :I want you

to practice firing at this target. Your life may well depend on how accurate you are with your weapons. As you practice, make sure you retrieve your spear darts. You probably won't have the opportunity to obtain new ones for a long time.:

Lena seems to take my mother's lecture about our lower place on the ocean food chain seriously. She grabs a speargun and a quiver and starts firing away at the buoy. At first she's rusty, but I'm relieved to see her old skill return to her. Robry and I practice as well, but I'm not sure it's necessary, because both of us have spent hours each week snorkeling through kelp forests shooting fish for our families' suppers, so . . .

While we're practicing, Gillian loads the zode with our packs and her own gear.

:That's enough for now,: she tells us. :Is anyone hungry? If you surface, you'll find you can still breathe air for short periods of time.:

Warily, I surface and take a breath. My mother is right. I can still breathe air, but now it feels dry and weird in my lungs.

Gillian hands us big thick ham sandwiches made with Alicia's wonderful bread. With a shudder, I wonder what I'll be eating in a few weeks. Somehow I doubt there's much fresh-baked bread where we're going. The idea of eating raw fish for the rest of my life, however long that's going to be, is beyond depressing.

"That's strange. I don't feel the least bit thirsty," Robry declares after he's halfway through his sandwich.

"That's because your body needs less water now. It can filter out the water you do need from the fish you'll be eating, just the way dolphins do," Gillian tells us.

When we finish the sandwiches, she checks her watch. "The tide should be low enough to get the zode out of here in another half hour. I'm going to come with you as far as Tyler's Cove just to make sure you get off all right," she says, and her gaze lingers on me.

"In the meantime, I want you to put these seasuits on over the swimsuits you're wearing now," she continues in her usual brisk way. "Both were designed by our scientists to function much like the slick skin of marine mammals, reducing drag as you swim. They also contain a light, strong polymer mesh that should protect your arms and legs from coral cuts and jellyfish stings."

She hands us the suits. After I wiggle into mine, I find it's surprisingly light and comfortable.

Next she hands each of us two dive knives, one to wear on a utility belt at our waists, and one in a sheath we strap on our calves. Then we don seapacks and adjust their straps so that they fit snugly and don't interfere with our swimming. Our spear quivers buckle onto the side of the packs so we can easily reach more spear darts.

Even though I'm still furious with her, I'm impressed

with the amount of thought my mother's obviously put into preparing each of us for travel in the open sea.

:It's past time we left here,: Gillian declares with another uneasy look up the tunnel. Then her gaze goes distant.

:The dolphins say the north cove is free of boats. They're eager to see the three of you now that you can stay underwater longer than they can,: she adds with a smile.

My mother goes first in the zode. She orders Lena to follow her, then Robry, with me bringing up the rear. We hold our loaded spearguns at the ready. The tide is just low enough for the zode to scrape under the craggy entrance to the cave. I realize it's a still, clear night when I surface on the other side. The pod is there, and the dolphins are overjoyed to see us.

Mariah heads straight for Lena and swims tight, happy circles about her.

:She missed me!: Lena says.

:Of course she did,: I say. :She never understood why you stopped coming to swim with her.:

I never understood, either, but this doesn't seem the right time or place to get into it with Lena. We pause long enough to introduce her to Tisi. As he butts against her playfully, I see Lena smile. I'm glad the dolphins can distract her. I know she's just lost everyone she cares about.

My throat tightens when I remember that I will be saying good-bye to Cam soon. I don't know if I'll ever see him again. I don't know how long I will survive in the sea. I don't know how long he will survive living away from it, but Cam is strong and stubborn.

:a big boat comes.: Densil's words break in on my thoughts. :it sounds like the dark one with the big motors,: he warns us from the mouth of the cove, where he's keeping watch.

It must be a Marine Guard cutter. A cold wave of fear surges though me, leaving me feeling shaky and breathless. My mother is the first to react.

:Right. The three of you help me get the zode behind that big rock. I'll hide with it, and then you are going to dive for the bottom and stay there until that boat goes.:

I hear Gillian issue rapid orders to the dolphins as well. :Mariah, take the pod inside the cave. If they see you surface, they may guess we're nearby. Densil, stay where you are and don't let them see you.:

My heart is in my mouth as we push the black zode toward the large rock, kicking as fast as we can. Once it's hidden directly behind the rock, Gillian slips into the water and holds the zode steady.

:Go, and don't you dare surface, even if they find me. The latitude and longitude of your father's colony is marked on charts in each of your packs. Now dive!:

My pulse racing, I slip beneath the water and kick for the bottom of the cove. Robry and Lena have found a big rock slab to hide under, and I join them, keeping a wary eye out for eels.

I can hear the deep-pitched rumble of the cutter's engine and feel the vibrations from its powerful screws churning through the water. Then those engines cut back to idle, and the big boat glides into the cove.

Seconds later, a brilliant light dances across the surface above our heads. They must be using a searchlight to sweep the cove. Will they spot the zode? No matter how angry I am with my mother, I don't want the Marine Guard to take her away.

chapter ten

:ROBRY, WHAT ABOUT OUR locater chips?: I ask him in a panic. :They might have tracking equipment on that boat!: Instinctively, I touch where the chip is embedded. I wince because my left armpit feels so sore.

:That's why we're hiding under this rock. It might help block their sensors. Plus, there's easily fifty feet of water over our heads.:

:That was quick thinking, Robry,: my mother says, breaking in on our mental conversation. :But I removed your locator chips while you were sleeping. You'll need to keep an eye on your stitches. We designed you to heal quickly, but your wounds can still get infected.:

Her mental tone is awfully calm for someone with only a rock between her and a trip to a work camp.

:Are you all right?: I ask her. :What about your chip?:

:Mine is buried in the last heel of Alicia's bread in our kitchen, where Hycault is welcome to find and choke on it.:

I chew my lip. My mother has truly burned her bridges. Removing a locator chip is a serious crime. If they do find her, she's heading to a work camp for sure.

:I think they're moving on now,: she reports, and moments later we hear the powerful engines start up.

I relax only when I can't hear or feel the vibrations from the cutter anymore. I glance at Robry and Lena. They are both pale.

:Do you think they were looking for us?: Lena's mental tone is subdued.

:I bet they're searching for fisher folk who decided to try to run rather than move inland,: I tell her, but I'm not sure my words make any of us feel safer.

After Densil reports that the Marine Guard cutter has moved on well to the north of us, we begin carefully working our way along the coast to Tyler's Cove. Lena and I travel beside Gillian's zode while the dolphins swim in a protective formation around us. Robry keeps darting down to the ocean floor to look at fish and shells. He flushes a large, harmless angel shark out of the sand and laughs when it startles us.

:This is so much better than swimming with a snorkel!: he exclaims. :I can't believe I can see everything so well!:

I'm glad one of us is happy. I've never loved night diving, even though my parents insisted that I do plenty of it. Under a dive torch, the colors of reefs and marine creatures become brilliant, but I can't forget that sharks and squid are constantly on the prowl in the dark.

:I wish you three would head straight out to sea right now,: Gillian says, and I can sense the strain in her mental tone. :Hycault may already have troops combing the coastal hills for us.:

:But I have to see Cam one more time!: My chest tightens at the thought of heading off into this dark, dangerous ocean without saying good-bye to him.

Then an awful possibility occurs to me.

:Can I even talk to him now? How long can I breathe at the surface?: I don't want to say good-bye to Cam if it's going to be like my nightmare where I became a monster that's half fish and half human.

:Your lungs can function for a brief time out of water, but then they will begin to labor.:

:You mean I'll be just like a fish out of water, flopping around and gasping for air.: I can't bear the idea of Cam seeing me that way.

:No, your lungs should work better than that, but you may start to feel light-headed after several minutes above the surface.:

:We are close to the cove now. Do you think my parents will come?: Robry asks me.

With a pang, I remember that Robry is about to lose his whole family. At least I'll see my mother as she supervises our "transition," as she calls it, to our life in the ocean, and

I can look forward to seeing my father again—if I can bring myself to forgive him by then.

:I doubt it, dartling,: I reply sadly. :I heard Gillian tell Cam to come by himself. At least you can see him one more time.:

Robry stops exploring. Instead he swims quietly beside me, his face set. We reach the entrance to Tyler's Cove at four thirty a.m., according to my marine watch, which means we have over an hour until sunrise. I'm tired, but I don't feel the least bit sleepy. I'm too worried about whether or not Cam made it past the Marine Guard.

My mother sends the dolphins ahead of us to check for boats. They report back that there's just one small dinghy drawn up on the cove's only beach. Gillian insists that we leave our fins, seapacks, and spearguns at the bottom of the cove, where we can retrieve them safely, just in case we have to leave here in a hurry.

After we surface at the entrance to the cove, I look toward the beach. A shadow detaches itself from the rocks beside it. Even from this distance I can tell it's Cam. I tense when I realize there are two more people with him. Lena's parents have come as well.

"I told them it was dangerous for everyone," Cam says to Gillian the instant she beaches the zode, "but they insisted on coming."

Lena hurriedly splashes out of the water. For all her talk

of being angry with her parents, she throws herself into her mother's arms. I follow her out of the water more slowly. I'm trying to get used to breathing air again. My mother was right: I can breathe it, but it feels dry and strange, and there's not nearly enough oxygen in it.

Lena and her mother are crying now, and Lena is speaking angrily to her father. I turn away to give them privacy.

Cam is talking with Gillian. I hear the tension in his voice. "I don't think we were followed, but I can't be sure. There're soldiers everywhere now."

"We have to make this quick, then," my mother declares, even as she scans the steep hillsides around the cove.

"Robry, you can say good-bye first," I say thickly. I need more time to pull myself together. Now that I'm here with Cam, I don't want to cry all over his shirt.

Robry looks at me and nods. I retreat back toward the surf so that they can be alone. Cam talks urgently to him, his hand on Robry's shoulder.

I think I'll always remember them that way: Robry standing there in a wash of moonlight, trying to be brave and looking like a smaller version of his big brother. Then Cam gives Robry a long hug. It's as if he's trying to pass on the love and caring of their entire family.

Robry splashes past me into the water, staring down at his feet, his face wet with tears. Suddenly, I'm facing Cam all by myself. I walk out of the surf to be closer to him.

All at once there's such a big lump in my throat that I have to struggle to speak. "What are you going to do?"

"I'm sailing south once I drop off Lena's parents. I might try to start a sail-making business with some of my cousins on the other side of the border."

I frown, thinking of the armed patrol boats he must pass in his tiny sailboat.

"Promise me that you'll be careful," is all I can think to say. I feel tears well up in my eyes. Gillian altered my body in so many other ways; why didn't she plug up my stupid tear ducts while she was at it?

"Nere, there's a chance I will see you again," Cam says, his dark eyes intent. "If you ever need help, get word to me through the smugglers. I'll come."

I can only nod, afraid to trust my voice. I must look miserable, though, because moments later, he hugs me. I bury my face in his shoulder, his arms tighten around me, and finally I feel safe.

"No matter what happens, I'll always love you," he whispers in my ear. I close my eyes. Do I love him back? I just know Cam is more important to me than any friend I've ever had. I open my eyes and raise my face to him, and then he kisses me. I realize I've been waiting forever for this. Cam's lips are soft and he smells like salt water and fresh sea air. I wrap my arms around his neck and kiss him back.

"There they are!" Hycault's exultant shout rings out over the little cove, and we freeze. I look up just in time to see dozens of soldiers charging down the hillside directly toward us.

chapter eleven

I STARE AT THE SOLDIERS stupidly until Cam shoves me toward the water.

"Run!" he yells. Then he turns to face the rush of men. He pulls a knife from a sheath at his belt and tries to block their path to me.

"Cam!" I shout.

Even as I watch, he's hit by a blast from a solar rifle. He staggers and drops his knife.

"No!" I cry, and struggle to reach him. But someone's holding my arms.

"Nere, there's nothing we can do!" Robry yells. He and Lena are there, dragging me toward the water.

"You've got to come with us. He'd want you to get away," Robry insists, but I can hear the tears in his voice.

Somehow Cam is still standing. The soldiers are on him now. He punches the first one in the face and knocks a second one off his feet. But a third raises the butt of his rifle and slams it into Cam's head. He crumples to the sand.

Stumbling backward into the sea, I hear the hiss of solar

shots hitting the waves all around us. It's hard for me to see past the tears that flood my eyes. Vaguely, I'm aware that the soldiers have surrounded Lena's parents. But where's my mother?

I see a soldier aim his rifle at me. His red sighting beam blinds me. I brace myself and close my eyes, expecting to be seared.

The red light against my eyelids abruptly disappears. I open my eyes. My mother has stepped between me and the soldier. She looks over her shoulder and sends me a motherly smile with no scientist in it.

Robry wrestles me down into the water. Before my head goes under the waves, I see the beam of killing light from the soldier's solar rifle slice through her.

I'm screaming and choking on bitter seawater as I dive for the bottom of the cove.

:We've got to swim deeper to avoid that solar fire and get back to our equipment,: Robry urges Lena and me.

I barely hear his words while I swim after him. I can't believe my mother is dead.

We reach the equipment we stashed in a pile at the bottom of the cove. With shaking hands, I drag on the fins that Robry thrusts at me.

:the big boat is here. divers are jumping into the water,: Densil warns us. :they have spearguns and tows that pull them fast!:

:We've got to get past those divers and under that cut-ter. Our only chance to lose them is if we hide in the kelp forest outside the cove,: Robry tells us.

Quickly, I relay his words to the dolphins.

:we will pull you to the kelp,: Mariah declares, her mental voice remarkably calm.

:we can swim faster than their tows,: Sokya adds, smug as always.

:your mother comes later?: Mariah asks me. I realize the dolphins must not have seen what happened onshore.

:She's not coming later. They killed her.: I'm careful to send her only the words and not the terrible image of Gillian's death. I know Mariah loved my mother, and I don't want that image to haunt her, too.

I sense the shock and grief erupting in Mariah's mind. She and five other dolphins appear moments later.

:little one, I am sorry.: Mariah nudges me gently with her beak. :but we have no time now to be sad.:

Robry hands spearguns to Lena and me. :Clip these to your seapack,: he orders. :You're going to need both hands to hold on to the dolphins' fins.:

I'm amazed and grateful that he is thinking so quickly. My mind feels like it's full of sea sludge.

I look toward the mouth of the cove. The glow of the divers' powerful torches creates halos of brightness in the dark water. The divers are spreading out to cut off our only escape route. The cutter's search beam flashes across the waves over our heads.

Suddenly, Densil and his older sister, Halia, are on either side of me. :grab hold,: Densil orders, and for a change I obey him. Mariah and Ricca tow Lena, and Kona and Nika pull Robry.

As soon as I have a firm grip on their dorsal fins, Densil and Halia surge forward, their powerful tails thrusting against the water. It's a good thing that I've got a strong hold on them. Here beneath the waves, the force of the water pushing against me is much stronger than when a dolphin team pulls me at the surface.

We race forward and the deep bass rumble of the cutter's engines grows louder and louder. Now we are so close I squint against the brightness of the divers' lights. I can barely make out the dark shapes of the divers holding them. One jerks the light around to shine it on me. They've spotted us!

:Faster, Densil, Halia!: I urge them. The dolphins sprint forward, aiming for the largest gap between the divers. I feel the rush of spear darts and hear their high-pitched whine as they slice through the water all around us. *Please, don't let the dolphins get hit.*

All at once we are past the divers. The dark hull of the cutter looms overhead, its propellers slicing through the water, and then we slip under it as well. Our dolphin teams race on toward the black waters beyond the cove. A few more spear darts hiss after us, but we're already out of range.

I glance back. Some of the divers are following us, and the tows they're using are faster than any I've seen before!

My shoulders and arms begin to burn from the strain of being pulled through the water by Halia and Densil, and my fingers cramp from holding on to their dorsals. The rumble of the cutter's engines grows louder and louder until it seems to fill the water all around us. The boat catches up and then keeps pace over our heads. Someone aboard must be tracking us with sonar. I keep seeing odd flashes of light along its black hull.

:They're firing solar rifles into the water, hoping to hit us,: Robry informs me grimly. :But I don't think their solar fire can reach us at this depth. If we split up in the kelp, there's a chance we can lose them.:

:But the dolphins have to breathe soon,: I remind him.

:I know. I think we're almost there.:

I glance back. I can tell by the brighter glow from their torches that the divers are getting closer.

:We made it!: Robry shouts.

Within moments, we're surrounded by tall, swaying stems. I've never been so happy to see a kelp forest in my life.

:Leave us here, and go breathe,: I tell Densil and Mariah, :but be careful to surface far from that boat.:

Seconds later, the dolphins are gone.

:Come on, we've got to work our way deeper into this kelp,: Robry tells Lena and me.

We follow him down into the forest, swimming as fast as we can. I'm amazed at how well I can see my way through the dense plants. In the daytime, kelp forests shut out much of the light, and at night they are incredibly dark.

:Stay clear of the fronds,: I warn Lena. :You can't let your seapack get tangled.:

:We need to find a cave or an overhang along the bottom where we can hide from their sonar,: Robry says as he swims swiftly along.

I look back and see a faint glow through the dense kelp fronds. The divers have reached the edge of the forest.

Robry follows my glance. :At least they can't use their tows in here. Their props would get jammed with kelp fronds in no time.:

:Let's split up. They're less apt to detect our body masses that way. Swim north and try to find a good hiding place,: I tell the others.

We head off in three slightly different directions, swimming fast. I head deeper into the forest until I'm skimming along between the holdfasts that anchor the towering kelp stems to the sea floor. After checking the compass on my dive watch, I head due north. Crabs scuttle away from me, startled by my presence.

It's eerie swimming through the silent black forest by myself. I've always dove and snorkeled with a partner before, particularly at night. Occasionally I scare up an orange Garibaldi fish that startles me as much as I startle it before it darts away into the depths of the kelp.

Just when I feel like I'm all alone in this vast, dark ocean, Robry's mind touches mine. :I can't see the divers' lights anymore.:

:I can see three to the south of me,: Lena reports. :And they're moving fast even without their tows.: Her mental voice sounds anxious and tired.

I pick up the pace and contact Robry on a private send. :The sun's going to rise soon. We can see the divers coming now because of their lights, but they'll be able to turn them off in a few minutes. Then we won't have any warning before they get close.:

:I know,: he says. :We've got to find a hiding place soon.:

The sea grows lighter. Several long, low rock ridges cross the ocean floor below me. Daylight begins to filter down through the dense stems. The back of my neck tingles as I swim past kelp fronds. I can imagine a spear dart piercing me at any moment.

And then I see the dark gash of an opening under a rock overhang, mostly covered by kelp holdfasts. I dart forward and peer in carefully.

:I found a cave big enough to hold all of us!: I tell Lena and Robry.

:Great,: Robry says. :But now, how do we find you?:

I send them images of the rocky ridges and the cave mouth. My heart lurches when I realize neither image is specific enough to help them find me in this maze of kelp.

chapter Twelve

TRYING NOT TO PANIC, I rack my brain for a quick way to find Robry and Lena and show them where I am. The light is getting stronger by the minute. Shivers trace down my back when I picture what could happen to Lena and Robry if those divers find them.

I have to call Densil and Sokya. :The divers still hunt us. Find me, and then find Lena and Robry and lead them back to me. I found a good place to hide.:

:we come,: Densil says. :our mother stays with the pod to nurse the little one.:

I tell Robry and Lena to be on the lookout for the dolphins while I keep a lookout for Marine Guard divers. Just a few minutes later, Sokya darts up to me, whistling and squeaking happily over her accomplishment.

:my brother has found the small male and brings him. I go find the female who makes you angry and sad.:

Sokya flashes away. Does Lena really make me angry and sad? I stare after Sokya in surprise. That's the problem with using telepathy. I know the dolphins often sense more than just the words and images I send them.

Densil appears with Robry and then dashes off to help Sokya.

:How are you?: I ask Robry. His face is pale, and there are purple shadows under his eyes. The shadows I see in his eyes worry me more.

:Tired. You?:

:Tired, too.: I shut him off from the images I don't want him to see that still replay in my mind. If I try to talk about Gillian or Cam, I'm afraid I'll lose it.

:Do you want to watch for those divers, or do you want to clear out the cave?: I ask.

:I'll clear out the cave,: he says quickly. Robry knows I don't like small, dark places.

:Be careful. I spotted at least one moray in there.:

:After what we faced tonight, tackling moray eels sounds pretty tame,: he says with an effort at a smile.

He takes off his pack. Holding it and his speargun in front of him, he cautiously enters the cave. Soon, three long morays with dead gray eyes swim their sinuous way out of the dark opening and disappear into the kelp. Suddenly, Robry starts swearing.

:Are you all right in there?: I look into the cave and see that a large moray with evil-looking teeth has clamped its jaw onto the corner of Robry's pack. Robry whacks it twice with the butt of his speargun. At last the big eel gives up the fight. I barely have time to duck out of the way before it arrows past my head.

:Is that it?:

:I think we'll be sharing quarters with a small octopus

that doesn't want to leave, and there are three spiny lobsters on the floor I want to catch. At least we can have lobster for dinner later,: he says, trying to sound cheerful.

I don't have the heart to tell him just how disgusting raw lobster sounds to me. I turn around to watch for Marine Guard divers. Sokya appears between the kelp stems, Densil right behind her, towing Lena.

:this female let go of my fin twice,: Sokya complains. :divers saw us. they chased us, but we were faster.:

:we will lead them away. one of us will come back and keep watch,: Densil says.

:Thank you,: I tell them both.

The dolphins disappear into the kelp. My mother was right. We never could have survived our first hours in the sea without them.

:I hope you've found a place I can sleep for the next two days,: Lena says. She looks ten times worse than Robry. Her face is pale, her eyes are red, and her whole body slumps with exhaustion.

Robry pops his head out of the cave and grins at us. :A hammock awaits you.:

I force myself to swim in after Lena. I try to ignore how small the cave feels as its black walls close in around me. I see that Robry has already strung up his own hammock.

:Can I sleep in that thing?: Lena asks him.

:Sure.:

:Thanks, kid,: Lena says and heads straight for the hammock.

:You should probably eat something first,: I tell her, but Lena ignores me. She pulls off her seapack and fins, drops her speargun, and crawls into the hammock. Seconds later, she's fast asleep.

Frowning, I pick up her gear and wedge it into a crack in the cave wall so it doesn't drift away. After taking two food pouches from my pack, I pull out my own hammock and stash my equipment in another crack.

:We should eat, and then one of us should keep watch,: I say to Robry, and hand him a food packet. Now that we've found safety of a sort, exhaustion slams into me. I can hardly find the energy to chew the fish bar I find in my packet.

:The dolphins will keep watch for us,: Robry says. :We both need to rest.:

:Aren't you afraid they'll accidentally lead the divers here?: I ask, fighting a huge yawn. :Now Hycault and the Marine Guard must know the dolphins are helping us.:

:I think Sokya and Densil are smart enough not to let themselves be seen,: Robry replies thoughtfully. :The divers probably spotted them this time because they were helping Lena.:

I glance over at Lena, deep in an exhausted sleep.

:Do you think she's strong enough to survive down here?: That's just one of a dozen worries whirling around in my mind while I tiredly set up my hammock.

:Are any of us?: he asks me in return.

I grimace as I lie down and tie myself into the hammock. It's a good question, and I don't know the answer.

~ ~ ~

It's nighttime when I wake up. For a long, terrible minute, I have no idea where I am. Why is there a dark rock wall above my head? I take a deep breath. I'm startled when I feel cold water flow down my windpipe and enter my chest. Then my memories come flooding back. I remember my mother holding my head under the waves until seawater came rushing into my lungs. I see Cam stagger when the solar blast hits him, and then the soldier clubs his head, and Cam falls to the sand. I try not to picture the moment they killed my mother, but it's no use.

Now I know exactly where I am and why I'm here in this close black cave. I shut my eyes. Tearing sobs rise up inside me. I cover my mouth with my hands in case the sound carries to the others. If only James were here. Maybe he'd understand the mixed-up pain and anger clawing at my insides. But my big brother isn't here, and I've never been so alone.

I cry until my head aches and I run out of tears. At last I drift off to sleep again.

When I wake up, it's lighter inside our cave. I check my watch and see it's actually seven in the morning. I've just slept for almost twenty-six hours. I wonder if my body is still recovering from its transformation.

Robry is cutting up a lobster and methodically sucking the meat from its legs. I sit up in my hammock, and he smiles at me.

:Are you ready for some breakfast?:

To my surprise, I realize I'm so hungry, even raw lobster sounds good.

:In a minute, maybe. I'm still half asleep. Is Lena awake?:

:I am now, thanks to you thinking so loudly,: Lena says grumpily. :And I am NOT going to eat raw lobster. Don't we have some sort of food bars in our packs?:

I glance over to see Lena is sitting up in her hammock, glaring at both of us balefully. Her long hair floats around her in a tangled cloud.

:Yes,: I tell her. :But you're going to have to get used to eating raw fish. Those food bars will run out eventually.:

:I'll wait for eventually, thank you very much.: Lena glances around the cave and rubs her eyes. :Where's my seapack, anyway?:

:I wedged it in that crack over there. You've got to tie your stuff down when you go to sleep, or it could drift away.:

:Do I look like I want to hear a lecture right now?:

Do I look like I want to deal with your attitude right now? :Lena, if you want to survive in the sea, you've got to look after your own equipment.:

Her face tightens, but I'm relieved when she doesn't keep arguing with me. I take the dead lobster that Robry hands me and start picking the raw meat from its tail with my dive knife.

Lena gets out of her hammock and fetches her pack. :So what's our plan?:

I glance over at Robry. :We do need to start figuring out a plan.:

:I've been looking through our seapacks,: he says slowly. :Your mother left each of us a packet of instructions. I . . . I think maybe she guessed we might have trouble getting away, and that something might happen to her.:

:So what do her instructions say?: I ask, fighting to keep my mental voice steady.

:I haven't had a chance to read them carefully yet, but she planned for us to hide in that old freighter that sank off the north coast of Santa Cruz Island. She knew we'd need time to adjust to living in the sea, and the *Alicante* was the safest place she could think of.:

Robry looks down at his hands. :That's also where the rest of us are supposed to rendezvous,: he adds after a moment.

:The rest of us?: Lena asks quickly.

:There are at least fifty more kids like us, from villages and towns up and down the coast of the southern sector, who were . . . altered like we were. If there was a government crackdown, their mentors were supposed to complete these kids' transformations and send them to this wreck for training. Then, when we're all fit and ready, we're to travel to the colony up north that Dr. Hanson has been building for us. The first generation of the Neptune Project.:

The idea that we're all part of some kind of giant science experiment makes me want to slam the dead lobster against the cave wall. I can tell from Lena's expression that she feels the same way.

:I don't think we can stay here for long,: I admit when my anger recedes a little. :Too many Marine Guard boats cruise these waters.:

:I agree,: Robry says. :Maybe we should head out to the Channel Islands. Mostly just smugglers sail that way, and there'll probably be fewer fishing boats there now.:

I sense his pain at the thought of what has happened to his family before he closes his mind to us.

:But what are we going to do after that?: Lena asks. :Are we really going to try to swim the length of the Western Collective to find some colony we don't even know exists?:

:I think getting to Santa Cruz will be enough of a challenge for now,: I reply. Twenty-five miles of sea lie between us and the Channel Islands. :Later we can decide if we want to try to find my father.:

I take a minute to check in with the dolphins.

:Densil, Sokya, are you near here?:

:I watch your cave,: Densil replies promptly.

:What are the divers and boats doing?:

:all the divers left the water. now the boats are stopping outside the kelp.:

This news makes the hair on the back of my neck rise. Why are the boats still here? Why aren't the divers in the water looking for us?

I swim to the entrance of the cave. Sunlight filters down through the towering columns of greenish-brown kelp overhead. The fronds sway and wave gently, moved by stray currents. It is so peaceful here. I've always liked swimming through kelp in the daytime. The redwoods are long gone now, but I've seen pictures of them. I can understand why people say kelp beds are like the redwood forests of the ocean.

Suddenly, I hear a deep, muted roar that vibrates through the water and fills my ears, and the cave begins to shake. I reach out to steady myself. Robry and I stare at each other in shock.

:Robry, what's going on??? Is this an earthquake?:

The roar subsides, but seconds later another rumble rips through the water. I feel Densil's pain and panic. His hearing is a hundred times more sensitive than ours.

:This is no earthquake!: Robry cries. :They're launching depth charges into the water!:

chapter Thirteen

A LARGE PIECE of rock breaks loose from the cave roof. It just misses Robry's head before it crashes to the floor. I don't want to be buried alive! I lunge for my seapack and hammock. Desperately, I reach for Densil with my mind.

:Densil, leave now! We'll call you when it's safe. Tell the others to stay away. Hurry!:

:I go!:

I long to bolt out of this dark, tight cave. But I can't leave my equipment. With shaking hands, I take down my hammock and thrust it into my pack. Robry and Lena are scrambling to gather up their gear as well. Another depth charge detonates nearby like a muffled clap of thunder. Moments later the water feels denser, and my ears ache. That explosion definitely was closer than the other two.

:We've got to get out of here. Does everyone have everything?: I glance back at Lena, making sure she has her speargun and seapack.

:We should split up to avoid getting detected by sonar,: Robry declares before we venture out.

:Stay as close to the sea floor as you can,: I add. :And duck under rock ledges if a boat starts following you. Let's swim on a heading of three hundred and five degrees and join up again in two hours.: If we're still alive in two hours.

:Lena, do you remember how to use the compass on your dive watch?: I ask because I don't want to think about the odds against us.

She nods, her face pale.

:Good luck, you guys!: I grip my speargun tightly and swim out of the cave first.

A cloud of sediment kicked up by the depth charges envelops me. The water is so murky that even with my genetically altered vision I have problems seeing more than a few feet ahead. I take a bearing on my compass and start swimming north and west as fast as I can.

An instant later, another depth charge goes off with a bass roar. The current from the shock waves spins me upside down, and my ears pop. The cave must have been protecting us from most of the force of the explosions. I right myself and keep kicking as fast as I can, threading my way through the violently swaying kelp. I glance back to check on the others, but Robry and Lena have already disappeared into the cloudy water.

:We need to get away from here before they drop one of those things right on top of us!: Robry gasps.

:I hope the dolphins got away in time,: I say while I concentrate on swimming faster.

:I hope *we* get away in time!: Lena chimes in.

Massive rafts of kelp plants torn loose by the blasts block my way. I have to swim more slowly to keep from getting tangled in the mangled stems. The only good news is that the depth charges have created such a mess down here, it's going to be harder for the boats' sonar to get a fix on us. I flinch when I come face-to-face with a dead sea lion caught in the kelp.

Another explosion sends the kelp dancing.

:That one felt like it was farther away,: Lena says hopefully.

Abruptly, I come to the end of the forest. I peer upward, looking for the dark hulls of Marine Guard boats, but it's useless. I can only see a few feet in any direction. That's not good news if I run into a shark, but then again, any sea creature that can swim is probably leaving here as fast as it can.

I take another bearing off my compass. My speargun at the ready, I dart out of the kelp. My blood pounds in my ears while I swim swiftly and keep as close to the sea floor as possible. Kicking hard, I keep waiting for a charge to explode right over me. A few minutes later, I check in with Robry and Lena.

:I'm out of the kelp,: Lena reports, :and I haven't seen any boats or divers.:

:I'm afraid I'm in trouble,: Robry says, his mental voice tense. :Divers with tows found me right after I left the kelp.:

:I'm on my way.: Even while I swim in the direction Robry took, I realize it is going to be almost impossible for me to find him in this cloudy sea.

:Densil, Sokya, we need you to find Robry. Divers are after him!: I call to them desperately.

:we come,: Densil replies at once, cool and calm as always.

:Nere, don't try to help me,: Robry protests. :There're too many of them.:

:I'm not going on without you!:

:I'm coming, too,: Lena says, breaking in on us.

:Lena, you shouldn't. At least one of us should get away.:

:How long do you think I'd last down here without you guys? Besides, I've always liked the kid.:

I swallow a lump in my throat as I race through the sea. My legs burn from the effort of kicking so quickly and for so long. :I like him, too.:

I hit a patch of water with better visibility and my heart freezes. Through sheer luck, I've found him. Above me, Robry is surrounded by eight divers who have lethal-looking spearguns trained on his body. They are herding him toward a big black net.

Lena appears at my side while I'm checking to make sure my speargun is ready to fire. :This isn't good,: she says, taking in the situation at a glance. Then she checks to make sure her own speargun is ready. Lena's always had guts.

:We could die doing this,: I warn her.

:I didn't think we were going to last long down here anyway,: she says with a shrug. But her face is pale.

:Let's go.: I charge through the water, my pulse hammering in my ears. At least we have surprise on our side. The divers are so focused on forcing Robry into the net that none of them notices us until we're close enough to shoot our spearguns.

I take aim at the nearest diver. I wish I could just shoot him in the leg or arm, but it's easier to hit a man's body. Besides, he and his crewmates were trying to blow me up a few minutes ago.

I fire, and the diver jerks as my dart pierces his shoulder. Quickly, I reload and move in closer, picking another target. I fire again, trying to imagine I'm shooting at a big grouper instead of at another human being. Again my spear dart goes home. Lena's first shot misses, but her second takes a third diver in the leg.

The men see us now. They turn and aim their spearguns at us. Lena and I are in serious trouble.

Suddenly, Densil and Sokya appear. The dolphins are a blur of motion, biting the divers' air hoses and slamming the men with their tails. Something burns across my thigh, but I manage to shoot a fourth diver in the shoulder. I reload but don't shoot again, afraid I might hurt one of the dolphins.

There are so many clouds of bubbles streaming from cut air hoses, I can't see what's happening. Then I realize that the divers are heading for the surface, towing their injured with them. They're giving up!

Robry darts to the bottom to search for the speargun they made him drop, and Lena and Sokya help. Now that the fight's over, I realize the graze on my leg stings horribly. I pull a pressure bandage from the first-aid kit in my pack and wrap it around my thigh.

I keep an eye out for sharks as I work. They can smell tiny amounts of blood, and I don't want one following me along with Marine Guard divers.

:I found my speargun!: Robry cries.

:Let's get going,: I reply, as a small mako shark appears from the east. I lead us north and west. We need to get back to a rockier area, where we'll have a better chance of hiding from the boats' sonar.

We swim hard, with Densil and Sokya alternating pulling us through the sea, but I can hear the deep rumble of large boat engines closing in fast. The big cutter passes directly over our heads. Then it slows, and several more divers with tows splash into the water ahead of us.

Robry, Lena, and I look at one another in despair. It's daylight now, and we have no place to hide from the Marine Guard's sonar or their divers this time.

chapter fourteen

SHOULD I CALL the whole pod to help us? The dolphins would be easy targets for Marine Guard divers in the daylight. But we're easy targets, too. The divers are starting to spread out in a large circle around us. Densil and Sokya drive through the water, towing us south now, where the divers haven't had a chance to close the circle.

Suddenly, a large dolphin appears in front of us. I blink when I realize it's towing an older boy who's wearing fins but no dive gear, just like us. His dolphin stops in front of me, and the boy takes a seapack from his back and pulls something from it.

:You look like you could use a little help,: he says with a cocky smile.

I stare at him in astonishment. He has dark eyes, pale skin, and long black hair caught back in braids.

:My friends are coming, but this should give those air-breathers something to think about in the meantime.:

After punching a button on a round metal device, he places it in his dolphin's mouth and points upward. A second later, the dolphin darts toward the boat.

:Come on!: the strange boy calls as he starts swimming

away from the divers and the cutter, back in the direction he came. :We don't want to be here when that magnetic mine goes off. Your dolphins don't, either.:

As I follow him, I warn Sokya and Densil, :Swim away from here, fast! There's about to be another explosion.:

:we go!: Sokya cries, and she and Densil dart away.

:Who *are* you?: I ask, while I struggle to keep up with him.

:We'll have time for introductions later,: the boy says, and fires his speargun at the first diver to close in on us. The boy's weapon has greater range than mine. His dart takes the diver in the belly.

I glance back. With a cold rush of fear, I realize Lena has fallen behind us. Another diver with a tow is closing in on her fast, and his speargun is trained on her.

:Lena, dive!: I cry, even as I kick upward to get a better angle for a shot.

Startled, she twists downward, and I shoot, praying I don't hit her. I catch the diver in the arm, and he veers off. Robry wounds a third diver in the leg, and the rest retreat for now.

:Nice shooting.: The boy grins at Robry and me both, revealing white, sharp teeth, and then he glances at a watch on his wrist.

:Cover your ears,: he orders. I just have time to cover mine before I hear a muffled roar from the mine detonating.

I'm spun upside down. My ears ache and all I can see for a very long minute is air bubbles.

:Whew, what a ride!: The strange boy sounds excited rather than scared. :That should teach those landlivers not to mess with us.:

:Is everyone all right?: I ask Robry and Lena.

:I'm still here,: Robry reports shakily as he floats up beside me.

:I think I'm here, no thanks to this maniac,: Lena says sharply as she joins us. I can tell the moment she gets a good look at the boy, though, because her resentful expression disappears in a heartbeat.

I leave Lena to her staring while I search the waters around us for divers. I'm relieved to see they're surfacing. I hope the cutter has a big hole in its hull and its crew will be heading for shore shortly in lifeboats.

:more swimming humans like you are headed your way,: Sokya warns me.

Swimming humans like me? I love my dolphins, but sometimes I wish we could communicate more clearly. I look to the south, and I spot a group of kids swimming toward us. I reload my speargun and raise it just in case.

:Those are the friends I mentioned. You don't need to be frightened,: the strange boy says to me.

:I'm not frightened,: I say, lying through my teeth. :I just like to be prepared.:

:That is always a wise thing to be in the sea,: he says solemnly, but when I glance his way, I see laughter in his eyes. Nothing about this situation seems the least bit funny to me.

When they draw closer, I see they are equipped much like we are, with fins, seapacks, seasuits, and spearguns. The group seems to be swimming in a set formation. Quickly, I count two girls and three boys.

While the rest hang back and eye us curiously, a muscular, stocky boy who appears to be their leader swims forward. The closer he gets, the tougher he looks. He has cool, pale blue eyes; his blond hair is cut short; and he has a livid red scar across his right cheekbone. This boy's skin is tanned, as if he'd lived much of his life in the sun. Even without reading his thoughts, I can tell he's furious.

:You used another mine, didn't you, Dai? Now we only have four left.:

:At the time, it seemed like a good idea.: The dark-haired boy looks bored.

:I'll say.: I'm not surprised to hear Lena speak up for our rescuer. :We had a cutter and eight Marine Guard divers after us, and they were about to shoot us full of spear darts.:

:Well, maybe it was necessary to use that mine,: the stocky boy admits after a long moment, :but don't disobey my orders again.:

Dai sends the blond-haired boy a disdainful salute, which makes his face tighten.

:My name is Kyel,: he says to us, all business. :We're members of the Neptune Project, and we're heading for the rendezvous point off Santa Cruz Island. We'll be safer if we travel together. We can talk on the way there, but we need to get moving before more boats come.:

He stares at the bandage on my leg. :Are you bleeding? We can't afford any shark attacks along the way.:

Does he think I'm a complete idiot? Kyel is starting to annoy me. :I've got this cinched down pretty tightly,: I tell him shortly.

:All right, then. I'll lead off, and we'll swim in a close formation. If we hear any boat traffic, we scatter to avoid sonar detection. You:—he nods to me—:swim beside me and tell me about your group.:

I want to salute him like Dai did. I feel as if I've just joined the military.

Kyel leads off, I swim beside him, and the others follow in a diamond formation behind us. Lena and Robry join the rest, and Dai brings up the rear, his big dolphin swimming at his side. I am impressed with how carefully everyone in the new group seems to be keeping an eye out for trouble.

:are you safe now?: Densil asks me. I can tell from the weakness of the contact that he is some distance away.

:We are fine. Thank you for helping us save Robry.

Please, go hunt and play with the others.:

:we will tell you if more boats come.:

:How long ago did you complete the transformation?: Kyel asks me just as I finish my private conversation with Densil.

:Maybe we should start with some more names.: I'm surprised to find myself countering him.

Kyel's mouth twists in impatience. :All right. You know I'm Kyel, and you've already met Dai. That's Thom back there.: He motions to a big, strong, homely boy with short brown hair and large hands who is swimming next to Lena. Thom smiles shyly at me, and then his gaze is drawn to Lena, who, of course, is busy peering back at Dai.

:That's Tobin swimming across from Thom.: I look over and meet the thoughtful gaze of a redheaded boy with green eyes, who is studying me just as carefully as I'm studying him.

:Then there's Ree, and Tobin's little sister, Bria.: Kyel gestures carelessly to the two girls. Is he going to be one of those boys who thinks girls are worthless?

Ree stares back at me with cool dislike. She's a striking girl with a strong nose, broad shoulders, and muscular arms. She wears her long black hair in multiple braids. I'd guess her ancestors came from Old Mexico. I wonder what I've done to have antagonized her already. She and Lena are going to get along great. Tobin's sister, a pretty little girl about Robry's age, with long brown hair and big hazel eyes, smiles at me brightly.

I glance back at Kyel and realize he's waiting for me to tell him our names. :I'm Nere Hanson. That's Lena McFadden and Robry Cruz,: I add.

Kyel is studying me more intently than ever. :You wouldn't happen to be related to Mark Hanson, the guy who's building a colony up north for us, would you?:

:He's my father.:

:So you must know all about the Neptune Project.:

:Actually,: I say tightly, :I only found out about it two days ago when we went through the transformation. Before that, I swear I'd never heard a word about the Neptune Project.:

Kyel looks like he doesn't believe me, but I'm relieved that he doesn't press me further. :Did you have any trouble after you transformed?:

:Soldiers came when we were still on land. We got away, but my mother was killed.: I have to pause for a moment. I still can't believe my mother is dead. Every time I have to talk about her, I'm afraid I'm going to fall apart. :We've been dodging Marine Guard boats and divers ever since. What about you?:

:We transformed twenty days ago down in San Diego. We've been working our way north up the coast since then.:

I blink as I absorb his words. So these kids have been in

the sea for almost three weeks now, and they had to travel past the drowned city of Los Angeles, with all its polluted water and dangerous debris. I'm impressed they've survived this long.

:Were there more of you originally?: Kyel asks me next. Maybe it's just his way, but I'm starting to feel like I'm being interrogated.

:We're the only kids from Goleta, if that's what you mean.:

:I was told there would be at least fifty of us, but you're among the few we've encountered so far.:

:It's a big ocean. There could be dozens of us heading toward Santa Cruz, and we might not find one another until we get there.:

:Or the others didn't get away. We know that a group of kids from Vista didn't make it.:

:How do you know that?:

:Because we found one of them dying outside the harbor there. Soldiers came before the Neptune transformation was complete, and executed the kids and the scientists in charge of them. Before she could tell us any more than that, the girl died of her solar wounds.:

I shiver when I remember how close Robry, Lena, and I came to meeting the same fate. Kyel starts to ask me more about our first two days in the water, but I sense a commotion behind me. I stop swimming and look back.

Lena is curled up in pain, and Tobin is at her side.

:She has a bad leg cramp,: Tobin tells the rest of us. :I think she's pretty tired.:

:We don't have time to wait for her if she's not strong enough to keep up,: Kyel declares. :They could send another ship this way anytime.:

:We can't just leave her,: I contradict him indignantly.

:If you travel with us, you place yourself under my command,: Kyel says, his face starting to flush. He raises his speargun until it's pointing directly at me. :And I say we leave her.:

chapter fifteen

I'M AWARE THE REST of the group has clustered around us, watching the confrontation between Kyel and me. My blood is hammering in my ears. I scan the faces of our new companions, but it's hard to tell what they're thinking. They can't agree that Kyel is right to leave Lena behind! Robry shifts until he's floating beside me. I draw comfort from his quiet support, as Kyel continues to point his speargun at me.

:It's obvious she isn't as strong as the rest of us,: Kyel says coldly. :She'll just slow us down. I say we leave her behind.:

:Maybe you should just shoot her yourself, Kyel,: Dai suggests, looking bored again. Lena stares at him in horror. I think Dai's kidding, but I'm not absolutely sure.

Thom, the big, homely boy speaks up. :Maybe we could go a little slower.:

:All the way to Santa Cruz? She's a liability. I'm fairly sure these two can keep up with us:—Kyel gestures to Robry and me—:but she can't.:

I don't really want to stand up for Lena, but someone has to. :We need to slow down or let our dolphins give Lena a tow. We aren't as fit as you are. We haven't been traveling in the sea for weeks like you have.:

Kyel stares at me. :You have dolphins?:

:Well, yes. They're off hunting right now.:

:That changes everything,: Kyel says, and lowers his speargun. :If your dolphins help her to keep up, she can stay with us.:

I didn't realize until then that I'd been holding my breath.

:Lena,: I say to her quickly on a private send, :do you think you're strong enough to take some tows from the dolphins?:

:Yes!: she replies, her face pale.

I call Kona and Mali and ask them to help Lena. In the meantime, Tobin massages Lena's cramping calf muscle.

:How many dolphins do you have?: Kyel asks me. His expression is cool and calm again. I can't believe he's going to act like that confrontation never happened. I decide to follow his lead, but from now on, I know that I'll never be able to trust him completely.

:We have twelve, but one is just a baby.:

:The kids from Vista had a pod, but the Marine Guard slaughtered them all. I've never worked directly with dolphins, but I see how they could be a big help to our mission.:

Kyel looks like he's thinking hard. I'm afraid that he's imagining all the ways he can use the dolphins, but the idea of Mariah and her family being under his control gives me the chills.

Kona and Mali streak down from the surface to join us. Even though they are two of our older dolphins and are both mothers, they still have lots of energy. They come and swim happily around Robry, Lena, and me before they greet and investigate each of our new companions. I can tell they are watching Dai's dolphin, but they don't interact with him. Maybe his sheer size intimidates them.

:Our dolphins are ready,: I tell Kyel curtly. It's hard not to stare at the speargun he had pointed at my guts just a few minutes ago.

We start off again. The dolphins alternate pulling Lena and swimming to the surface to breathe.

Kyel asks me about our escape from Goleta, and I tell him and his companions everything that's happened to us in the past two days.

:You did well, particularly for such a small group,: Kyel admits when I finish.

His praise gives me enough confidence to make two suggestions. :If we could swim a little closer to the surface,: I say quickly, :the dolphins won't use as much energy going up to breathe. And the rest of the pod has found a strong current heading northwest a little to the north of here. If we could ride that, we'd make better time.:

Kyel's face tightens at my suggestions, but I'm relieved when he heads closer to the surface and leads us north. Soon we hit the current Mariah told me about, and for a few hours we double our speed until the current peters out.

Three times that morning we hear boat engines in the distance, but no boats come within sonar range of us. We stop at midday in a rocky canyon, where there are plenty of places we can hide if a boat does appear. Ree and Thom go off foraging and return with two large kelp bass they shot for our lunch. I'm not thrilled about our menu, but I don't want to hurt Thom's feelings. So when he offers me a slice of very fresh bass, I take it. His face falls when Lena looks disgusted by his offering and pointedly starts eating a fish bar from her seapack.

Our new companions have developed a practical system for eating. Any sort of food in the ocean instantly attracts dozens of live hungry fish, and sometimes they can't tell the difference between dead fish and human fingers. I see four of Kyel's group eat while the other two watch for scavengers and keep them away.

Lena nibbles at her fish bar just a few feet away from me. Robry drifts over and joins us as we eat. The raw kelp bass actually tastes so good, I devour it in several bites.

:Thanks for standing up for me back there,: Lena says grudgingly.

:You would have done the same for me.: I shrug off her thanks while I wonder if that's true.

:I can't believe Dai suggested they just shoot me.: Lena sends Dai an angry glare, but he's oblivious. He's sitting by himself while he eats, a remote look on his face.

:I'm pretty sure he was making a joke,: I say, and at that instant, Dai looks over at me, his expression quizzical.

:I didn't think it was funny,: Lena says.

:Me neither,: Robry offers. :But I think he was trying to help you, in his own twisted way.:

:Twisted is right. I'm not sure I like him or Kyel much,: Lena says darkly.

:I'm not sure I like Kyel, either,: I admit. :But he is right about one thing. We are safer if we travel together.:

:Until he points a speargun at you. If he threatens any of us again, I vote we make our own way to Santa Cruz,: Robry declares, and Lena nods.

:I totally agree,: I reply.

We start off again as soon as we finish eating. The dolphins take turns helping Lena keep up. We travel throughout the afternoon until my legs are burning from kicking constantly. I notice that Bria is starting to look as tired as I feel. Even though I don't want to tangle with Kyel again, I'm just about to suggest we rest when Ree asks him to stop.

Kyel frowns, but when he looks back at Bria, he agrees. While everyone gets food from their packs, I swim over to Bria. Ree looks at me suspiciously, but I ignore her and smile at the little girl.

:Would you like some help from a dolphin?: I ask. I noticed her face lit up when she met Kona and Mali earlier. :My friend Ricca is one of our gentlest dolphins, and I know she'd be happy to give you some tows. I'll ask Mariah to come, too, and you can meet her calf.:

Bria brightens, but she looks to Tobin for permission. I can tell they are exchanging thoughts on a private send. Then Bria beams at me and says, :I'd love to meet Ricca and let her pull me, if she doesn't mind. I can't believe I get to swim with a dolphin. I'm going to feel just like a mermaid!:

:You already look like one.: I smile at her. With her big eyes and delicate features, Bria reminds me of the mermaids in one of my mother's rare old picture books. I reach out to my dolphin friends, who have fed well on a large column of sardines they found a few hours ago. Mariah is eager to see me and happy to ask Ricca to help Bria.

This time the entire pod comes along with Mariah and Ricca, curious about the other humans Robry and I have met. Wanting to start off on the right foot with the rest of our companions, even if Kyel and I haven't, I make a point of introducing everyone to each member of my dolphin family.

:This is Mariah. She's the leader of this pod. She was a calf when my mother was a little girl, and the two of them grew up together. This is her youngest calf, Tisi. Mali, Mona, and Ricca are her nieces; and Sokya, Halia, and Kona are her daughters. Pani, Nika, and Laki here are her grand-daughters, and Densil is her son.:

I can't help but notice that everyone is grinning as the

dolphins come in close. Dolphins just have that effect on people. Even Kyel cracks a smile as little Tisi swims around our group upside down in the water, showing off in his excitement over meeting new people.

Because Kyel is smiling, I decide to go for it and risk another suggestion.

:Most of the dolphins are fed and rested right now. Maybe we could practice taking dolphin tows. I can make sure the pod pulls us in the direction we need to travel. I think we should only use the dolphins to help those of us who are the most tired. But in emergencies, the dolphins can help us all get away from danger much faster than we can swim on our own. Hanging on to a dolphin, though, takes some practice.:

Kyel frowns as he considers my idea.

:Very well,: he says at last. :We can all practice as long as we don't get distracted from watching out for trouble.:

:The dolphins will let us know if there's any danger heading our way,: I promise him.

Quickly, I pair each person with a dolphin, trying to match personalities and strength. Because he's the strongest and the biggest, I assign Densil to pull Thom. Our next strongest dolphin is steady Kona, and so I ask her to tow Kyel. Since Mariah already knows Lena, I think they'll make a good team. Then I assign happy Pani to Ree, hoping she can handle Ree's attitude. Mali, who is both strong and quite a flirt, is excited when I ask her to tow Tobin. Nika, one of Mariah's younger granddaughters, is playful and sensible at the same time. She has been friends with Robry for years, and I know she will take good care of him. Gentle Ricca makes Bria grin when she tickles the little girl with her beak.

Since I'm used to Sokya and her tricks, I ask her to tow me. Dai already has his big dolphin, and I have a hunch the two of them could teach me plenty about dolphin handling. After I show everyone the best way to hold on to the dolphins' dorsal fins, Sokya and I lead off to the northwest, with Tisi, Halia, Mona, and Laki swimming in circles around us. I look back and see grins on everyone's faces as they practice being pulled by their sleek, powerful dolphins.

As Sokya tows me swiftly through the sunlit sea, I realize I'm grinning, too. I've always loved dolphin rides at the surface, but being towed below the waves is like flying through a whole new world. Sokya pulls me up and over rock ribs and past the edge of a kelp forest. We skim across a sand flat, startling a large torpedo ray hiding on the bottom. Minutes later we cut through a big school of salema and send the surprised fish flashing away from us in glinting swirls of gold and silver.

With the pod's help, we make good time over the next hour. Then I send them off to rest, except for Mariah and Ricca, who stay to help Lena and Bria. Working with the dolphins has helped to cheer up everyone. I notice, though, that the tension in our travel group increases as the light in the ocean fades.

:Dai,: Kyel suddenly orders, :send Ton out to search for a place where we can spend the night.:

I watch Dai give a series of hand signals, and the big dolphin speeds off. It never occurred to me to ask the dolphins to help find us shelter. With their ability to echolocate, they probably can do a better job of finding caves and overhangs than we can.

Kyel orders us to swim in a tighter formation and to keep our spearguns at the ready. I can tell my new companions are frightened as the sea darkens. Although I feel uneasy, too, I wish I could make them understand that the dolphins fear the same predators we do. Mariah and the rest of the pod will warn me if something dangerous approaches us.

:These people haven't spent as much time in the sea as you obviously have,: Dai says, suddenly breaking in on my thoughts. :I tried to tell them that Ton would warn us of danger, but they don't believe me.:

:It'll probably take some time before they learn to trust the dolphins.:

:That's their problem,: Dai says with a shrug. Before I can ask him how he came to work with Ton, the big dolphin comes back and bobs his head at Dai.

:I'm going to check out what Ton found for us,: Dai tells Kyel.

Dai heads off, kicking incredibly swiftly for someone who just spent his whole day swimming through the sea.

The group draws even closer together after that. Everyone is on the lookout for sharks, which do become more active at night. Ree and Bria in particular keep glancing around them, their faces pale. It's hard for me not to feel tense when everyone seems so scared.

As the last of the light vanishes, true night turns the water black all around us. Now I can only see twenty feet ahead of me. My legs feel like lead. I hope Ton and Dai find a place for us to get safely settled for the night, and find it soon.

chapter sixteen

:NERE, PLEASE TELL KYEL that Ton's found a protected overhang big enough to hold us all,: Dai contacts me. :I'm sending Ton to bring you all back here while I clear out a couple of wolf eels.:

:Why don't you tell him yourself?: I ask. I've already made a lot of suggestions today, and I'm pretty sure Kyel is getting tired of them.

:Because Kyel isn't a very strong telepath. He has problems hearing my thoughts over longer distances.: I can feel Dai's exasperation with Kyel and me in his mental tone.

:I'll tell Kyel for you,: Tobin offers, and I smile at him gratefully. Moments later, Tobin relays Dai's news to everyone. Ton appears soon after that and leads us to a large overhang he's found at the end of a rocky canyon. The overhang is deep enough to protect us from sonar detection, and the canyon is narrow enough to give us some defense against predators.

Kyel inspects the overhang carefully. I grow impatient as I watch him. I'm beyond ready to eat and hit my hammock.

At last Kyel declares, :All right. This looks good. Let's set up camp.:

He assigns Thom to keep watch while the rest of us put up our hammocks. Ton returns from a quick foraging trip looking quite pleased with himself. He presents to Dai the big yellowfin tuna in his mouth. Dai makes short work of filleting the yellowfin with his knife while Ton chases away greedy scavenger fish. Ton swims off with the carcass while Dai comes around and offers each of us strips of tuna.

Once again, Lena refuses the raw fish, but Robry and I thank Dai and take some. I'm hungry enough to eat just about anything, but in the midst of wolfing down the raw fish, I can't help remembering the ham sandwich my mother gave us right after our transformation. Now I wish I'd eaten it more slowly.

Robry meets my gaze as we eat. :I miss my mother's bread,: he admits.

:I think she must be the best baker in the southern sector,: I say as my mouth waters at the memory of her crusty, warm bread.

:I miss everything we ate on land.: Lena sighs wearily as she eats another fish bar.

I look out into our little canyon. Its walls are covered by sea fans, spiky purple anemones, lush red algae, and ostrich-feather hydroids. Densil and Sokya have swum down to meet Ton. I can tell from Densil's behavior that the bigger animal intimidates him. Sokya, however, seems quite taken with him, nipping and rubbing against him and inviting him to play. Ton swims after her slowly as if he doesn't quite know how to respond to her antics.

Eating the yellowfin has given me more energy. I swim out into the canyon to say good night to the dolphins. While I study Ton, I realize his body is crisscrossed with scars. Most wild dolphins have scars from shark attacks, but Ton looks like he's been through a war.

:We have survived some rough times together.: Dai swims over to join me. His cool expression warms as he looks at his dolphin. Ton watches me just as carefully as I watch him. Every dolphin has his or her own personality, just like people. I sense that Ton is intelligent, serious, and reserved, like Dai.

:He's beautiful. I've never seen such a big Pacific white-sided, though.: I study Dai's profile as he watches his dolphin. With his dramatic cheekbones, strong jaw, and brooding dark eyes, he looks like one of those male models I've seen in the old glossy magazines. His thick black hair is caught back in several long braids all tied together that reach to the middle of his back. Now that we are floating side by side, I realize he's quite a bit taller than me; and he's strong, in the long, lean way swimmers are.

:Deep-sea dolphins grow bigger than your coastal dolphins,: Dai says abruptly, and I can sense him raising shields around his mind. I feel a little insulted by those shields. I'm not planning to pry into his thoughts.

:You're strong enough to pry if you wanted to, though.: Dai surprises me by reading my surface mind.

:Now who's prying?: I ask him indignantly.

:I am,: he says with a shrug. :You should shield your mind more tightly if you don't want me to read you. You broadcast and read more strongly than anyone here. You're by far the strongest telepath in this group, except for me.:

:How can you tell?:

:I could hear your thoughts as clear as day the moment the Marine Guard boats starting dropping depth charges on you. I knew your group was in trouble, and that's when I told Kyel we needed to hurry to your rescue.:

:I'm glad you did. I was about to call our dolphins, but I hated to do it. Some of them might have been killed trying to save us.:

:You should have called them anyway. Dolphins are here to serve us.:

I stare at him in surprise. :Do you really feel that way?: I ask.

:Humans are the most important species in the ocean.:

:I'm not sure we're any more important than other intelligent species down here. At least dolphins didn't mess up the whole planet the way we did.:

:What humans did in the past doesn't matter. The ocean is ours to conquer and explore.:

:Well, if we conquer and explore it as thoroughly as we did the rest of our world, the oceans are in big trouble.:

I turn away from him and head back under the overhang. I'm surprised to see Tobin hovering nearby. Has he been listening in on our argument? It's hard to tell from his impassive expression.

:Kyel sent me to check on your leg,: he says simply. :I'm what passes for a medic in our group. I can treat your wound for you.: His gaze goes to the bandage tied across my thigh, and his face colors. With his fair skin, it's really obvious when he blushes. :Unless you'd rather look after it yourself.:

:I'm sure you'll do a better job than I can,: I reply. I've never really liked dealing with my own blood.

I swim over to a nearby rock and try not to wince as I take off the pressure bandage. A curious zebra perch comes up to investigate, and I shoo him away with my hands. That's when I notice Dai is staring at my injury. His face strained, he abruptly turns and swims away into the dark ocean. Maybe he likes blood even less than I do.

Tobin's expression is thoughtful as he studies the wound. :That's a nice little graze you picked up today.:

:I'm lucky it's not worse,: I admit absently. :I thought that diver had me for sure.: I smile when I see that Robry and Bria are playing with Sokya and Ree is helping Lena untangle and braid her hair. I'm glad to see our groups are beginning to mingle.

:For someone who was in a real fight, you seem pretty cool about it. Dai said you handled yourself well.:

I close my eyes against the memory of the men I shot. They were trying to kill me, but I hope none of them will die.

:I don't think it's sunk in yet. None of this has—not really.: I open my eyes and look at Tobin. :We haven't been in the water as long as you have. I haven't had time to think.:

:It's probably better that way,: he says with a grimace. His expression surprises me. Until now, Tobin seemed the most cheerful of our new companions, except perhaps for smiling Bria.

Tobin holds a tube of antiseptic cream next to my graze. :This is going to sting a little.: He glances at me, his gaze apologetic. I realize suddenly that his eyes are an amazingly deep green color. They remind me of the bright moss that grew on the stones below the little shower that Cam made for my mother and me.

Thinking of the shower makes me think of Cam, and I look away from Tobin and stare hard at my feet. I flinch when he smooths the salve on the graze. It stings like crazy.

:So how did you end up as the medic?: I ask him, to keep my mind off the pain.

:My mother was a nurse,: he says as he works gently and quickly to cover the entire graze with salve. :I used to help in her clinic.:

:*Was* a nurse?:

:She died in the last famine.:

:I'm sorry.:

:I'm sorry, too. Bria and I miss her. She was amazing. Somehow, even in the worst times, she managed to make us feel safe. I didn't realize until too late how little she had been eating to make sure we had enough.:

The guilt and sadness I hear in his voice makes me want to cry for him.

:There, the worst is over,: he declares in a lighter tone. :I'm just going to put a fresh bandage on it now.:

I steel myself to peer down at my wound. I'm surprised to see it's already starting to heal. My mother was right about our heightened healing abilities.

:Thanks for fixing me up. And I guess I should thank the Neptune scientists for keeping me from oozing blood down here.: I glance at the hammocks tied under the overhang where the eight of us will be sleeping tonight. :I still can't believe all of this. . . . When did you find out that you were engineered to live in the sea?:

:My mother told me the truth when I was twelve,: Tobin admits. :What about you?:

:Exactly two days ago,: I say bitterly.

Gillian, why didn't you trust me with the truth? This would have been so much easier if I'd known that someday I'd have to give up my entire life on land.

:I'm not sure it made it that much easier for Bria and me to know ahead of time what was going to happen to us. We're still pretty landsick right now.:

:What do you miss the most?: Somehow, being around Tobin is calming, and I don't want him to stop talking just yet. As I study him, I realize I like his face. He has even features, a stubborn chin, and a nice smile. :Or is it too hard to pick the one thing you miss the most?:

:No, that's easy. The one thing I miss more than anything else is music,: he says promptly. :Sound down here is too muffled. The ocean is quiet compared to our life on land. I guess I can hear more than I expected to, like the whisper of sand slipping against sand along the bottom— or dolphins whistling, sawing, and clicking—but sea music isn't the music I know. And now I'd better report back to Kyel. He might have more chores for me.:

:Who made Kyel boss, anyway?:

:Actually, we did, two weeks ago, in an election,: Tobin says with a crooked grin. :He beat Ree by two votes, and she's still sore about it. Kyel knows more about fighting than any of us. His father was a soldier before he went AWOL and started fighting with the Western Resistance. Kyel's lived with a guerrilla band up in the San Gabriel Mountains since he was little. He can come on kind of strong sometimes, but so far he's done a good job of keeping us alive.:

:I'll have to take your word for it. Thanks again for fixing up my leg.:

:You're welcome. And by the way, I have to agree with Dai,: Tobin adds with a smile that lights up his green eyes. :I definitely think your life is worth more than a dolphin's.:

Thanks to Tobin, I'm in a happier mood as I go to my hammock. Before I climb into it, Kyel informs me that I'll have sentry duty for two hours in the middle of the night. Looking at his set expression, I realize I don't want to try convincing him that we'll be safe with the pod sleeping nearby. Dolphins literally sleep with one half of their brains awake at all times, so I know the pod will give us plenty of warning if a big predator comes calling.

Irritated, I climb into my hammock and tie myself in. I'd love to get a good night's sleep, but I just don't have the guts to challenge Kyel again so soon.

:Robry, how are you doing?: I ask as he settles himself in the hammock next to mine.

:Tired,: he admits. :But I think I'm glad we joined up with Kyel's group. I like Bria.:

:I like her, too.:

I want to ask Robry how he's really doing, but he looks so tired, I decide to let it go for now.

:G'night, Nere,: Robry says sleepily.

:Good night, dartling.:

As exhaustion sucks me down into sleep, I'm aware of the vast, dark mass of water that separates me from the sky and the stars I've always loved.

chapter seventeen

REE CURTLY WAKES ME UP at midnight so that I can take my turn keeping watch. I swim back and forth across our canyon, my speargun at the ready. Shivers go down my back when I see a big rust-colored octopus engulf a lobster and gobble it up. I hope nothing comes along and gobbles me up.

I told Tobin that since my transformation, I've had no time to think. All alone doing my sentry duty, I suddenly have too much time.

I wonder where Cam is tonight. I refuse to believe they executed him. The Western Collective needs strong, healthy young men. But how badly was he hurt by that solar blast? If they've sent him to a work camp, I hope he won't cause trouble. He has to stay alive.

I don't want to think about how my mother died. Instead I try to focus on a happy memory of her. I smile when I remember how excited she would get when one of our young dolphins learned a new behavior, or how James could make her laugh with his stupid jokes. I also remember the smile she sent me right before she saved my life.

I know she loved James and me, but I still can't believe she did this to our bodies.

A flash of motion startles me, and Densil is at my side, watching me curiously with his intelligent dark eyes.

:why are you sad?:

:I miss my mother.:

:we all miss her, too. why are you angry?:

I blink at his question, but I suppose I shouldn't be surprised. Densil and I grew up together. He's always been able to read my moods even better than Cam or Robry.

:I can't believe my mother changed me so that I would always have to live in the ocean.:

:you do not like the sea?:

:It's not my home.:

:it is now,: comes his practical reply. :I am happy you are always going to live in the sea,: he adds, flipping his head for emphasis.

:Thanks.: I have to smile at his enthusiasm. :But I think it's going to take me a while to get used to that idea. You should be resting with the others.:

:I will sleep when you sleep,: he says simply, and for the rest of my watch he brings me shells and starfish and funny little green crabs that make me laugh, and I no longer feel so sad and lonely.

I'm relieved when my two hours are over. Densil returns to the pod, and I go to wake up Tobin. He's placed his hammock on the outside of Ree's and Bria's, probably to make sure that a shark will eat him before it eats the girls. He looks so peaceful sleeping that I hate to wake him.

:Tobin, you need to get up now,: I call to him, but he's too sound asleep to hear me.

At last I resort to shaking him gently. He starts and sits bolt upright in his hammock. His hand goes to the knife at his belt as he looks around wildly.

:Tobin, it's all right. Nothing's wrong. It's just time for you to relieve me on sentry duty.:

His eyes focus on me, and his alarm fades. He rubs his face with his hands. When he lowers them, he looks embarrassed.

:It's going to take me a while to get used to waking up to this,: he says with a grim nod toward the black ocean all around us.

:I know.:

:Sweet dreams,: he calls as I swim back to my hammock.

I raise my hand to acknowledge his words, but I'm afraid my dreams will be anything but sweet.

~ ~ ~

The ocean is just starting to get gray when Dai wakes me from a troubled sleep. :Kyel wants everyone up, pronto,: he says as I glare at him sleepily. When I don't move right away, he grins, grabs my hammock, and starts shaking it.

:All right, I'm getting up,: I say crossly before he can dump me out of it.

:Guess you aren't a morning person. By the way, who's Cam?:

:Someone I knew on land,: I reply without thinking, and then I wake up enough to wonder how Dai knows anything about Cam. :You've been eavesdropping on my thoughts again,: I say accusingly.

:I didn't have to eavesdrop. You're a noisy dreamer. I can't help hearing you.:

:Oh,: I say, wondering if I should apologize, but Dai is already turning away from me. I hope my nightmares didn't keep him awake all night.

We are a quiet group as we pack up our hammocks and eat a quick breakfast of halibut and lobster. Somehow, raw fish is tasting better to me. Maybe my body is starting to crave the kinds of food I need to eat down here to survive.

We head out for Santa Cruz right after breakfast. If we make good time we could reach the island by tonight. Making good time is painful, though. My legs feel stiff as logs when I begin kicking with my fins. I glance at Lena. If my legs feel this sore, she must be in agony. Her face is pale, but she doesn't complain to anyone. Maybe she's afraid that Kyel will threaten to leave her behind again.

We make good progress much of the morning, riding a

strong current the dolphins find for us. Near noon, Mariah, who is off hunting with Tisi and the rest of the pod, suddenly calls me.

:the big boat is heading toward you!:

By big boat, I know she means another Marine Guard cutter. My heart races while I relay her news to Kyel. There's nothing but sandy bottom below us. Quickly, I ask the pod about the terrain around us.

:The dolphins say there are rocks ahead, maybe a quarter mile away,: I tell Kyel and the others.

:We'll have to split up and sprint for them, using the dolphins,: Kyel decides quickly. :After the pod gets here, Bria and Lena will come with me. Ree, Thom, and Tobin, you stay together. The three of you:—he gestures toward Dai, Robry, and me—:spread out, but stay in visual contact with one another.:

After a long, agonizing minute, the pod arrives. Now I'm glad I suggested that everyone practice being towed. Without my asking, the dolphins go straight to the person they worked with yesterday.

:We must reach the rocks before the boat reaches us,: I tell Mariah and Densil, and they tell the others in excited whistles and sawing sounds. Wasting no time, we head off in our different groups.

I can tell that the dolphins are having fun racing one another with their human partners against the approaching boat—except for Mariah and Densil. They understand we could be killed or captured if that boat finds us.

I try to keep my body still and straight so that I create as little drag as possible while Sokya tows me. Dai's and Robry's dolphins are keeping pace with Sokya. The others have disappeared in the cloudy water. I listen hard for the sound of engines in the distance, and then I hear them. Is that boat in sonar range yet? When will the sand below me change?

There! I see the first dark ribs of rock appear on the ocean floor. Sokya starts angling downward.

Suddenly, a piercing scream rings in my head. I think it's Bria!

:shark!: Mariah calls to me a second later, and I feel her panic and fear for little Tisi, who is never far from her.

Sokya starts whistling and sawing wildly.

:Go!: I tell her as I swim for the rocks. I'm sure I can find some crack where I can hide. Right now I want Sokya to help Mariah and Bria. Sokya dashes away with Nika at her side. I hope Bria is all right.

I see that Robry is swimming hard for the rocks, too. Where are Dai and Ton? I can't see them anywhere. I feel a sharp stab of disappointment. I thought we could depend on Dai. But what do I really know about him, anyway?

:Nere, head north!: Dai calls me. :Ton's found a hiding place for us. It'll be a pretty tight fit, but I think it'll work. I'm sending Ton to find you.:

Seconds later, Ton streaks up from the rocks. He turns around when he knows we've seen him, and leads us back the way he just came.

The sound of the engines is growing louder. We don't have time to reach Dai's hiding place. We are going to be in sonar range any moment.

chapter eighteen

DESPERATE TO ESCAPE that boat's sonar, I reach out to Ton. I don't know the signal Dai uses to ask him for a tow. Instead, I try to send him an image of what we need, the way I communicate with Kona or Ricca, who can't use human words.

I can tell that Ton is startled by my mental contact. An instant later, though, he swims between Robry and me.

:I think he's willing to give us a tow,: I gasp to Robry.

We both grab on to Ton's dorsal. The big dolphin surges forward through the water, pulling us down toward the rocks much faster than we could swim on our own.

:In here!: Dai calls. I look to my left. Dai is waving to us from a narrow, horizontal gash in the rock wall. As Ton pulls us closer, I see that Dai was right: it is going to be tight.

:I'll go first. I'm the smallest,: Robry offers, and he flashes past me, takes off his fins, and wedges himself into the back of the cleft.

After taking a look at Dai's long legs, I slip off my own fins and settle myself next to Robry. I try to send feelings of gratitude to Ton as Dai sits next to me. Ton bobs his head at me before Dai sends him away with a hand signal.

I close my eyes and reach out to Sokya.

:Is everyone all right?:

:no one was hurt. together we made the big shark go away.: She sounds pleased with herself, as always.

I sigh with relief.

:Bria's fine,: Kyel reports to everyone moments later. :She's just a little shaken up. We were hunting for a place to hide, and we came face-to-face with a large shark. The dolphins chased it off. We're waiting under a large ledge. Is everyone else hidden from that boat?:

I overhear Dai, Tobin, and Thom all check in with Kyel. Everyone has found a place to hide, and not a second too soon. The bass vibrations from the cutter's engines fill the water all around us.

:Well, isn't this cozy?:

Dai is grinning at me. We are packed in so tightly, I realize our shoulders and arms are touching.

:I think I owe that boat captain a favor,: he adds, a gleam of mischief in his dark eyes. :I wouldn't mind if he decided to drive in circles over our heads for the next few hours.:

:I think your muscles would get a little cramped by then.: I nod at his long legs, which he's had to bend to fit into our hiding spot.

:The pain would be worth it,: he says, looking at me. I feel my cheeks heat up as I stare back at him. Is Dai actually flirting with me? No one's ever flirted with me before, but

I've seen boys flirt with girls at school. Lena seems so much more his type.

My gaze falls to a small black coral ring he's wearing on a thin black cord around his neck. Trying to hide how uncomfortable I feel, I ask, :What's that?:

He looks down at the ring, and his smile fades. :It's something my sister gave me a long time ago. I wear it to remember her.:

I sense the sadness he is trying to hide. :Did she die?:

:Yes. Did Cam?:

I close my eyes as pain sears through me. :I don't know,: I answer after a long minute.

:You can never be with him anyway,: Dai says matter-of-factly. :You breathe water now, and if he's still alive, he breathes air. The Neptune transformation is permanent. There's no going back to a life on land for you.:

My eyes fly open at Dai's cool statement. I clench my hand into a fist. I *so* want to hit him.

:You think I don't know that?: I manage to say instead. :I'm not a complete idiot.:

Before I burst out crying, I turn away from Dai to face Robry. The problem is, of course, that Dai's right, but I don't want to accept that he's right.

:How's it going over there, Robry?:

Robry is watching me with worried eyes. I was speaking on a private send with Dai just now, but Robry is aware that something has upset me.

:Other than the fact there's a lump of rock pressing into my kidney, I'm fine,: he says after a moment.

:Let's take a look at those charts and see what we can find out about the waters around Santa Cruz,: I suggest.

It takes some shifting around, and all the while I refuse to look at Dai, but at last I can reach into my seapack. Robry and I pore over the chart for the northern Channel Islands.

:It looks like there should be a strong current heading west along the northern side of Santa Cruz,: Robry says after he reads some of the notations written by hand around the edges of the chart. Those notations, I realize with a start, are in my father's handwriting.

I still can't believe Dad let me believe he was dead. I suddenly want to hit someone again, but I force myself to focus on the chart instead.

:If we can get in close to the shore, and if that current's still there,: I say to Robry, :we should definitely use it to shorten our travel time along the northern side of the island.:

:I think it's safe to go on now,: Kyel calls out to everyone. :The boat never slowed or changed course. I don't think its sonar picked up any sign of us.:

Just to make sure, I close my eyes and check in with Mariah. :Is the boat going away?:

:yes.:

:Is Tisi all right?:

:he is still scared and stays close to me. tomorrow he

will be brave again,: Mariah predicts with dolphin humor.

:I am glad he's all right. Thank you for helping us.:

:the strong boy put himself between the shark and the young female and Tisi. we are all one pod now.:

I open my eyes at her calm pronouncement. It's hard to imagine that Dai, Kyel, or Ree could ever become my family here in the sea.

While I've been talking with Mariah, Dai has unfolded himself from our hiding spot. Now he floats directly in front of it, refusing to move out of my way until I meet his gaze.

His eyes are serious when I finally look at him. :Nere, just for the record, I don't think you are an idiot, and Lena will never be my type.:

With that, he turns away, and we go to join the others.

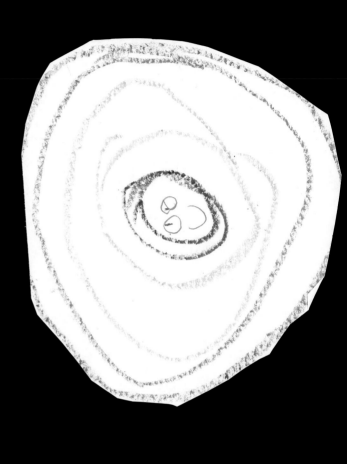

to Mommy

from Addy

chapter nineteen

AFTER EATING A QUICK MEAL, we head off again. Bria looks like she's been crying, and Ree and Tobin stay close beside her. I contact Mariah.

:The smallest female is still scared, just like Tisi. If a dolphin swam near her, she would feel safer.:

:we will take turns swimming by her,: Mariah promises, and playful Pani appears a short while later. After Pani swims several tight circles around her, Bria starts to smile. Pani settles in to swim beside her, and the little girl looks much happier. Tobin sends me a relieved salute.

I smile to myself. Then I realize Dai is swimming nearby, and he's watching me. His expression is puzzled.

:What?: I ask in exasperation.

:You worry about Bria so much already, but you just met her yesterday.:

:Yeah, so?:

:So, how can you care so much about someone you just met?:

:So, how can you be so irritating all the time?:

:Being irritating is just one of my many gifts,: he says with a mental laugh. I'm relieved when he falls back and swims next to Thom instead.

We draw even with the northeastern tip of Santa Cruz around three. During a brief rest stop I ask Robry to point out to Kyel that there should be a good current we can ride if we move in closer to the shore. Dai watches me with a knowing smile as Robry approaches Kyel with the chart. I think he guesses that I don't want to keep pushing Kyel with my suggestions.

:Nere and I found these notations on this chart,: Robry explains to Kyel. I wince when Robry mentions my name. :If we move in closer to the shore, we might be able to pick up a westward current that will help us.:

Kyel's cool gaze flickers to me. I think I see annoyance there, but all he says to Robry is, :That's good. We'll swim closer to shore, then. I'd like to reach that freighter by nightfall if we can.:

We find the current just where my father's notes said it would be. Even if we weren't swimming, the water pulls us along at three or four miles per hour. Swimming with it, I figure we are probably traveling at six to eight miles per hour.

The light is just starting to fade when the dolphins become agitated. I hear them whistling and sawing excitedly. I feel the hair rise on the back of my neck. They only act that way when they sense danger nearby.

:Mariah, what is it?:

:there are humans in the water ahead, and many sharks.:

:Keep Tisi close to you. Can you send Densil to scout and ask the rest of the pod to swim with us?:

:he goes. we come.:

Dai moves up beside me. His face is strained.

:There's blood in the water up ahead—human blood.:

I look at him in surprise. How does he know there's blood? Ton couldn't have told him, because dolphins can't smell. :Densil is on his way to see what's happening.:

:You'd better warn Kyel,: Dai tells me.

:Why don't you?:

:Because he likes and trusts me even less than he likes you,: Dai says tersely.

When the dolphins suddenly surround us, our companions look worried.

I suck in a deep breath. :Kyel, I think we may be about to run into trouble. The dolphins are upset. They say there are sharks and people ahead of us.:

:Everyone hold up.: Kyel snaps the command. We all stop swimming. The relentless current, though, carries us onward.

Swiftly, I explain to the others what Mariah has told me.

:They could be other Neptune Project kids in trouble,: Tobin says. :We're not that far from the rendezvous point now.:

:Densil says there are three young humans ahead of us.: I relay the information as he reports it to me. :Two are females and one is male. One girl is badly hurt and bleeding. The other two are fighting off several sharks.:

Kyel hesitates. :Will your dolphins fight the sharks if we try to help these people?: he asks me.

I bite my lip, afraid that what I say next could get my friends hurt or killed. :That's exactly what they've been trained to do,: I admit.

:All right, then. Everyone, make sure your spearguns are ready to fire and that you can get to more darts easily if you need them. Nere, ask your dolphins to tow us, but let's swim in a tighter formation with Bria and Robry in the middle.:

:If it comes to close-in fighting, sharks' most sensitive areas are their eyes, gills, and snout,: I can't help adding. :If you can hit one in any of those places with the butt of your dive knife or speargun, the shark might back off.:

My advice earns me an irritated look from Kyel while the dolphins start towing us quickly along with the current.

:Densil, we're coming. You be careful,: I tell him. My stomach tightens. I couldn't bear it if he got hurt.

:hurry! there are many sharks.: Densil's mental voice sounds strained.

I concentrate hard, trying to make contact with the frightened kids ahead of us. Suddenly, I touch the panicked mind of a boy I've never sensed before.

:Kalli, I'm out of spear darts!: I can hear him yell at his companion.

:Hang on! Help's coming,: I call out to him.

:Hurry! We can't last much longer.:

:There they are,: Dai cries, and he and Ton forge ahead of the rest of us.

:Dai, don't go charging off on your own! It's too dangerous,: Kyel calls after him angrily, but Dai's already disappeared into the darkening ocean.

A minute later the dolphins bring us to the edge of a desperate fight. A dozen sharks, big and small, are circling around three figures in the water. A girl is wildly firing spear darts at the approaching animals while a boy slashes out with a dive knife at the ones that come in close. An injured girl, her eyes closed, floats between them. I wince when I see the spear dart protruding from her shoulder.

Ton and Densil are already fighting the larger sharks. Our dolphins leave us and quickly join the fray, all except for Mariah, who hangs back with little Tisi at her side.

Gripping my speargun tightly, I sprint after the dolphins. I realize Dai has already shot three of the biggest sharks. Two makos he wounded are thrashing about, and a long blue is sinking toward the ocean floor. A few smaller sharks follow it downward and start tearing it to pieces. Other sharks keep trying to get at the injured girl.

Robry and I are faster than the rest. I'm first to reach

the boy. I shoot an eight-foot great white in the mouth, but it keeps coming, close enough for me to look into its cold, dark eyes. I hit it hard on the snout with the butt of my speargun at the same time that Densil rams it from the side. The shark swims off, my spear dart sticking out of its mouth. I reload, and Robry shoots a small mako before it can bite the injured girl. Kona rams it in the belly, and the mako struggles away. The other girl is still firing wildly. I knock her speargun upward before she can shoot at Kona.

:THE DOLPHINS ARE ON OUR SIDE!: I yell at her. :If you can't tell the difference between a shark and a dolphin, stop shooting!: Then I hit a persistent little whitetip on the snout with my gun. I glance at the others.

I'm shocked when Dai plunges his knife into one of the big injured makos. Sharkskin is incredibly tough. Dai must have a sharp knife and be phenomenally strong. He spins away, as graceful as an old-time ballet dancer, and guts the other one, easily staying clear of its thrashing tail and wicked teeth.

Abruptly I realize we have killed or chased off all the sharks, except for the ones that are busily tearing to pieces the dead and wounded sharks beneath us. It's hard not to stare down at the frenzy. Even Kyel looks stunned and fascinated by it.

Dai swims up to us, his hands covered in shark gore. He's breathing hard, and his gaze is wild. :More sharks will be here any moment. You've got to stop her from leaking blood:—he jerks his head toward the injured girl—:or leave her before you all get torn to shreds.:

:We can't just leave her here,: the strange boy says angrily. I realize that he looks Asian and is maybe a year or two older than me.

:I can stay with her and bandage her wounds, but I'll need some time,: Tobin says with a calm that helps to steady all of us.

:The dolphins can't fight off sharks for us all night long,: I protest.

:I've sent Ton to find shelter,: Dai says quickly. :If you can get inside a protected place, you can hold off the sharks while Tobin tries to save her. When Ton gets back, he and I can lead the others to the freighter. It's just five miles from here.:

Dai's so comfortable in the ocean, I'm surprised he isn't volunteering to stay with the injured girl through the night. It's going to be dangerous for whoever ends up helping her.

Kyel glances toward the surface and then seems to make up his mind. :We're losing the light quickly now. We'll follow Dai's plan. Who's willing to stay and help Tobin?:

:I'll stay with Sara,: the strange boy volunteers at once.

The other girl looks like she's about to fall apart. :I can't do this anymore. I'm sorry, Penn, but I just can't. I want to go with the others.:

:It's all right, Kalli,: he says.

There's a long, awkward moment while Kyel waits for someone else to volunteer.

I see Robry straighten up beside me. I don't need to read his mind to know what he's about to do. Before he can volunteer, I say quickly, :I'll stay.:

:I'll stay, too,: Thom offers immediately after, his face pale but determined.

:That's decided, then.: Kyel nods.

Ton comes rushing back and bobs his head at Dai. We follow the big dolphin closer to shore, Thom and Penn towing the unconscious girl between them. Ton leads us down to some sort of vessel lying on the ocean floor. As we draw closer, despite the sea growth covering it, I can tell it's a large yacht.

:Don't stay in any rooms with windows,: Dai warns us. :A big shark can break the old glass easily.:

:If we can close off a big cabin or stateroom, this should work well,: Tobin says.

:You be careful tonight, Nere,: Robry tells me in a private send, his expression worried.

:I will be,: I promise him. :You be careful, too. I know Nika is going to keep a close eye on you for me.: I see Tobin go hug Bria, who looks very unhappy that her big brother is staying behind.

:Good luck,: Kyel says briskly. :We'll come and check on

you first thing in the morning.: He turns his back on us and heads for the freighter.

Robry follows the rest. I watch him go, suddenly feeling very lonely. Then I spot two long, narrow blue sharks swimming their sinuous way toward us across the bottom. I swallow hard and turn toward the sunken ship.

chapter twenty

AS THE OTHERS LEAVE, I contact Mariah and
tell her what we've decided to do. She sends a third of the
pod to protect the group traveling to the freighter. I'm not
too worried about them now, having seen Dai in action
against the sharks. He and Ton are like a small army in
themselves.

I'm much more worried about us. I ask the rest of the
pod to keep sharks away until we can get settled safely inside
the old yacht.

The others look at me expectantly. I'm annoyed that
they seem to want me to decide what we do next. :All right,
two of us should probably check out the yacht, and two
should keep watch and take care of Sara.:

Tobin looks me straight in the eye. :I need to talk to
Penn about how she was hurt and how long ago.:

That makes sense, and I don't think Tobin is trying to
dodge the dangerous job of checking out the wreck. He was
the first from our group to volunteer to stay with Sara.

:Okay, Thom, I guess that means you're with me,: I say
as I start looking for a way into the yacht.

:And Nere, the faster I can bandage her shoulder, the

better,: Tobin calls after me. :She's lost a lot of blood.:

:I know, but we need to make sure there's nothing living inside this thing that could hurt her worse.:

Thom and I split up to find an opening into the yacht. Looking at the amount of algae, seaweed, and barnacles growing on her hull, I'd guess this yacht sank just twenty or thirty years ago. If Ton hadn't found her for us, though, we probably would have swum right over her and never guessed she was here. As I study the yacht, I realize I'm looking at her top deck. She must have sunk upright and settled on the bottom, leaning against some rocks.

:Nere, I think we can get inside through this hatchway,: Thom calls to me.

I swim over to the open hatch he's found forward on the yacht. I hesitate while I stare down into the black interior. Robry and I have explored dozens of wrecks together, but they always give me claustrophobia. And I meant what I said to Tobin. You never know what you are going to find living inside a wreck.

:I can go first,: Thom offers, but I can tell from the way he's gripping his speargun that he's nervous.

:Have you ever been inside a wreck before?:

He shakes his head.

:I'll go first, then. Make sure that you have your speargun ready, and that you can get to your dive knife in a hurry. Even some smaller fish can get territorial.:

My heart beats faster as I force myself to swim down through the narrow hatch, and then I'm in a long, dark passageway. I head slowly toward the stern until I reach a large, open room. Suddenly I'm enveloped in a blinding silver cloud of sardines!

Most of the small fish dart toward the stern and disappear, but a stream of fish slips past me toward Thom. I hear him swear behind me in surprise, and then the school is gone.

Looking around the big room, I realize we must have reached the main dining salon. There is a big table along one side and the moldering remains of sofas and chairs.

:I can't believe the money they must have had, to own such a big boat,: Thom comments as he swims up beside me.

:Maybe they were corrupt government officials,: I say, studying the layout of the salon. :We could put Sara on that table and let Tobin work on her here, but this salon has too many windows.: I turn around swiftly. I know she may be running out of time. I swim toward the stern and find a large open hatch that leads to the top deck.

:This must be the way that school of sardines just escaped. This opening also means sharks can reach us, unless we barricade ourselves inside a cabin somehow.:

:Let's try the cabins toward the front,: Thom suggests.

:I'll check the upper ones if you'll do the lower ones.:

:All right,: Thom says simply.

I'm starting to like Thom very much, I decide as I swim my way toward the bow. I can tell he's scared, but he's still doing what needs to be done. Carefully, I check out each of the dark cabins. A big crab startles me when it scuttles across the floor and slides from sight under a sagging bunk.

:The cabins on this upper deck all have big windows,: I call out to Thom.

:Crikey!: I hear his mental exclamation, and then I hear a muffled thump.

:Thom, are you all right?:

My pulse racing, I twist around and kick my way as fast as I can down to the lower passageway. There's a commotion in a cabin on the left. Through a cloud of sediment I see Thom is literally wrestling with a big gray grouper. The wide, ugly fish already has one of Thom's spear darts sticking out of its mouth. Even as I watch, Thom gets his dive knife out and stabs the big fish in the belly. The grouper twitches several times as it sinks to the floor of the cabin.

:That thing almost scared me out of my skin,: Thom admits shakily as he pulls his knife free. :It charged the second I looked in the doorway.:

:I told you some fish get territorial. Usually groupers aren't aggressive, but he must have thought this cabin was his.:

:That's a grouper? That is one ugly dude. He's even uglier than me,: Thom tries to joke.

:At least we don't have to worry about hunting for supper tonight. Thanks to you, grouper's definitely on the menu.:

Thom nudges the dead grouper with his foot. :Hear that, you big ugly sucker? You're dinner.: Thom looks up from the grouper and seems to remember our mission.

:The cabin at the end looked pretty good,: he tells me.

I swim forward and find a large triangular-shaped cabin that must occupy much of the bow. It only has two small portholes, and best of all, there's a large bed on one side, where Tobin can treat Sara.

Thom waits for me outside in the corridor :Can we shut the door to this?: I ask him.

He peers at the old worm-eaten wooden door beside him and tries to swing it shut. It disintegrates in his hands. :Guess wood doesn't last very long down here,: he says with a shrug. :I think I saw a big metal one back there.:

I swim past him and discover there is indeed a thick metal door, probably made to seal off this part of the yacht in bad weather. I try shoving it, but the door doesn't budge. I'm afraid the seawater has corroded the hinges too badly.

:Let me try,: Thom suggests.

He braces himself against the wall and puts his feet on the edge of the door. He straightens his legs, his face twisting with effort, and moments later the door swings shut.

:That's great, but . . .: I say to him. :Now we need to get that door open again.:

152

He responds with a shy smile, and then he pulls the door open.

:We're all clear here,: I call to Tobin. :You can bring Sara down the main hatch by the stern. We found a big cabin where you can treat her.:

I swim to the top deck and glance around quickly. Mali and Densil are keeping an eye on the two blue sharks that are now swimming together in slow, lazy circles around the yacht.

There will be even more sharks soon. When Tobin pulls that spear dart out of Sara's shoulder, they'll scent her blood. My parents taught me that sharks can smell a single drop of blood diluted in hundreds of gallons of water.

As I show Tobin and Penn the way to the forward cabin, I reach out to Densil. :We should be safe now. Thank you for helping fight the sharks. Be careful tonight. Don't rest too close to this place. More sharks will come.:

:we are always careful. we hope the girl will live.:

Even though I thanked him for what he did, I know dolphins don't really understand gratitude. They just do what needs to be done, like Thom.

chapter twenty-one

AS SOON AS Tobin and Penn place Sara gently on the bed, Tobin pulls off his seapack. Thom glances at the spear dart sticking out of Sara's shoulder and quickly looks away.

:Maybe I'll go see about closing that door and cutting us some grouper,: he suggests.

:That sounds like a good plan,: I tell him while I shed my own seapack, fins, and speargun. As I wait for instructions from Tobin, I study the unconscious girl. Her face is incredibly pale, but I can see that she's pretty. Her brown hair is cut short, which emphasizes her delicate features.

:Put your pack under her feet,: Tobin tells me as he pulls out a big first-aid kit from his seapack. :She's in shock, which means we need to warm her and get more blood to her head and organs. Penn, I need you to share your body heat with her. Lie down next to her uninjured side and stay as close as you can.:

While Penn is getting settled next to Sara, Tobin bends a chemlight until the divider seal cracks and the chemicals inside it mix and begin to glow.

:Here.: He hands the chemlight to me. :Fix that someplace above us so I can see better.:

As I hang the chemlight from the edge of an old light fixture hanging from the ceiling, Tobin sets to work. He wraps a pressure bandage around a nasty shark bite I hadn't noticed on Sara's right thigh.

:We'll stitch that up later,: he tells me on a private send. :If she survives my pulling that dart out.:

:What are her chances?:

:Not good.: Tobin's expression is grim. :Penn says she's been bleeding for hours. She was shot escaping from Marine Guard divers, and then she had to swim hard after that. They also just went through the Neptune transformation a day ago, which means her body is still coping with massive physiological changes. She needs a major blood transfusion, but I don't even have a blood substitute with me.:

:Is there any way we could give her some of our blood?:

:Even if by some miracle one of us had her blood type,: he replies as he readies a bandage for her shoulder, :we'd need sterile tubing to deliver that blood. IV needles I have, but no tubing, sterile or otherwise.:

I can sense the frustration he's feeling, but he continues to work calmly and steadily, doing his best to save her with what little he has.

Carefully, he uses a pair of surgical scissors to cut Sara's torn seasuit away from her shoulder. Then Tobin asks Penn to sit Sara upright and hold her there. When her head lolls back, Penn tucks it gently against his shoulder.

:I'm about to pull the dart out,: Tobin tells us. :Nere, as soon as I do, I want you to press these pads down hard on both the entrance and exit wounds while I strap her up as fast as I can. Penn, there's a good chance the pain of the extraction is going to wake her up. You need to keep her still and calm while we get this bandage on her.:

Penn's face is white with strain, but he nods to show he's ready.

Tobin grips the dart with both hands. :Here we go.:

Slowly and steadily, he starts pulling on the dart. Just as he predicted, Sara groans, her body tenses, and her eyes flick open just as the dart comes free and he tosses it away. Bright red blood starts flowing from both of the wounds. I'm scared by how much there is. Kneeling on the bed in front of her, I place the two bandages on her shoulder and press them hard.

Sara looks around wildly, her chest heaving. I can only imagine how strange it would be to wake up in a wrecked yacht.

:Where am I? God, my shoulder hurts.: She looks at me accusingly.

:Shh, Sara,: Penn reassures her. :They're just trying to help you. They need to get your shoulder bandaged before you lose any more blood.:

Tobin is working swiftly and deftly, wrapping a bandage under her armpit and over her shoulder, trying to keep as much pressure as possible on the pads on her wounds.

:I'm glad you're here, Penn.: Sara makes a brave effort to smile at him. :I thought I was just having some bizarre nightmare,: she says as she looks around the cabin and her face crumples. :But it's all real, isn't it? We're still in the ocean. They shot me, and then the sharks came. I feel so dizzy.:

:We're going to lay you back down in a moment, and then you'll feel better,: Tobin tells her.

:Who are you?: Sara cranes her head to look at him.

:My name's Tobin,: he says. :I'm a medic.:

I can tell that the quiet confidence in his tone reassures her.

She lays her head on Penn's shoulder and closes her eyes. I look at the pad under my fingers. Tobin hasn't covered it completely yet with his bandage. His eyes narrow when he sees the blood spreading across the pad and seeping out behind it.

:The spear dart must have sliced an artery,: he tells Penn and me on a private send. I sense the anguish in his mind, but his face shows little of what he's feeling. :She didn't bleed out right away because the dart kept pressure on that cut.:

:So when you took the dart out . . .: I can't bear to finish the thought.

:I killed her.:

:Tobin, you had no choice.:

:I know, but she's going to die in a few minutes just the same. Penn, I'm so sorry.: Tobin ties off the bandage and quickly finds a syringe in his med kit. :You don't need to keep pressing on those pads now,: he tells me, and I move away from the bed.

Penn looks stricken as he searches Tobin's face. :You're sure there's nothing else you can do?:

:I can try to make her a little more comfortable.:

Sara is breathing harder and harder now. :It feels like I'm not getting enough oxygen,: she says. :I think the transformation didn't work. There must be something wrong with my lungs.:

:Shh, the transformation worked just fine,: Tobin tells her as he gently straightens her right arm.

:What's that?: I can sense the panic she's fighting to control.

:I'm going to give you an injection. It will help you relax and feel less anxious. This will sting a little.:

:All right, then,: she says and bites her lip. The drug takes hold quickly, and her body begins to relax. :Penn, I feel so cold.:

Penn gathers her more tightly against him. I realize he's crying, and I look away from his face. Sara cuddles closer even as her lungs continue to heave.

After a long minute her eyes open, and she looks straight at me. :I'm dying, aren't I?:

I think for a moment. If I were her, I'd want to be told the truth.

:Yes,: I say.

:I don't want sharks and fish to eat my body. Please, swear that you'll bury me on land.: Her mental voice is growing weaker, but I'm amazed by her strength and courage. I think Sara and I could have been friends.

:I swear,: I say.

She turns back to Penn. :You mustn't be angry about this. I know you are going to want to fight them because of me, and I don't want you to do that. Promise!:

:I promise,: he says.

She relaxes in his hold and nestles her head against him once again. I glance at Tobin. He is watching Sara die, his gaze achingly sad. I wonder how many people he's watched die before. He looks so lonely and helpless that I step closer and slip an arm around his waist.

Wordlessly, he leans into me.

A short while later, Sara's chest stops heaving. After Tobin waits a long minute more, he reaches out and takes her pulse. He draws a deep breath, and I slip away from him.

:She's gone,: Tobin says.

Penn's grief fills the cabin with a psychic pain so sharp it makes my head pound.

chapter twenty-two

:ANYONE WANT SOME GROUPER?: Thom sticks his head in the door a short time later. He takes in the scene at once, and his smile fades.

:She didn't make it, did she?: Thom sees the answer to his question in our eyes.

:We'll all need to eat later, though,: I manage to say through my tears.

Penn wants to stay with Sara for now. Tobin and I decide to leave him alone with her. We slip into the cabin across from where Thom killed his grouper. Side by side, we sink down on what's left of the bed, and suddenly I realize I'm exhausted. Thom drifts in a little while later and sits across from us.

I glance sideways at Tobin. He looks even more tired and sad than I feel. :You did everything you could,: I tell him. :It's more than the rest of us knew to do.:

:It wasn't enough.: He leans his head back against the bulkhead and closes his eyes wearily.

I hear scraping and knocking against the hull. I shudder when I realize those must be sharks, trying to get at us.

:Someone needs to stay awake,: I say, fighting to keep

my eyes open. :Just in case one of those sharks breaks through a glass porthole on this deck. Only a small shark could get through those openings, but even small sharks can do some damage.:

:You two sleep first,: Thom says. :I'll keep watch.:

:Thanks,: I say. I lean my head against the bulkhead, let my heavy eyelids close, and feel Dai's mind reaching out to mine.

:Nere, are you all right? I sensed that something scared you a minute ago.:

I'm surprised at how strong his mental touch is across such a distance.

:We're not in danger. I just don't like listening to the sharks banging against the hull of the yacht.:

:It's probably blues. They're persistent idiots. Did the girl make it?:

:She died after Tobin pulled out the spear dart.:

:I'm sorry.:

:I'm sorry, too. Is everyone all right there?:

:They're fine. Robry shot a nice white sea bass for dinner. He's almost as good with a speargun as I am.:

:He might actually be better than you.:

:I doubt it. I hope your dreams are happier tonight. Try dreaming about me, and they will be.:

:Right. Good night, Dai.: Warmed by this odd interchange, I fall asleep almost instantly.

~ ~ ~

I wake in the middle of the night to find I've been sleeping with my head on Tobin's shoulder. Careful not to disturb him, I ease away from his side. He's frowning as he sleeps. I'm sorry his dreams aren't happier, but I'm very glad he's here. Now I've seen him in action, I know Tobin was meant to be a medic, or even a doctor. I don't much like Kyel and Ree, and Dai completely confuses me, but I'm glad that we met up with Thom and Tobin.

I find Thom shooting spear darts into an old chair he dragged out into the passageway.

:It was the best way for me to stay awake,: he says with a shrug. :And I need to get better with this thing.:

:It's your turn to sleep now.:

:I'm ready to rack out. I left some grouper fillets in that metal box there.:

:Thanks.:

After Thom goes off to sleep, I make myself eat one of the fillets. Then I go check on Penn. When I enter the forward cabin, Penn is wide awake and sitting next to Sara's body. His face is pale but composed.

:You should eat something and get some rest. The other guys are sleeping in the cabin down the hall,: I tell him gently. :She'd want you to look after yourself.:

:I don't want her to be alone.:

:I'll stay with her. I'm on sentry duty, but I can do it from here easily enough.:

After a moment, he gets up. :All right. I'll try to sleep, but I don't think I could eat anything right now.:

:She was very brave.:

:She always was the brave one, even when we were little,: Penn says as he looks at her. :If anyone had the guts to survive down here, it was her. But the Western Collective stole that chance just like it stole so much else from us.: The hatred in his tone worries me. I want to remind him that Sara didn't want him to be angry, but I don't think he'll listen to me right now.

Penn swims out of the cabin and leaves me with the dead girl he loved.

I pick up my speargun and make sure it's ready to fire. I have no problem staying awake. The occasional bang of a hungry shark hitting its head against the side of the yacht is enough to keep me alert. Plus, I have to think up some way to fulfill my promise to Sara. Burying her on land isn't going to be easy.

Tobin wakes up at six a.m., when the ocean is starting to lighten. He comes to find me, looking grumpy. :You should have woken me to take my shift.:

:I figured you had a rougher time last night than I did.:

:I don't think last night was much fun for any of us. This morning won't be, either, if there are a hundred sharks waiting out there to have us for breakfast.:

:Mariah will tell me when the others come back from the freighter. Between all of us, I think we can chase those sharks away.:

Tobin studies me curiously. :You really aren't scared down here, are you?:

:What do you mean?:

:You and Dai, it's like you've lived in the sea all your life. Most of us are scared out of our minds, but you look like you were meant to be here.:

:I don't know about Dai, but I'm plenty frightened down here. I'm probably more comfortable in the water just because my parents were always taking me diving and snorkeling. The dolphins help, too. I know they'll warn me if there's danger. A lot of being scared is not knowing what's out there. Thanks to Mariah and her family, I do know.:

:Even if you do know, I still think there's lots down here to be scared of.:

:Maybe staying scared will help us stay alive. Now, let's go get some breakfast.:

:Let me guess. We're having more grouper,: he says without enthusiasm.

:Grouper and some kelp. You need to have your greens.:

:I'd rather have a cup of hot coffee with some milk.:

:In your dreams,: I reply as I fetch some kelp fronds I

tied to my seapack yesterday. I don't know much about our new metabolisms, but I'm guessing we shouldn't try to survive entirely on raw fish.

It feels strange making jokes about breakfast with Sara lying cold and silent in the next cabin, but somehow the rest of us have to keep going.

Dai contacts me soon after Tobin and I have eaten grouper and some very spongy kelp. :We're all on our way to escort you back to the freighter.:

:I'm not sure Penn and I are heading there today,: I respond.

:Why?: Dai sounds intrigued.

:Before she died, Sara asked me to make sure we bury her on land. It's safer to do that at night, and we're a lot closer to land here than we'd be at the freighter.:

:A land burial is not exactly in Kyel's plans for today. This should be interesting.:

:You don't have to sound so happy about it.:

:I'm not happy about you risking going out on land, but I am happy that we joined up with you. Before that, Kyel was irritated with me all the time. Now he's mostly irritated with you. That makes my life much easier.: On that cheerful note, Dai closes his mind to me.

The group from the freighter arrives an hour later. Working together, Ton and my dolphins manage to chase away the twenty or so sharks that are circling the yacht. Thom pushes open the door that closes off the lowest deck, and we meet up with the rest of the group in the large dining salon.

:Are you ready to travel to the freighter?: Kyel asks us right off. I wince and look away from Penn. Kyel should have said something to him first about Sara.

:I'm not going to the freighter until Sara is buried properly on land,: Penn declares. :You can all go ahead, but I have to do this for her.:

:I'll stay and help you,: I promise Penn.

Kyel looks at the two of us as if we're crazy. :She's dead. Does it really matter what happens to her body?:

:She didn't want the fish to eat her, and I promised her I wouldn't let that happen,: I try to explain. :A promise is a promise.:

:It's a stupid promise if it can get you killed,: Dai says to me impatiently. :It's dangerous for you now up at the surface. What's the difference between her body being eaten by crabs in the ocean or worms on land?:

I look around and see that I'm not the only one shocked by his callous words.

:Maybe there isn't a big difference,: Robry speaks up, :but I think we're really arguing about how we're going to live down here. We should take time to bury our friends when it's not too risky for the rest of us.:

:I agree with Dai,: Kyel says flatly. :Going back on land means an unacceptable amount of risk for us at any time.:

:Maybe we should put it to a vote,: Lena suggests.

:It doesn't matter how your vote turns out,: Penn says with a wild look in his eyes. :I'm going to bury Sara on land with or without your help!:

:All right, then,: Kyel says, fighting to keep control of the situation. :A small volunteer burial detachment can remain here today, and tonight you can bury her body and rendezvous with us back at the freighter in the morning.:

In the end, Penn, Tobin, Thom, and I decide to remain at the yacht while the rest return to the freighter. As the others get ready to leave, Dai still seems angry about my choice.

:Just be careful up there.: He glowers at me. :I'll be listening for you, and if you run into trouble under the water, Ton and I will come.:

~~~

Tobin, Penn, Thom, and I spend most of that day sleeping in the wreck. When night falls, we head for land with Sara's body wrapped in kelp. The dolphins guard us while Penn and Thom go ashore to pick a burial site. After they return to the water to reoxygenate properly, they tell Tobin and me where to dig.

When I walk out of the surf and take my first deep breath of air, it feels harsh and dry in my lungs. I have to reach out my arms to steady myself because I've lost my sense of balance. Reluctantly, I face the truth: my parents have changed me so completely I no longer feel at home on land.

Tobin and I find the gravesite Penn has chosen, beneath a hardy scrub oak. There, we dig at the sandy soil with sticks until we grow so hot and out of breath that we have to return to the sea. We take turns with Thom and Penn until the grave is deep enough, and then we all troop ashore to finish our sad task.

Thom and Penn gently lower Sara's body into the grave. We stand there awkwardly. I look at Penn, wondering if he wants to say anything, but he can only stare down at Sara's body, his face wet with tears. Tobin clears his throat. "I could sing a song for her, or a hymn."

"Sara did go to church," Penn gets out. "And sometimes I went, too, just to be with her. She always liked that one about joy."

Tobin frowns, and then his face clears. "Do you mean 'Ode to Joy'?" He hums a bar of it, and Penn nods to show that Tobin has the right one. Tobin tilts his head back and launches into the old hymn. Even though he has to pause from time to time to catch his breath, he has a fine, rich voice, and the song he sings is beautiful.

As I listen to Tobin, I feel like I'm saying farewell to my life on land along with saying good-bye to Sara. Tears slip down my cheeks, and they aren't all for the dead girl at my feet.

"I'll cover her up now," Thom offers when Tobin is finished.

Tobin and I take Penn back to the shore while Thom fills in the grave. Penn is still crying, but he seems more at peace.

chapter twenty-three

AS WE RETURN TO THE SEA, I can't help panting, and my lungs feel like they're on fire. The moon emerges from its thick cover of clouds and floods the beach with silver light.

Tobin tenses beside me. "Nere, there's a man down at the south end of the beach. I think he's watching us."

I look to the south, my heart pounding. There is a single dark figure standing absolutely still, facing our direction.

"I don't know what he's doing out here, but he looks way too interested in us," Tobin says. "We'd better get out of here, fast."

Tobin sprints for the water, and Penn and I follow on his heels. Maybe Dai was right after all. Maybe we were stupid to do this. We'd all be so much safer if *no one* knew we were here on Santa Cruz.

I dive into a wave and let the cool seawater flow down into my dry lungs. Thom joins us shortly. Surrounded by the dolphins, we head for the yacht. As I swim, I worry about the man I saw on the beach. I wonder who he is and if he'll report to the Marine Guard that he saw a group of young people who disappeared into the sea.

Thom, Penn, Tobin, and I spend the night in the wreck. We leave the yacht at first light. By midmorning, we reach the place where Neptune Project survivors from all along the southern coast are supposed to rendezvous—the wreck of the freighter *Alicante.*

The old cargo freighter looks much the way I remembered her from a research trip we took to Santa Cruz when I was ten. The ship sits upright against a rock reef in fifty feet of water. She was a big vessel with a raised wheelhouse. Fifty yards from her stern is the start of a large kelp forest, which gives us a good escape route if we come under attack. Even though she sank just twenty years ago when her drunken captain ran her into a shoal, her rails and hull are already covered with a thick growth of sea fans, barnacles, algae, and seaweed.

Bria and Robry rush out of the freighter to greet us, and Kyel follows them more slowly. :Welcome to the *Alicante* Hotel,: Robry says with a grin as he gestures to the wreck. :It's the very best in undersea lodging.:

Kyel orders Robry and Bria to show us around. Talking excitedly, they give us a tour through the wheelhouse, crew cabins, crew mess, and hold. My parents did choose a good spot for us to hide out. Because the *Alicante* is a relatively young wreck, her bulkheads are still in good shape and strong enough to offer us protection from predators and sonar sweeps.

:You won't believe what we found in the crew's mess,: Robry announces in a dramatic tone. The gleam in his eyes gives me some warning. I fall back and let Tobin, Penn, and Thom go ahead of me into the mess. A second later, Bria pops out of a dim corner holding a big dead crab in front of her, waving its pincers in the boys' faces. All three of them jump in surprise while Robry and Bria giggle in triumph.

:Dudes, that was so not cool,: Thom complains, but he smiles at their trick.

:I'm going to get you for that later,: Tobin promises his little sister, which just makes her giggle harder.

Finally we manage to convince our laughing guides to continue with our tour. I leave my seapack and speargun in the large crew cabin that we're using as the girls' dormitory.

As soon as we've finished exploring the wreck, Kyel calls a meeting in the wheelhouse. As we find places to settle, Kyel watches us, his expression serious. I realize I've only seen Kyel really smile twice. The first time was when he met the dolphins, and the second was when Kona gave him his first tow. Kyel's solemn air makes him seem older than the rest of us; though I'd guess he's only a few years older than me. Maybe if I'd spent most of my life fighting the Western Collective, I'd look older, too.

:Now that we're all here, we need a plan,: Kyel begins. :I think we should take turns swimming patrols every day. We all need to get more fit:—Kyel's gaze lingers on Lena—:and ready for our long trip north to Dr. Hanson's colony. These patrols will also prepare us to deal with trouble out in the open ocean.

:Furthermore, I think we need to teach one another useful skills while we wait for more Neptune kids to make it here. Dai and Robry, you two can teach the rest of us how to shoot our spearguns more accurately. I'll teach a class on hand-to-hand combat. Tobin, I think you should teach us as many of your medical skills as you can. Nere, you need to teach us how to communicate with the dolphins. Right now, if something were to happen to Nere or Tobin, we'd be in big trouble.:

I feel my cheeks heat while I stare back at everyone. I understand that they need me because of the dolphins, but I can't help feeling glad that I'm important to this group. I've spent so much of my life being invisible.

:Robry actually knows most of the hand signals I use,: I point out, :but I'd be happy to teach them to everyone anyway.:

:Good.: Kyel nods. :No one should leave the freighter without a partner and without letting me know. We'll have one person up here in the wheelhouse on the lookout for danger at all times. I'll take the first watch. Everyone rest up for an hour, and then we start our training.:

Feeling like I've just been dismissed from class, I head for the girls' dormitory. I need to figure out what to do with my hair. For days it's been floating around me in a tangled mess.

I fetch a comb from my seapack and set to work. After five minutes of tugging at the snarls, I'm swearing and ready to give up. Maybe I'd be better off wearing it short down here. I yank my knife from its sheath and I'm about to saw off the first piece when Lena, Kalli, and Ree swim into the cabin. Clearly they've already become friends and allies, just like Robry and Bria.

:What do you think you're doing?: Ree asks me with a surprised look at my knife.

:I'm going to cut off my stupid hair,: I say. :It's just one huge knot now, and it keeps getting in my way.:

:That's what you get for rushing off to fight sharks and bury people,: Lena says with a shrug.

:I guess so,: I say, trying to act as though her words and tone don't sting. I take a deep breath and start sawing at the first big tangled lock.

:Stop!: Kalli cries, and grabs my wrist. :We can help you get this mess untangled, unless you really want short hair.:

I study Kalli. Her skin is brown, her eyes are large, and she has a long oval face framed by thick dark hair caught back in several braids. She's tall and skinny and built like a distance runner. Her expression is friendly. I remember she didn't want to stay with Sara when she was dying, but maybe she didn't really know her. Their first day in the sea must have been terrifying.

:I'd rather keep my hair long,: I admit, :if I can figure out a way to keep this mess out of my face and out of the way.:

:Ree's got that all figured out,: Kalli says. :She braided mine for me last night, and it turned out great.:

Kalli's many braids do look pretty, and practical. She has them tied in two sets, one on either side of her head.

I look at Ree. :I can do yours, too,: she offers grudgingly.

:That's all right,: I say, feeling my face start to burn. :I can figure something out on my own.:

Kalli sends Ree a long look. :I'm sure Ree wouldn't mind.:

I can tell Ree does mind, but Kalli wins out. Even Lena ends up fetching a comb. Soon, among the three of them, they have my hair untangled, and Ree deftly begins to braid it. Even though I still feel uncomfortable with the girls, I can't help closing my eyes and enjoying the touch of Ree's hands on my head. Bria floats in after a time and hands Ree ties she's cut from a thin black cord she found in her seapack.

It's easier after Bria comes. She chatters away happily to all of us, and even Lena is nice to her. I try to pretend we are a group of girlfriends. I've never been part of a group before. There would have been six of us if Sara had lived. I can't forget her face.

I open my eyes, and my gaze finds Kalli. :I'm really sorry about Sara.:

:I am, too,: Kalli says. :But I didn't know her well. She lived two villages down the coast from me. I just saw her a few times at gatherings. It's much harder for Penn. They grew up together.:

:Was there supposed to be more of you?:

:There were seven in our group originally. Somehow the secret police found out about us, and soldiers came right as we finished transforming. Only three of us made it out of Oxnay Harbor. I watched my cousin Ter get cut down and killed by soldiers with solar rifles.:

I can feel the grief and horror roiling in her mind. :I'm sorry,: I say. I want to tell her about Gillian and Cam, but I just can't. Instead I ask, :Did you always know you were a part of the Neptune Project?:

:My mother told me when I was eleven, just after I almost died from a lung attack. I think she knew how much I needed to know my lungs would be better some-day. That's when I started to dream about living in the sea. I read and learned everything I could about oceanography. It's amazing down here, but I never thought it would be this hard. . . .: Kalli's mental voice trails off.

:*Her* mother only got around to telling us three days ago.: Lena breaks in on our conversation and nods at me.

Something in me snaps. :That would be the same woman who died when she stepped in front of a solar blast to help you, Robry, and me get away,: I remind her fiercely.

Lena's gaze falls before mine. Abruptly, she spins away and leaves the cabin.

:Whew, what's between you two?: Kalli asks.

:She used to be my best friend.:

:What happened?:

:I don't know,: I say bitterly, and it's true. Did she stop being my friend because she wanted to become popular at school, and she had to dump me to make that happen? Or was there something more? I used to catch her gazing at me reproachfully, but I can't remember doing anything, ever, to hurt her.

I'm very aware that Ree is standing behind me, listening in on our conversation as she braids my hair. I wonder what Lena has told her about me.

:We can tie your plaits into two clusters, or all together, like Dai's, if you want,: Kalli suggests after an awkward pause. :Ree is almost finished now.:

As if the sound of his name had summoned him, Dai pops his head in the door. Tobin, I see, is right behind him.

:What are you doing?: Dai asks us curiously.

I almost laugh at the effect he has on the other girls— even Bria. They all sit up straighter and smile at him.

:We're trying to keep Nere from cutting her hair off,: Bria tells him cheerfully.

:I'm glad to hear it. That would have been a terrible crime.:

Kalli laughs and Bria rolls her eyes. I would guess Ree is grimacing. I sit there as stupid as a giant clam, painfully aware that I'm blushing, and wishing that Dai would just go away.

:Your wish is my command,: he tells me on a private send.

:Stop reading my mind!:

:Stop thinking so loudly about me, and I will.:

I'm relieved when Dai and Tobin do go away, and Ree finishes tying back my new plaits all together.

:Thank you,: I tell her, but she's already turning away from me. She leaves the cabin, probably to find Lena.

Kalli purses her lips as she studies me, and then she smiles. :I think that style suits you. It emphasizes those incredible cheekbones of yours.:

I smile back at her. I didn't know I had incredible cheekbones. I never really liked looking in a mirror, but for once, I wish I had one.

Just then, Kyel calls us all to the cargo deck, where we work on hand-to-hand fighting for the next hour. Demonstrating various moves with Dai as his partner, Kyel shows us several ways to protect ourselves and to wound and disable divers. Kyel is clear and patient, even with Lena and Bria, who are the slowest to understand the various moves he wants us to practice.

In the middle of their demonstration, Dai uses a move

that Kyel isn't expecting, and Dai's knife ends up against Kyel's throat. For a long, tense moment, the two of them stare at each other. I can sense the dislike and distrust radiating from them both. I'm relieved when Dai lowers his knife, and they both go on with the demonstration as if the moment never happened.

Near the end of our lesson, they have us spar with a partner, using our knives still sheathed. I work with Robry, who is as quick and hard to hit as a little eel. We both earn words of praise from Kyel and from Dai.

:All right, Nere.: Kyel startles me when the hour is over. :You're up next. Teach us all about your dolphins and how they can help us to survive.:

Suddenly, everyone's eyes are on me. I gulp and wish I were anywhere else but here.

chapter twenty-four

AS I STARE AT EVERYONE staring at me, I decide that fighting a shark might be easier than trying to teach a big group like this. I reach out to Mariah and ask her to wait nearby to help. But I still can't think of what to say. My stomach tightens and the awkward moment seems to stretch into forever.

Ree grins maliciously and leans her head closer to Lena's. I bet they are exchanging thoughts about me on a private send. I feel my face start to flush.

:Maybe you could begin by telling us how you call the dolphins to you,: Tobin suggests with an encouraging smile.

:Well, it depends on who I need to call.: I focus on his face and pretend I'm just talking to him, and suddenly it's easier. :With most of the dolphins, I just send them a feeling that I need them, but with Mariah, Sokya, and Densil, I actually tell them in words what I want them to do.:

Dai looks stunned. :Your dolphins can communicate to you in English?:

:Well, yes, mostly because of Mariah. She was orphaned as a calf and grew up with my mother, who is—I mean was—a strong telepath.: My cheeks burn hotter over my stumble, but I make myself keep going. :They played together all the time, and somehow Mariah learned our language from her. She taught it to Sokya and Densil. The other dolphins in the pod just don't seem interested or able to pick it up. I use hand commands or send visual images to them.:

:Will we be able to communicate telepathically with Mariah?: Kyel asks me intently.

:We'll have to try and see. I'm going to call Mariah down here, and one at a time, you can try asking her to come to you. She'll let me know if she can understand your thoughts.:

I call Mariah and explain to her what we're trying to find out.

:I hear the youngest female, and she understands me,: Mariah replies promptly as she swims down from the surface with Tisi at her side.

I look at Bria in surprise. :Mariah says she's already been talking with you.:

Bria blushes and looks uncomfortable at becoming the center of attention. :I started hearing her words in my mind that first day when Kyel and I saw the shark. She told me the dolphins were my pod now and they would make sure I stayed safe.:

:This is great!: I tell her. :I'd like to start teaching you how to work with all of them right away.:

:I'd love to,: Bria says, her eyes shining.

Kyel looks pleased. He knows now that if something happens to me, he still has a way to communicate with the dolphins.

:All right,: I say, :let's see if she can understand anyone else.:

One by one, different members of our group try to call Mariah to them. She hovers in the water next to me while Tisi plays with an orange puffball sponge nearby. Dai tries longer than anyone else, frowning with effort, but Mariah can't understand him.

Just when I'm sure no one else in the group will be able to speak to her, Mariah surges through the water and gently pokes her beak into Tobin's belly.

Tobin's face lights up, and he reaches out to scratch her melon. :She just told me she likes to be scratched right here. She says she can understand me almost as clearly as she can understand you.:

From the way Mariah remains with him, I can tell she likes Tobin. Next, I call all the dolphins, and they go to the human partners I've already assigned them. I ask joyful Laki to work with Penn, and sweet-tempered Mona to work with Kalli. I show everyone the basic hand signals the dolphins know for fetching, finding, protecting, and towing. At the end of my hour, I tell everyone to go off and play with their assigned dolphins.

Before long, Robry and Nika get a wild game of tag going. Towed by our dolphins, we chase one another over and around the *Alicante* and in and out of the kelp forest nearby. Although I've played tag with Robry and the dolphins before, it's much more of a rush when so many of us are darting and twisting through the kelp. I grin when I hear Bria shriek with laughter as Kyel and Kona manage to tag her. Everyone joins in by the end except for Dai. He just watches, looking perplexed and increasingly bored.

:Tomorrow we can work on sending your dolphin partners visual messages,: I say, happy to see that most everyone is smiling as we wrap up the session.

The humans stop to eat. After lunch, Kyel sends us out in teams of three and four to go on patrol with our dolphins. I sigh when I find I've been assigned to patrol with Ree, Thom, and Robry. Thom and Robry I can work with, but I'm not looking forward to a whole afternoon of swimming around with Ree.

Kyel tells us to skirt the eastern tip of the island and patrol the waters to the south. He orders us to report any contacts with boats but to make sure we stay out of sonar range.

The first two hours of our patrol pass smoothly enough. I'd forgotten how beautiful the waters around the Channel Islands are. We pass steep rock walls covered with pinkish-red gorgonian sea fans and carpets of delicate orange and white brittle stars and neon-colored nudibranchs. Robry spots a family of sea otters playing in the kelp. Even Ree ends up smiling as we pause to watch the bright-eyed animals twisting and diving as they chase one another.

We make it to the tip of the island without encountering any boats or danger. We slow our pace as we approach the series of rocky pinnacles and shoals that form the most northeastern tip of Santa Cruz.

As we thread our way through those pinnacles, I think I hear a boat engine, and I ask our group to stop. I tell Sokya to go find it and tell me what type of boat it is.

:What are we waiting for?: Ree asks me impatiently.

:I hear a boat out there somewhere.:

:Well, I don't hear anything, so it can't be very close.:

Robry speaks up. :I hear it, too.:

I look uneasily at the rocky shoals and towers all around us. :Sound can do strange things underwater,: I warn Ree. :That boat is probably miles away, but surf, surge, and shoals like this can really distort sound waves.:

Ree starts swimming forward. :I don't want to hang out here all day. I just want to get this *stupido* patrol done.:

Thom and Robry stay with me. :You should wait until Sokya checks back with me. . . .: I call after Ree.

Seconds later, Sokya arrows toward me, whistling and sawing in fear.

:net! net! net!: she cries and sends me a chilling image

of a seine net rushing through the water. The rest of the dolphins start whistling and clicking wildly. They are terrified of fishing nets.

:Ree, get back here! There's a fishing boat out there pulling a net. Sokya, Densil, Nika, Pani—get back by these rocks!:

:You're crazy.: Ree turns around to face us. :I still don't hear anything.:

I spot the tall black net rushing toward her. :Ree, swim toward us! Swim back to us, NOW!:

Startled, she looks over her shoulder and finally sees the net. She sprints toward us, her legs kicking wildly, but it's too late. The fishing net sweeps her up and drags her away.

chapter twenty-five

:SOKYA, I NEED A TOW NOW!: I call as I kick desperately after Ree.

:but the net—: Sokya protests, and I can sense the terror in her mental voice.

:It's already passed us. I promise it won't catch you. But it has caught my friend. Please, Sokya, before it's too late.:

The fishing boat is traveling so quickly, if we don't catch up to it in the next few minutes, Ree will be beyond our help. Her panicked shouts buffet my mind.

Sokya appears beside me, and I catch hold of her fin.

:We're coming!: I call after Ree. Then I urge Sokya, :Swim fast! We've got to catch up with that net.:

I concentrate on hanging on to her dorsal and making my body as streamlined as I can. Sokya surges through the water, her powerful tail propelling us forward.

I can see the net now. It's like a giant black spiderweb spun across a huge expanse of sea.

:Take me close to Ree, and I'll catch hold of the net.:

:I try,: Sokya says, but I can sense she is straining. Soon she will run out of air in her lungs, and she will need to surface. We *have* to catch the net before then, or poor Ree will be crushed by the fish caught in the net or captured by the fishermen, who will probably turn her over to the Western Collective.

I don't like Ree, but I can't leave her to be crushed or captured.

With a final burst of speed, Sokya pulls me right up below Ree. I let go of Sokya's fin and lunge forward. I wrap my fingers around a section of net. My arms jerk, my shoulders pick up the strain, and suddenly I'm being towed forward through the water on the outside of the big net.

:Go breathe, and then please stay close,: I say to Sokya while I struggle to pull myself closer to Ree. :We may need your help to get away.:

It's hard to keep my grip against the power of the water rushing at me. I feel like I'm fighting a strong riptide. Ree had the sense to get out her dive knife, but she's having problems sawing through the thick strands. The force of the water keeps pushing her body against the net.

Holding on tight to the net with one hand, I work my dive knife free of its sheath on my belt. I hook my left arm through the net and set to work on a section next to the one she's cutting.

:Thanks for coming,: Ree grits as she saws away.

:We can't afford to lose our best hair braider,: I say while I focus on slicing through the thick black fibers.

Ree keeps looking over her shoulder as frantic fish dart

past her. A big green sea turtle is clawing at the net below us.

:I can't believe all the stuff they've caught in this thing,: Ree says shakily. :I think there's a pretty big shark in here, too.:

Moments later, she lets out a startled yelp and drops her dive knife as the frantic turtle bumps into her leg. I glance down and realize it was forced upward because the net is getting smaller. The fishermen must be winching it in.

Robry and Nika appear beside me. Agile as a monkey, Robry catches hold of the net and lets go of Nika's dorsal.

:Ree dropped her knife and we're running out of time,: I tell him breathlessly. :Try to cut through that section there.: I point, and Robry sets to work on it. Our dive knives are incredibly sharp, and we're sawing at the net just inches away from each other's hands.

As the net tightens, the frightened creatures inside it are forced closer together. Ree turns, sets her back to the net, and uses her speargun to fend off the turtle and a bat ray that are frantically ramming their heads against the net right next to her.

The last strand separates in my section. Immediately, I start on the section Ree was cutting.

:Nere, they're pulling us up now,: Robry warns me.

:I know. Keep cutting.:

:I can see the boat!: Ree cries in panic.

Folds of the big net begin to close in around us. If we're

not careful, Robry and I could get tangled in it.

:I'm through!: Robry yells.

I push harder on my knife, and a second later, it severs the last strand. Now there's a good-sized hole in the net.

:Ree, turn around!: I shout.

Robry and I force the opening wider, and Ree tries to thrust her head and shoulders through it. Her broad shoulders catch. I'm afraid she can't possibly fit. I yank the net over her right shoulder; she kicks and twists desperately, and she's free.

Robry and I let go of the net, and we watch as it continues to constrict, forcing the frantic sea creatures inside closer and closer together. A few frightened mackerels slip out through the hole we cut, but the turtle and the bat ray are pinned against the sides by the rest of the catch. The turtle will probably drown before it's hauled out of the water, and the bat ray will be crushed.

:Let's get out of here before they pick us up on sonar,: Robry says unsteadily.

:Right,: I say as I sheathe my knife with trembling hands. They're going to be sore later. I ask Sokya and our other patrol dolphins to tow us out of the boat's sonar range. As we hurry back the way we came, I grow angrier at Ree.

We see Thom and Densil rushing toward us. That's when I realize cutting Ree free probably only took us a few minutes at the most. Thom smiles shyly at her.

:I'm glad you aren't going to end up in a can of tuna fish. Are you okay?: he asks her.

:I'm a little shook up, but yeah, I'm okay, thanks to these guys.: She sends a sideways look at Robry and me. I wonder if that's as close as she's going to get to thanking us.

:I'm sorry I couldn't catch up with you in time to help out.: Thom looks embarrassed. :I think I'm a lot for him to tow.: He nods to Densil.

I can't hold in my anger a moment longer and turn on Ree. :Rushing ahead like that was incredibly stupid. We all could have gotten killed just now.:

Without another word, I swim past her and head for the pinnacles and shoals at the tip of the island. We stop there to rest. After a quick, tense discussion, we decide we've done enough patrolling for one day.

When we start heading back to the *Alicante*, Robry and Thom take the lead. Ree falls back to swim along beside me, but I do my best to ignore her.

:You've got every right to be mad,: she says after a while. :I was *muy estúpida*. Thanks for coming after me anyway. I owe you big-time.:

:You don't owe me anything,: I reply shortly. I want to go back to ignoring her, but she looks so sorry I say, :Listen, it's okay. We've got to look after each other down here.:

:Yeah, well, you seem to be looking after everyone else better than we're looking after you.:

Her words make me uncomfortable. :I think I've just spent more time in the sea than the rest of you, except maybe for Dai.:

:Speaking of Dai, I thought I really liked him, but he's barely talked to me since we met up with you, except to tell me to take out my silver hoops before a barracuda bit my ears off.:

I stare at Ree. Does she think Dai likes me?

:I just wanted you to know, I've decided you can have him. He's one of the most *guapo* guys I've ever seen, but there's just something really off about him. Kyel's more my type anyway.:

:Kyel?: I can't hide my surprise. Somehow I can't see Kyel being into any girl.

:Hey, even tough guys need girlfriends. Kyel just doesn't know he needs me yet,: Ree says with a smile that lights up her whole face. :But here's some advice. Flirt and have fun with Dai, but Tobin's a better bet for you in the long run. You're the smart, quiet type, and so is he.:

I feel my cheeks starting to burn. :Um, I think we need to figure out how to survive down here first.:

I'm *really* relieved when Ree gets off the topic of guys and starts talking about her past instead. She tells me she was a *Chica Malas*, a girl from one of the gangs who roam the hills above the drowned, tyrox-ravaged city of LA. Her father was a genetics professor, which Ree thinks is how she became part of the Neptune Project. Her dad was arrested and taken away when she was so young, she barely remembers him. When her mother and her little sister, Isa, died in the last famine, Ree joined the gang to survive.

:I still miss Isa,: Ree admits. :She could be a real pain, like when she was always begging me to play with her, but she was my sweet little *amiga*, too. When Bria smiles, she reminds me of Isa so much sometimes . . . .: Ree stops speaking for a moment and looks away from me before she resumes her story.

:Then this weird young guy showed up and hung out with our gang for a while. He told me he knew why my eyes and my lungs were so weak. My lung attacks were getting pretty bad, so I agreed to go down to San Diego with him. There in his secret lab, he gave me some lung meds and told me all about the Neptune Project. He'd already found Tobin and Bria. Kyel and Thom showed up a few weeks before we went through the final transformation together.:

:And what about Dai?: I try to sound casual.

:He met up with us a few days before you did, just south of LA.:

I blink. I thought he'd been a part of Kyel's group from the start. :Was there anyone with him?:

:Just that big dolphin.:

:Did he say where he came from?:

A familiar male mind touches mine. :If you're that curious about me, Nere, just ask.:

Dai swims out to meet us, his expression tight. With a start, I realize we are almost back to the *Alicante*. There's a challenge in Dai's gaze that makes my stomach clench.

:All right,: I reply. I don't like his eavesdropping on my private conversation with Ree, but he looks so angry that I decide to wait until later to call him on it.

:We have to report to Kyel, but then I do want to hear your life story,: I declare while I carefully close my mind to him.

And I want to know how, exactly, you came to have a deep-sea dolphin and learned how to kill sharks with your dive knife.

chapter twenty-six

KYEL CALLS A MEETING in the wheelhouse so everyone can hear about the patrols. Thom, the official leader for our patrol group, matter-of-factly reports what happened to Ree. Robry and I receive some curious looks by the end of his report, and Dai gives me a mock salute. After Thom finishes, Kyel nods to Robry and me.

:Nere, Robry, that was quick thinking. Now we know we need to watch out for fishing nets. And Ree, now you know you've got to stay with your travel group.:

Then Penn reports in for his patrol, and it's clear from the start that he's excited about something.

:We found a Marine Guard vessel anchored in a natural harbor ten miles to the west of here. It's the *Defender*, the same one that chased Sara, Kalli, and me out of Oxnay. She has at least twenty crew aboard her.:

I draw in a breath. It is *not* good that a Marine Guard vessel looking for Neptune Project kids has turned up here.

:I think we should go back there tonight and sink that ship with a mine,: Penn declares, his dark eyes smoldering with hatred. :I bet they won't be watching for us on their sonar scopes at night.:

:You might as well walk right up on the beach of Santa Cruz and tell the Western Collective that we're hiding out here,: Tobin speaks up. :The Marine Guard knows we have mines now, and if we sink this ship, they'll guess we did it.:

:But these are the same men who killed Sara,: Penn says angrily. :We can't let them get away with murder.:

:This is an excellent chance to strike at our enemy with only a small possibility of casualties,: Kyel adds, so calmly that a chill goes down my back.

:But that's not our job,: I burst out. :Our job right now is to learn how to stay alive down here. We can't fight every Marine Guard vessel we come across.:

:Penn, I know they killed Sara, but sinking this ship isn't going to bring her back,: Lena adds quickly.

Ree straightens up and crosses her arms. :Kyel, *mi amigo*, you're not leading some guerrilla group that's dedicated to bringing down the Western Collective anymore. Me, I'm dedicated to staying alive for another twenty-four hours, and based on my mess-up with that net, survival's a big enough challenge for us right now.:

:I agree. Going after Marine Guard boats is a crazy idea,: Kalli adds.

:Have any of you actually read the information in our seapacks?: Robry asks, his expression earnest. :The mission of the Neptune Project is not to attack boats or to try to topple any government. Our mission is to establish a colony in the sea and build something new and better under the waves. We risk all that if we try to fight the Collective's ships while there's still so few of us.:

Kyel's face is impassive as he considers our words. :My primary mission has been and will always be to take down the Western Collective. It's a corrupt, rotten regime responsible for the careless deaths of millions. We'll head out for the *Defender* as soon as it's dark.:

The fanatical light in his eyes seems oddly familiar to me, and suddenly I remember the way my mother looked when she was talking about the Neptune Project.

:Kyel, I'm sorry,: Tobin says, :but you and Penn are dead wrong to go after this Marine Guard boat. If you're determined to ignore us, I propose we hold another election for leader right now.:

He looks at each of us and adds, :And I nominate Nere Hanson.:

I stare at Tobin. My stomach starts twining and twisting like an octopus. Is he crazy? I can't possibly lead this group. If Kyel, with all his years of guerrilla training, has difficulty getting this group to follow orders, I don't stand a chance. I have problems just leading a lesson on how to work with dolphins.

:I think Nere would be a good leader for the following reasons,: Tobin declares. :She thinks fast, she has the guts to act on her decisions, she knows the ocean, her dolphins give her vital information that has already helped save lives, and, most importantly, she understands that our survival in the sea comes first.:

:I second that idea.: Lena stuns me by agreeing. :She knows more than any of us about the sea, and she has the common sense not to go around blowing up boats.:

I look across at Dai, hoping he might volunteer to lead us, but he's just watching our heated exchange and smiling as if we're entertaining him.

Then I glance at Kyel. His expression is cool, but there's a muscle ticking in his cheek. :I agree to another election. I don't want to be your leader if I don't have the support of the majority,: he says tightly.

:You don't need to hold any election,: I say before this craziness goes any further. :I'm sorry, Tobin, but I couldn't possibly lead this group. Kyel has already shown he can lead us and make sound decisions in pressure situations.:

I force myself to meet Kyel's gaze. :Up until now, I think you've been doing a good job. I just don't think we should be attacking the Marine Guard.:

:So, if we elect you, you really won't act as our leader?: Tobin says.

I have to look away from the disappointment in his eyes.

:You'd be making a huge mistake,: I say.

:I don't believe that for a minute,: he counters.

:Maybe *you* should be our leader,: I suggest. :You always seem to know how we feel and what we need.:

Tobin's mouth twists. :Kyel's a better choice than me. If I had to decide in some tough situation who has to risk his or her life, I'd hesitate until I got us all killed.:

:I don't believe that for a minute, either,: I say, remembering how decisive he was when he was fighting to save Sara's life.

:You should,: Tobin counters. :Medics are all about saving lives, not deciding who might have to die.:

Then Tobin addresses the entire group. :New plan—Kyel should continue as our leader, but we vote on whether or not we attack the Marine Guard ship. At the start, we agreed that we would vote on the really big, important issues.:

After hesitating briefly, Kyel nods. :All those in favor of trying to sink the Marine Guard vessel, raise your hands.:

I look around at our group, and only Penn and Kyel raise their hands. Kyel glances across the wheelhouse at Thom, clearly expecting him to raise his hand, too.

:K-man, I hate the Collective as much as you do,: Thom says with a shrug, :but I'm tired of fighting. Maybe the best way to beat them is to make something really good down here.:

Kyel swallows, and I can tell Thom's vote has shaken him. :All right, who wants me to continue as your leader?:

We all promptly raise our hands except Dai. Kyel looks around, and when he realizes the vote is almost unanimous, his face relaxes a little.

:Right. I will continue to serve as the group's leader, for now. Kalli has the next watch. My patrol brought in a fresh grouper everyone can eat for dinner. This meeting is adjourned.: With that, Kyel swims from the wheelhouse all alone. Thom looks after Kyel, his expression troubled. After shooting me a quick grin, Ree follows Kyel.

The rest of us head for the crew's mess, where we cut up Kyel's grouper and a bunch of seaweed Kalli gathered for us. Swimming hard works up an appetite, but I can't get excited about more raw fish and seaweed.

:God, I miss bread,: Lena says after she takes a nibble of green wakame. Clearly she has finally run out of fish bars from her seapack.

:I miss milk and cake,: Bria chimes in.

:I miss ice cream,: Robry says with a sigh. :I only had it twice, but I'll never forget it.:

:I miss eating without fish trying to snatch my food from me,: Kalli says as she shoos away a persistent little rock wrasse.

:Get this. When I was a little kid,: Thom tells us, :I loved sushi more than anything. My Japanese grandma used to go down to the docks and trade the vegetables she grew for fresh fish. She could make flowers and shapes out of that fish, some seaweed, and just a little bit of rice. It was such a big deal when we got to eat her sushi that I used to wish I could have it every single day.:

:So, I guess they're right when they say, 'Be careful what you wish for.': Tobin grins at him.

:That's pretty much what I think every time I eat down here now,: Thom replies, making such a wry face at his grouper that we all end up laughing.

After we eat, I swim closer to the surface to visit with the dolphins before night falls. I check each of my friends to make sure they haven't picked up parasites or cuts. I've just finished looking over playful Pani when Dai swims up to join me. Suddenly I feel breathless, which makes me furious.

I glance at Dai, and then look away. He reminds me of a statue of an angel I saw once in an old chapel. He has the same severe, beautiful features. Except that I can't imagine an angel looking as disdainful or mocking as Dai can look.

But I sense that he isn't in a mocking mood now. :You should have said yes today when they wanted to make you their leader,: he says bluntly. :Tobin was right. You would do a better job of leading this group than Kyel does.:

:I told everyone the truth. I don't want the job.:

I'm very aware that Dai is studying me. :You really don't think you could do it, do you?:

:Isn't that obvious?: I say, refusing to meet his gaze. Instead I call Densil and start checking him for parasites.

Dai keeps after me. :But this is what you've been training for all your life.:

:Maybe my parents did train me to live in the sea, but

they didn't train me how to lead anyone, much less a group like this. I can't tell experienced fighters like Kyel or Thom what to do. Until this afternoon, Ree would have beaten me up if I'd given her an order, and Lena probably would've laughed at me.:

:But after what you did for her today, Ree won't beat you up, and Lena wanted you to take over Kyel's job.:

:You don't understand!: I turn to face Dai, frustration boiling up inside me. :I'm used to being nothing in the village where I lived, and nothing at the school where I went. My parents were so focused on their precious research, sometimes I was nothing to them, too. I barely know how to talk with people my own age, much less get them to follow my orders.:

:You'd be surprised how well I do understand,: Dai admits. :But you're wrong if you think you aren't important to this group. You may not talk much to the others, but they like and trust you already.:

:If you say so,: I say with a shrug, trying not to show how much his words mean to me. :I'd really rather talk about you now, instead of me.:

:What do you want to know? I'll answer exactly five questions,: Dai says. His expression is wary, but there's a hint of a smile in his eyes.

:So, number one is, who are your parents? You already know all about mine.:

:My father is a marine biologist,: he replies, looking bored. :My mother was a geneticist, but she died when I was so little, I don't remember her. I've lived on research vessels most of my life, which is why I don't always know the right thing to say to people, either.:

I study Dai as he talks. He's shielding his emotions, and I get the strong impression that he's choosing his words carefully.

:Okay, here's question two. When did you find out you were actually a part of the Project?:

His eyes narrow at that, and for an instant, his shields waver. I sense the sharp, sudden pain my question causes him.

:You're just like me. It hurt to find out you'd been bred for a purpose,: I say softly.

He smiles, but there isn't any humor in his eyes. :I shouldn't have been so surprised. The sea has always come first with my father. I found out when I was ten, though, so I've had some time to get used to the idea.:

:How did you know where to join up with Kyel's group?:

Dai raises one eyebrow. :That's three. You only have two left.:

:Technically, I answered part of the last one for you, so we're still on two.:

He sends me an exasperated look. :Technically, I don't think you count so well. My father had been in touch with

Neptune Project scientists. He knew the kids from the southern sector would head for the Channel Islands, and he sent Ton and me down the coast to look for them.:

And Dai made that trip all by himself. A sudden suspicion takes hold of me. :When did you actually go through the transformation?:

Dai hesitates. :When I was ten,: he admits at last.

I stare at him. :How old are you now?:

:Fourteen. So, yeah, I've been part fish for four years now.: He says the words defiantly, but I can sense the vulnerability behind them.

:You should be leading this group, not Kyel or me,: I say, shaking my head. I can't believe Dai has survived in this dangerous ocean for four years already.

:That's not going to happen, Nere. This group doesn't like or trust me, and I don't think I particularly like or trust them.:

:But why did you have to go through the transformation so young?:

:I think my father was excited about it, and he wanted to make sure it worked.:

There it was again. Even though he tried to hide it, Dai radiated such strong psychic pain when he spoke of his father that I couldn't help shivering. How could a father do that to his son? Rather than continuing to upset Dai, I decide to change the subject.

:How did you start working with Ton?:

Dai smiles at the mention of Ton, just as I thought he would. :That's question number seven, by the way, but I never mind talking about Ton. He was orphaned as a calf. He and I grew up together, much the way you and Sokya and Densil did. But he never learned to communicate in English. I still can't believe that you can actually talk with Mariah. I communicate with Ton through visual images, just like you do with the other dolphins.:

:Mariah's contact with other dolphins was limited when she was a calf, and I'm not sure she really understood she was a dolphin instead of a human at first. Take into account that my mother was a powerful telepath, and you can see how she may have accidentally taught Mariah words in English while she was first learning them herself as a small child.:

:I wonder if Mariah could teach Ton to talk with me.:

:I'll ask her,: I say, trying to hide my misgivings. I'm not sure Mariah really can talk with Ton, or at least, not in the sense Dai means. I don't think dolphins think or communicate with each other in words at all. They use images, feelings, and a wide variety of sounds, some of which human ears can't even hear.

Hoping to change the subject, I point out that it's getting dark, and we both swim back down to the freighter.

:Nere, I think we need to keep an eye on Penn,: Dai says soberly before we enter the wreck.

:What do you mean?:

:I don't think he's given up on the idea of attacking that ship.:

I want to scold Dai for listening in on other people's thoughts again. But maybe he's not worried about Penn because of something he overheard telepathically. Thinking about the end of the meeting today, I realize Dai may be right. Penn didn't look happy about the way the vote turned out.

I shudder when I think of what could happen to us if he decided to go off and attack that ship on his own.

chapter twenty-seven

OUR NEXT FEW DAYS on the *Alicante* fall into a routine. In the mornings, we rotate through a series of classes on fighting, speargun marksmanship, and first aid. I teach how to communicate with and care for the dolphins. And Kalli, who turns out to be an expert on sea plants, shows us what species and varieties we can harvest to eat.

In the afternoons, we patrol up and down the coast of Santa Cruz with the dolphins. I'm happy to see my companions are growing closer to the pod. Sometimes the dolphins even come down to the *Alicante* on their own, seeking out their partners to play. One afternoon I catch Kyel and Thom racing against each other with their dolphins through the kelp forest, which makes me laugh.

We all keep hoping other Neptune kids will reach the wreck, but so far, no one has. I worry about the lone man we saw on the beach after we buried Sara, and Dai and I both keep an eye on Penn. He does participate in our lessons and never mentions the Marine Guard vessel that continues to patrol the area and anchor nearby us at night.

I ask Mariah to help Ton communicate to Dai in English, and her response doesn't surprise me.

:the big dolphin doesn't understand my human words.:

:Could you please keep trying to teach him?:

:I try, but he thinks and talks like a dolphin,: she says, and I can feel the frustration in her mind.

:It's amazing that you can think like a human.:

:I am smart,: Mariah says, sounding so smug, I have to laugh. :and your mother helped me to learn,: she adds, grief coloring her tone, :when I was just a calf.:

I reach out and place a hand on Mariah's melon. :I miss her, too.:

~ ~ ~

During the day, I keep busy learning all the skills I can to stay alive. The waters around the Channel Islands are so beautiful and full of marine creatures, sometimes I actually like my new life. I have always loved the sea; I just never imagined I'd have to live in it forever.

I try not to think about what happened to my mother or what might be happening to Cam right now. But at night, when I struggle to fall asleep, I keep seeing them cut down by the soldiers at Tyler's Cove, like a slip of old video on continual replay, or I see poor Sara with a spear dart in her shoulder, surrounded by frenzied sharks. My dreams after I fall asleep are even worse.

One time when I wake up, Lena is there beside my hammock, shaking my shoulder.

:You were thrashing around and having a nightmare,:

she says. :I thought you'd rather wake up than be wherever you were.:

I look at the black ceiling of the wrecked freighter while I fight to catch my breath. Would I rather be here? :Thanks,: I manage to tell her.

:I have nightmares sometimes, too,: Lena admits. :You know, I am sorry about your mother. I'll never forgive her for what she did to me, but I'm sorry she's dead, just the same. And Cam, he's so strong. If anyone can survive a work camp, it's him.:

:I think you're right about that.: I almost manage a smile, but then I feel tears start to well. :What do you think of Kyel and the rest?: I ask quickly to change the subject.

:I don't like Kyel much, and I really don't like Dai, but I do feel safer being with this group.:

:I do too, even when things get tense. Robry feels the same way. We'll stay with them, then. And Lena, thanks for waking me up.:

:You're welcome.:

But the next day, Lena goes back to avoiding me, and I wonder if I dreamed our talk.

~ ~ ~

One afternoon, a small wooden sailing craft starts following the dolphins on patrol with Tobin and his group. Mariah tells the dolphins to submerge for so long, they lose the small boat, but the contact makes us all jittery.

We are surprised when the same craft appears just before nightfall and anchors in a tiny inlet directly ashore from the *Alicante*.

:Whoever it is, he or she seems way too interested in our dolphins,: Kyel concludes during an emergency meeting in the wheelhouse. :Nere, ask the pod to keep away from us for a day or so, and we'll stay close to the freighter tomorrow.:

The sailboat is still anchored in the inlet the next morning. We go through our usual morning classes, except dolphin training, and everyone is on edge.

We've just gathered to eat some lunch in the crew's mess when Penn, who's on guard duty, calls out to us. :Some guy with a speargun and fins just swam down from the surface! He's looking around the cargo deck right now.:

:Don't let him see you,: Kyel orders Penn. :Does he look like a Marine Guard diver?:

:No, he's not wearing scuba gear.:

:He could be another Neptune kid,: Kalli says hopefully.

:Neptune man, maybe,: Penn responds. :You should see the beard on this guy.:

:What's he doing now?: Kyel asks Penn after we've waited an endless two minutes.

:He's still looking around the cargo area. Wait, he's

heading back to the surface now. I'm pretty sure he can't breathe water.:

After we're sure he's gone, we all head for the wheelhouse in a hurry.

:Whoever he is, he just performed an impressive free dive,: Robry points out. :He swam down sixty feet and stayed at this depth for over three minutes.:

:I wonder what he was looking for,: Bria says, her eyes wide and worried.

:Maybe he wanted to scavenge something off the wreck,: I suggest. People have gotten so desperate back on land, some have become scroungers, searching through wrecks to find things they can eat, use, or sell.

:Well, whoever he is, we can't risk his seeing us,: Kyel says flatly. :We stay in the wreck for the rest of the day. He might be back.:

No one looks happy about Kyel's order. Most days we eat our meals inside the *Alicante* for protection from pesky fish who try to steal our food, and we sleep in her at night, but our wreck is a dark and gloomy place.

:Robry, you can give us another navigation lesson right now,: Kyel says. :Nere, you take the next guard shift.:

I nod and go fetch my seapack. I figure I can skim some of the Neptune Project information notes and keep an eye out for the free diver at the same time.

I'm in my second hour of guard duty when I spot the

mysterious diver kicking his way down through the water to the wreck once again.

:Hey, we've got company!: I call out to the group. :He's back. Everyone stay below.:

Suddenly I realize I'm in trouble. The free diver is heading straight for the wheelhouse!

My pulse thunders in my ears. The only access to the wheelhouse is from the outside, since the big hatch to the lower decks is corroded shut. If I try to leave, the diver is going to spot me for sure.

That means I have to find someplace to hide inside the wheelhouse, and I have to find it fast. I look around wildly. There are no lockers large enough to hold me. My only chance is to duck under the wide control board and hope he doesn't think to look there.

I dart under the control board, stretch myself out, and try to hold completely still. Ten heartbeats later, I see the flick of a fin as the diver enters the wheelhouse and starts prowling around.

I grip my speargun tightly. What am I going to do if he sees me? Will I have to kill him? He's bound to notice I have no scuba gear. He may mean us no harm, but we can't allow him to tell someone onshore that he's seen a girl on the *Alicante* who breathes water. But I don't want to kill anyone!

Please don't look under the control board. Please don't look here.

He whirls around—almost as if he heard my thoughts! My heart stops when he peers under the control board. I catch a glimpse of long shaggy hair and a bearded face.

Taking a deep breath, I raise my speargun and try to force myself to pull the trigger.

:Nere, don't shoot! It's me!:

I gaze into his eyes, and I realize I know this stranger.

:James?:

I lower my speargun in disbelief. With his long hair and bushy beard, my big brother looks like some sort of wild castaway.

:I thought I saw you on the beach last week, and I've been looking for you ever since. I've got to surface now. Can you come with me?:

:Yes, but it would be safer if I came to see you after sunset,: I say, struggling to overcome my shock. James must have been the man we saw onshore after we buried Sara. :And I have to tell the others where I'm going.:

I swim forward and give him a hug, even though I know James isn't big on hugs. I'm just so happy to see him. He pats my shoulder awkwardly.

:Are there other kids from the Neptune Project here?: he asks the instant I move away from him.

:Yes.:

:And the transformation worked on all of you?:

:Yes.:

I can't tell if it's pain or excitement I see in his eyes before he heads out of the wheelhouse and kicks swiftly toward the surface.

:Meet me at the *Kestrel* at ten o'clock tonight,: he calls to me, and then the blue water swallows him.

So the wooden vessel anchored nearby must be James's beloved sailboat.

:Nere, what's going on?: Kyel and Dai ask me impatiently at the same time.

:You can all come out now. The free diver is my brother, James.:

I realize I'm grinning as our group swims up to the wheelhouse. I'm so glad James is alive.

:Can we trust your brother?: Kyel asks the moment he sees me. :Is there any chance he's going to report us to the Marine Guard?:

:James hates the Western Collective as much as anyone. He used to talk about going off to join a group like yours. He finally ran away a year ago, but not to fight. We'd heard he was living out here on one of the Channel Islands, but no one's seen him for months. I . . . I thought maybe he was dead.:

:Why did he run away?:

I feel my face heat up. I'm embarrassed that I don't know what made my brother leave us. :I'm not sure. I know he and my mother had some awful arguments. He was always getting into trouble his last year at school. The only time he was happy was when he was off sailing in his *Kestrel*. That's the boat that's anchored near us now.:

:Was he supposed to be a part of the Neptune Project, too?: Tobin asks, his green eyes shrewd.

I remember what Gillian told me while I was going through the transformation. :I think maybe he was supposed to be. My mother said something about their making a mistake when they altered his genes.:

:In our group, there was a kid who didn't survive the transformation,: Penn says somberly. :After the scientists injected him with the virus, the gill filaments in his lungs didn't function properly, and he suffocated because he couldn't breathe either air or water.:

I feel myself getting angry all over again at my parents and the secrets they kept. I don't know if my mother tried to inject James with the virus and his transformation failed, or if somehow she knew beforehand that he wouldn't be able to transform.

:Kyel, I have to go to the surface and talk to him. I . . . I need to tell him about our mother.: I see him start to protest, so I add hastily, :Plus, James may have news of other Neptune kids and what's going on back home.:

After a long minute, Kyel nods. :All right. You can go tonight. Just make sure no one sees you while you talk with him.:

As our meeting breaks up, I realize I can't wait to see James, but it's going to be so hard to tell him about our mother. I also keep wondering . . . what sort of mistake did my parents make when they tried to alter my brother's genes?

chapter Twenty-eight

I LEAVE THE ALICANTE to talk to my brother right before ten o'clock. James is waiting for me in the water by the stern of the *Kestrel*. I hug him as soon as I surface, and he actually hugs me back.

"So, what's it like, breathing water and living in the sea?" he asks as we tread water side by side. His gray eyes are alight with excitement. His voice sounds rusty, like maybe he hasn't used it in a long time. His face and arms are deeply tanned, and his long brown hair is sun-bleached. His face looks thinner than I remember, and the beard makes him look much older.

"I've been so busy trying to stay alive, I haven't had much time to think about it. So far, it's mostly been hard and dangerous."

"I know it will get easier, and you have such amazing adventures ahead of you. Humans have barely begun to explore the depths of the sea. Think of all the places you can go now."

"James, there's something I need to tell you, and you're not making this any easier."

His smile fades. My throat starts to close up. Still,

somehow I manage to blurt, "Gillian's dead. She was killed helping Lena, Robry, and me get away."

James's eyes widen in surprise, and then he bows his head. They didn't always get along, but I know he loved her.

"How did it happen?" he asks, and I tell him about our transformation, the soldiers who came, and how she stepped in front of solar fire to save me. All the while, James looks at the water and cries silently, and I cry with him.

"That sounds like her. She was never afraid of anything," James says, his voice gone tight and rough.

"At least I can give you some good news. Dad's still alive."

James looks up at me at last. "I already knew that," he says, impatiently wiping his tears away.

"You did?"

"I found out when I came across a coded computer message he sent to her. That was one of the reasons Gillian and I argued so much. I thought she should have trusted both of us with the truth."

It takes me a moment to absorb his words. Then I explode. "I *can't* believe you knew that Dad was alive and you didn't tell me!"

"Gillian convinced me it wouldn't be safe for you to know. You're my little sis. I couldn't put you in danger."

"You still should have told me," I tell him fiercely. "You know I cried my eyes out for weeks and weeks after we lost Dad." I glare at him, but he doesn't look away. Finally my curiosity gets the better of me. "Have you heard anything from him since?"

"A trader I trust brought me a message from him three months ago. At that time, anyway, Dad was still alive."

Despite my anger at my father, I feel relieved. "So, I guess we really will have to try to get to his colony."

"It's not going to be an easy voyage. You'll have to cross a thousand miles of ocean."

"I know. I wish you could come with us."

"I do too, but the *Kestrel* might attract too much notice. I'd much rather swim under the waves with you, but that's not going to happen now." His expression turns bleak.

"Why didn't the transformation work for you?" I ask quietly.

"Gene splicing isn't an exact science, and Gillian and Dad were still learning when they worked on me. I'm like their flawed prototype. They managed to give me many of the traits I assume you have. My eyes see amazingly well underwater. My telepathy is strong enough to hear the thoughts of others, across short distances, anyway. But when Gillian injected me with the virus, the gill filaments in my lungs wouldn't activate. I'm lucky that I can still breathe air."

"You're right about that." I tell him the story of the boy who suffocated when his lungs didn't transform completely. "So the geneticists in the Project still made mistakes years after our parents worked on you."

James smiles crookedly. "So, little sis, you're still trying to keep the peace and make me feel better. Some things never change." Then his smile fades. "You should probably know there's something else that went wrong with me."

"What?" I ask, getting goose bumps from the seriousness of his tone.

"It has to do with my telepathy. My range is pretty limited, but I can hear every thought in every mind near me. In fact, I can't shut those thoughts out—at all. I don't seem to have the natural ability to shield that most telepaths have, which keeps them from going insane."

I draw in a breath when I realize what he's saying. "So when you're around people . . ."

"It gets incredibly painful after a while. That's why I'm better off out here, where there's almost no one to bombard me with their thoughts. There's another twist our parents didn't expect. Remember, Gillian was an incredibly powerful telepath. Somehow they magnified and mutated her abilities in me, and I became a controller."

I shudder at his words. During the Eugenics Wars, geneticists accidentally produced a handful of telepaths who could implant ideas and control thoughts in others. Those "controllers," as they came to be known, wreaked havoc until the nations of the world had them all hunted down and killed.

"That's what Mom and I fought about. I kept doing stupid

stuff like forcing my teachers to let me skip assignments. Mom was scared someone would figure out what I was doing."

"Are you sure you're a controller?"

James looks at me steadily, and my nose itches. Then, suddenly, I *have* to scratch it. I raise my hand, and the compulsion disappears.

My mouth goes dry. "Was that you?"

James just nods his head.

"Don't *ever* do that to me again."

"I swear I won't, but now you see why I have to live out here on my own."

It would be so tempting to make people do things. "You could end up controlling our whole government, but . . . maybe you'd be a good leader."

"But we can't be sure. I might become a power-hungry dictator," he says with a twisted smile, "and no one could stop me. That's why it's just safer for everyone that I stay away from people."

"There's got to be some way to switch off your telepathy. You shouldn't have to live out here by yourself forever." My eyes burn with tears.

"Yeah, maybe if I was willing to let someone perform brain surgery on me, but I'm not that desperate. Believe me, Nere, I can think of a lot worse places to end up. I've always loved these islands."

"Are you still angry with our parents?"

James sighs and shakes his head. "I was at first. But I know they did their best."

I stare at him in surprise. "You're not mad that they tried to alter you in the first place?"

"Nere, all I've ever wanted to do is live in the ocean," he admits, his gray gaze tormented. "Now the best I can do is live on it and dive in it every day."

Why did I end up with the life my brother desperately wanted? "I'd trade places with you in a heartbeat if I could."

"You're crazy." James shakes his head. "Down there, you can live free of the Western Collective, the Marine Guard, and all the wars, famines, and diseases humans keep inflicting on themselves. You can build something better, and someday you might even find a way to help the sea or save the whole planet."

"Right now we're having a hard enough time just staying alive." Quickly I tell him everything that's happened to us since we left land.

"There's been a Marine Guard vessel anchored at Diablo Cove for a week now," he warns me.

"We know. Mariah and the rest of the pod have been keeping an eye on it for us."

"How is the old girl?"

"She's still going strong, and very proud of Tisi, her latest calf. But she misses Gillian."

I'm starting to get short of breath. I'm about to tell James that I need to duck under the water when Dai's mental shout breaks in on my thoughts.

:NERE, Penn's missing! And so is one of the mines.:

:Someone's got to stop him. If he sinks the *Defender* he's going to bring every Marine Guard vessel within fifty miles down on us!:

:I know. Ton and I are on our way, but if we don't catch that sponge-brain, we're going to need to leave the Channel Islands fast. Kyel wants you back down here right away.:

:I'm coming. And Dai, be careful.:

:There you go, worrying about me again.:

:Don't be so full of yourself. I just want someone else around who can tell a mako from a great white.:

I break off the contact to tell James what's happening. His eyes widen as I talk.

"That idiot's brought you and me a world of hurt," James says angrily. "I need to get the *Kestrel* back to the cove where I usually hide her. I'm toast if I don't make it there in time. The Marine Guard will seize and sink her in a heartbeat when they realize she's not properly registered."

"I'm sorry."

"I'm sorry, too. I don't want to leave you, but the *Kestrel* is how I survive out here. Listen, Nere, we've got to talk more about the Neptune Project. I'm not sure Gillian told you everything. Before you go swimming off to find Dad, there's more you need to know."

"Okay, I have to go now, but I promise that I'll come back up here as soon as we're ready to leave. And maybe this is all a false alarm." Although in my heart, I know it isn't.

"Hurry. I can't afford to lose more than a few minutes."

I want to give James another hug, but he's already scrambling up the stern ladder on his sailboat. Fighting back tears, I dive under the water and head down to the *Alicante*. There, I find everyone is hurriedly packing up gear and getting ready to leave. I do the same, although I don't have much to pack except my hammock.

After I'm organized and ready to head up to see James again, Kyel calls me. I find him in the wheelhouse poring over charts. I'm surprised when he looks relieved to see me.

:I wanted to ask your opinion on our best route out of these islands,: he says. :I read topo maps back in the mountains all the time, but I don't want to risk our lives by misreading these.:

Studying the charts, I realize it probably wasn't easy for Kyel to admit he needed help. :We're too apt to run into rescue vessels if we head directly west,: I tell him. :We'll still have plenty of sea room to dodge Marine Guard ships if we head north and then west.:

:North and west it is,: Kyel says with a nod. :On our way here from San Diego we averaged twenty miles a day. If your dolphins can find us good currents, I think we can count on covering thirty miles each travel day. Which means we should be able to reach your father's colony in five weeks or so.:

:If we don't run into more trouble,: I say, thinking of all the dangers we may encounter between here and there.

:If we don't run into more trouble,: Kyel agrees soberly. :I'm more worried about what's going to happen to us if Penn sinks that boat. For what it's worth, I think you were right. There are too few of us to mount any sort of effective resistance against the Marine Guard. For now, I've decided that survival should be our primary objective.:

:I'm glad to hear that,: I say awkwardly, and try not to stare at the red scar on his cheek. I wonder if Kyel will always talk and think like a guerrilla.

I'm just turning away when Dai contacts me.

:Penn's gone and mined the ship,: he reports with disgust. :Ton and I almost caught him, but we were too late. The vessel is sinking now, and this moron and I are on our way back to the *Alicante*. Tell Kyel I'm willing to execute him for disobeying the group's orders.:

I think he's kidding, but he's furious enough with Penn that I can't be sure. Quickly, I relay Dai's news and offer to Kyel.

:Tell Dai not to kill him,: Kyel tells me. :But we'll have to decide what to do with Penn later if we can get away from here safely.:

:We could head out now and let Dai and Penn catch up to us,: I suggest to Kyel after I relay his orders. My stomach clenches when I think of the Marine Guard vessels that will probably be converging on Santa Cruz in a few hours.

:No,: Kyel says firmly. :We're safer if we travel in a single group, especially at night.:

I want to argue with him, but I can tell from his set expression that his mind is made up. :We'll have to use the dolphins carefully,: I say instead. :They could help us out of a tough spot, but they could also lead the Marine Guard straight to us.:

:We'll be careful, but Nere, I hope I don't need to remind you that humans are more important than dolphins.:

:Right,: I say, not bothering to hide my irritation as I leave the wheelhouse. That's one thing Dai and Kyel do have in common: they both believe that dolphins are expendable.

I kick for the *Kestrel*, hoping I can catch my brother before he leaves. I try calling James telepathically while I swim, but I can't reach him. When I surface, I see at once that the *Kestrel* is gone, and my heart sinks like an anchor. I know his boat is the only way he can survive out here. But while I watch the silver light from a quarter moon shimmer on the waves, still I wish I could have seen my big brother one more time.

Blinking back my tears, I dive for the *Alicante*.

Dai brings Penn to the wheelhouse a half hour later. We're all waiting for them and ready to travel. When Kyel begins to speak, his mental tone is so cold, I'm very glad I'm not Penn.

:Penn, you defied a decision made by this group and put us all in danger. You also stole one of the mines we may need to survive an attack by the Marine Guard.:

:But you wanted to blow—:

:We'll decide what to do about you later,: Kyel says, cutting him off. :Everyone, we are going to have to swim hard and fast and hope we can get away from here before the Marine Guard finds us.:

As Kyel turns and leaves the wheelhouse, I see Tobin give Bria a quick hug. She looks as pale and shaky as I feel. Our spearguns at the ready, we follow Kyel north with Mariah and half the pod swimming protectively around our group. The *Alicante* soon disappears behind us, swallowed by the deep, dark ocean.

chapter twenty-nine

WE'VE BEEN DRIVING HARD through the water for an hour when Densil contacts me. :two big boats come from the east. they move fast!:

:Ton sees one boat heading this way from the north,: Dai tells us seconds later.

:many fishing boats come, and they drag big nets behind them!: Sokya's mental voice is tinged with panic. She and Ricca have been patrolling the waters to the west of us.

Swiftly, I relay to my companions what's happening. I hope they can't sense the fear that's making me tremble. Clearly the Marine Guard is determined to catch us and make us pay for the destruction of the *Defender*.

:We'll all head north and try to slip past that single ship,: Kyel declares. :Nere, call back the dolphins. We'll need their help if this comes to a fight.:

I ask Mariah to tell the rest of the pod to return to their human partners as fast as possible. I can hear the deep throb of boat engines in the distance, and that throbbing grows steadily louder. I bite my lip while I scan the ocean floor. All I can see in any direction is sand.

Maybe we'll get lucky. Maybe the Marine Guard's sonar won't pick us up.

Five minutes later, our luck runs out. The first of the boats from the east cuts directly over us. I feel like I've swallowed a chunk of sandstone when that boat slows and begins to circle above us. We keep racing north, but a second boat soon joins the first, and then a dozen divers jump into the water with torches and powerful tows, blocking our way and creating a perimeter around us.

:We're going to have to fight,: Kyel warns us. :Form a circle, stay together, and try to make every spear dart count.:

The torches grow brighter and brighter, making me squint. Then the first of the divers is on us, and I don't have time to be scared anymore. I aim my speargun and hit the lead diver in the shoulder. As I quickly reload, I see Tobin's first dart just miss a man. Then Ree shoots another in the leg.

The dolphins streak down from the surface, where they went to breathe. They start biting air hoses and hitting the divers with their powerful tails. I don't dare fire a spear dart now, but I can't hang back and let the dolphins do our fighting for us.

I charge forward, and Tobin, Ree, and Bria are right beside me. Tobin rips the speargun out of one diver's hands and clubs him with it. I use my knife to cut a diver's air hose. Out of the corner of my eye, I see Bria boldly strip the mask from another man.

I glance upward, and I realize that one of the divers is lining up his speargun at us. But then Pani flashes by!

:NO, PANI, WATCH OUT!: I cry, and try to send her an image of a spear dart speeding toward her, but I'm too late. She jerks as the dart pierces her body.

Angrily, Ree fires a dart at the diver, but he's already out of range. We've broken their attack. The first wave of divers is retreating.

The spear dart must be lodged near Pani's heart. As I watch her eyes, I see the life fade from them. I choke back a sob. She's always been one of the happiest and sweetest of our dolphins.

Ree's face twists as she tries to hold Pani in her arms.

:Nere, tell me what we can do to help her!: Bria cries, hovering next to Pani.

:Sweetling, there's nothing. She's dying.:

:little one, her heart has already stopped,: Mariah tells Bria sorrowfully.

:Heads up. More divers are heading your way!: Kyel warns us.

I glance up and see a second wave of divers charging at our side of the circle. The closest diver aims his speargun at me. I raise my own speargun, but I know I won't be able to fire in time. I brace myself while I take aim, expecting to be hit at any instant.

Suddenly, the diver jerks, and he drops his speargun. As

he falls away from his tow, I see the spear dart in his back. Where did that come from?

I spot a wild figure coming up behind the divers, and then I see it's James! Using his homemade solar tow, he's snuck up behind our attackers.

Before they can react, he's shot another man, and the rest head for the surface, kicking frantically. Maybe he's planted some frightening idea in their heads to make them panic.

For one brief moment, I'm left staring at my brother across twenty feet of ocean.

:Thanks, big brother!:

:I've got to surface now. Nere, watch out for trouble on your way to Dad's colony. His message said they've been under attack.:

:Has the Marine Guard figured out where he is?:

:No, but he implied someone else is trying to destroy the colony. You be careful!: James turns his tow away and disappears into the black sea.

:Nere, there's a third boat up there now,: Tobin warns me.

I can't help looking after James. This is so unfair. I can't believe I've found my brother just to lose him again.

:Why don't they just chuck some depth charges down on us?: Tobin asks as we watch the glow from more divers entering the water over our heads.

The same question has been nagging at the back of my

mind. :Maybe they want to take some of us alive.: The moment I say the words, I realize they must be true. :Maybe they know we're telepaths, or maybe they've decided they need us to start their own Neptune Project.:

I swallow hard as I meet Tobin's gaze. If I'm right, being captured will lead to a future much worse than death.

:the fishing boats are close,: Mariah warns me. :their nets surround us now.:

Several new divers from the third boat charge at us.

:WATCH OUT, BRIA!: I hear Kyel shout. I twist around in time to see Kyel lunge between Bria and a diver. Kyel's body jerks as a spear dart takes him in the chest.

Bria raises her speargun and coolly shoots the diver who just shot Kyel.

:Ton's mined all three boats!: Dai shouts, and suddenly he's there, in front of me. :Send your dolphins away. The mines will blow any minute now!:

:Mariah, you all must go! Swim right above the ocean floor, and you should be able to avoid those fishing nets.:

:we go!: Within seconds, the dolphins are gone, racing away from the coming explosions that could deafen them. The explosions aren't going to be healthy for us, either.

:Everyone, swim north as fast as you can,: I call to our group.

I turn to help Kyel, but Thom already has him in a life-guard hold. Penn shoots the last diver in our path. We dart under the cutters before the mines detonate. I look back. Sweet Pani's body is already drifting toward the bottom. I force myself to look ahead. I can't bear to watch scavengers eat her.

:We chewed up their divers so badly, I knew they'd start tossing depth charges at us,: Dai says as he swims along beside me. :The mines were the only way I could think to stop them.: He actually looks a little uncertain.

:I don't think you had a choice,: I reassure him. :FASTER, EVERYONE!:

Seconds later, I see a flash behind us and hear a muffled roar. I'm spun upside down. Shock waves press on my entire body and eardrums. All I can see are bubbles in front of me. Then there're two more flashes, more roaring, and the water tosses me about like an orca playing with a seal.

My head is ringing when I finally regain my bearings. The night sea is so full of sediment now, we waste precious minutes trying to find one another.

:Is everyone okay?: Kyel calls out. I can hear the pain in his mental voice. :Report in to Thom and me. We're down here on the bottom.:

One by one, people find their way to Kyel and Thom. Tobin takes quick stock of our injuries. Kyel's wound is the worst. I can't bear to look at the spear dart sticking out of his chest. His expression stoic, Kyel floats quietly while Thom cradles his head and shoulders.

:Is everyone accounted for?: Kyel asks me.

:We're all here,: I reply.

Rather than pull out the spear dart, Tobin quickly wraps a bandage around Kyel's chest. Then he puts a pressure bandage on a knife cut Penn took along his right forearm, while Robry and Lena treat a spear dart graze across Ree's shoulder.

In the meantime, I call the dolphins. We'll need their help to travel swiftly and keep sharks away from Kyel. I ask Mariah to tell Halia she'll be towing Ree from now on.

:You should get going the moment Tobin's done treating everyone,: Kyel tells us. :And put some distance between you and those Marine Guard vessels. Leave me here. I'll just slow you down.:

:We can't leave you behind,: I protest.

:You can and you will. I'm fish food anyway.:

:He's right, you know,: Dai says to me. His words may be callous, but I can sense that he is as upset as the rest of us.

:We're not going to leave Kyel here to die by himself.:

:I can take him.: Thom breaks in on our argument. I know Thom is strong enough to carry Kyel, but Thom by himself is a lot of weight for Densil to tow.

:If you're determined to do this, then Ton and I can take him,: Dai surprises me by offering. :Ton's strong enough to pull both of us for a while.:

:I'm a waste of your time and energy,: Kyel says furiously.

:For once, K-man, just shut up,: Thom tells him. His big hands are gentle as he hands Kyel over to Dai.

Everyone seems to be waiting for me to give another order. :All right,: I say, squaring my shoulders. :We've got to get more distance between us and the Marine Guard. Remember, if you see a net, dive under it.:

After dividing us into three travel groups to avoid sonar, I lead off with Sokya giving me a tow. Dai follows me with Kyel and Ton in the middle, and Tobin brings up the rear. Almost right away we find a fishing net blocking our path, but it's not hard to slip under its bottom edge.

After we get past the net, I ask Tobin a question, even though I'm afraid to hear his answer. :Does Kyel have a chance?:

:No,: he replies, his mental tone somber. :That dart pierced one of his lungs. It's amazing he's still alive.:

Tobin's response hits me hard. Kyel seemed so indestructible. How can we go on without him?

:another net ahead!: Mariah warns us.

:Dive for the bottom!: I order. We dive to the sea floor and wait for the net dragged by two fishing boats to pass over us. I can tell the dolphins are terrified, but thanks to Mariah's firm control over the pod, they stay with us and don't bolt.

When the net sweeps past us, the dolphins surface to breathe, and then we travel on, making good time, considering that Ton is towing two humans through the water. After we're sure we're clear of the last of the fishing vessels and their nets, we turn west.

:Nere, we'd better stop soon. Kyel's not going to last much longer,: Tobin warns me a short while later. I glance back and see that Kyel is looking gray, and his chest is rising and falling rapidly.

:If Thom will take Kyel, I'll send Ton out to find a place where we can rest and hide,: Dai offers.

We pause long enough for our travel groups to join up again, and for Thom to take Kyel, who is barely conscious. Ton flashes off to look for a cave. Dai manages to keep up with us on his own.

As we drive through the night sea, I look back at Kyel, hoping he can hang on a little longer.

:Ton's found a good sea cave,: Dai finally tells me. :It's deep enough to hold us all.:

When we reach the cave, Dai goes in first and clears out several eels. All of us follow him inside except Penn, who lingers by the entrance.

:I'll keep an eye out for sharks,: he offers. He can't even look at Kyel. I wonder if he's sorry now that he mined the Marine Guard vessel.

:The dolphins will help you,: I tell him tiredly.

:I want to see Nere.: Kyel's mental voice is strained as he calls for me. I swim into the cave. Thom is holding Kyel, and the rest of the group is gathered around them. Bria and Kalli are crying. Ree's face is pale and set.

I blink back tears of my own as I go to his side. Kyel's pain-filled gaze focuses on me.

:You were right,: he says, his chest heaving. :Penn shouldn't have attacked that boat. I wanted to fight the Western Collective until the day I died. Now that's here, and everything I did and all the friends I lost, we didn't change anything. Maybe the best way to beat them is to survive and build something more free and fair in the sea. . . .:

He pauses to fight for breath. :Nere, there's something you have to promise me. When they hold another election and choose you to lead, you *have* to do it this time. You're their best chance of surviving. You'll be a good commander. You'll make some mistakes, but you'll do a good job. Promise me.:

Kyel's eyes stare at me, compelling me to answer. Even dying, he is one of the most formidable people I've ever met.

:I'll do it if they ask me,: I promise.

:Good,: he says, his mental voice growing weaker. :Where's Thom?:

:I'm here, K-man,: Thom replies, and Kyel searches for his hand. Thom reaches down and grips it.

:This is my final order. You are going to swim away from here and leave me to the fish and the crabs. I'm dead anyway, and I don't care what happens to my body.:

:All right. But we're not leaving until you're gone, K-man.:

:You always were one stubborn guy.: Kyel tries to smile at Thom, but he coughs up blood instead.

:Ree? I can't see. Are you there?:

She bends over him and presses a kiss on his forehead, and I think he is saying something to her on a private send. She straightens up, and Kyel grimaces, as if he's facing one last enemy. Then his chest stops heaving and his body goes slack.

After Tobin checks Kyel's pulse, he gently closes his eyes.

:He's gone,: he says simply.

Thom bows his head, and his big shoulders begin to shake. Ree slips an arm around his waist.

I bite my lip when I realize that everyone else is looking at me now.

chapter Thirty

:**I NOMINATE NERE** to be our new leader,: Robry says, his mental voice sad but firm.

Ree gives me a resigned look. :I think Kyel nominated her first, right before he died.:

:Let's put it to a vote, then,: Tobin says. :All those in favor of Nere taking over as our leader, raise your hand.:

The vote is unanimous. A heavy weight settles on my shoulders. Is this how Kyel felt every day? I still believe that they are making a huge mistake, but I have to honor the promise I made to Kyel.

:All right, I'll do it,: I say numbly. :I know I have to make the hard decisions, and in emergency situations, you have to follow my orders. But I also want to hear your suggestions. I can't do this quite the way Kyel did. We're still figuring out how to make this work down here, and I know you're all going to have good ideas.:

As acceptance speeches go, it's pretty lame, but I'm too sad and weary to think up anything better. I look at Penn's averted face. With a sigh, I realize he's one of the first problems I'm going to have to solve.

:Thom, please go through Kyel's seapack,: I say, trying

to sound sure of myself when I'm really just winging it. :Divide and pass around his equipment. I know Kyel didn't want a full burial, but I think we should do something for him before we leave here.:

I look at Ree's set face, and I add quickly, :Ree, you can help Thom if you'd like.:

Ree sniffs and nods.

:And keep an eye on Thom for me, will you?: I add on a private send. :If he looks like he's about to go for Penn, don't let him.:

:All right, but I'd like to pound Penn's face in myself. Kyel's death is all his fault.:

I close my eyes. I can picture big rangy Ree taking apart Penn, who is slight for a guy. :Try not to, okay? I think Penn understands that Kyel is dead because of him, and that's not going to be an easy thing for him to live with.:

:At least he gets to live. Kyel and my *querida* Pani didn't,: Ree says bitterly as she goes to help Thom.

Starting to get a headache, I decide that our next order of business is eating. :Dai, I want you and Ton to go find us some food.:

:We're on it, boss.: Dai salutes me, but I don't think he means the salute disrespectfully. I realize now that Dai mocks everyone equally. :I think shark's probably on the menu,: he adds with a meaningful look at a large mako that is circling outside the cave mouth.

:Good. Everyone else, stay in the cave and try to rest up. We'll head out in a half hour.:

I swim over to the cave mouth. The sea has started to lighten. It's morning now. Robry comes to float beside me. I watch as Dai kills the mako with a single shot through its right eye. After the shark stops thrashing, he tows it away.

:Thanks for the nomination, kid,: I tell Robry on a private send. :Remind me to do the same for you someday.:

:I know you don't want to do it, but Kyel was right. You're the best choice for the job.:

:Well, I meant what I said about the suggestions, especially from you. You're twice as smart as I am.:

Robry snorts at that. :I'm smart enough to know you're going to make some mistakes, and you're going to beat yourself up over them.:

:I'm counting on you to give me good ideas, and then maybe I won't make as many mistakes. So:—I force myself to add on a lighter note—:did I sound leaderlike just now?:

:Absolutely, Commander Nere,: Robry says with a grin. :I almost saluted you, too.:

:I'm really glad you're here.: I want to give him a hug, but I know that would embarrass him in front of the others, so I punch his shoulder lightly instead.

:I'm glad I'm here, too,: Robry says. He looks away from

me and studies the sea floor beyond our cave. :You know, it's been harder down here than I thought it would be, but it's also more beautiful.:

I follow his glance. The early morning sun shines down in rippling gold and greenish beams through the water, highlighting a rare group of purple hydrocoral growing on the rocky sea floor. A school of ocean whitefish swim by, their yellow tails glinting in the sunbeams. I'm glad Robry helped me to see how pretty this place is. I needed to see something pretty right now.

I call the dolphins and check them carefully for injuries. Kona has a spear-dart graze on her tail that I treat with antiseptic cream from my seapack. The dolphins are in a subdued mood.

:Mariah, I'm so sorry about Pani,: I say.

:I miss her. we all miss her,: Mariah says as she rests her head on my arm, and Tisi crowds in close for a rub.

Dai returns to our cave with some mako fillets and hands out strips of shark meat. I have no appetite, and I really don't like shark, but I make myself eat several bites, since I'm the leader now.

Kalli calls to Ree and Thom, who stop their sad work to join us.

:What is this, anyway?: Thom asks as he takes a strip from Dai.

:Shark,: Dai replies.

:Hey, it's nice to take a bite out of one of them for a change.:

We all smile at Thom's joke. I appreciate the effort he's making to cheer us up.

When we finish with our simple meal, Thom tells me, :We're pretty much done back there.:

:All right. Would you like to say something? You knew him best.:

Thom grimaces. :I'm not so good with words.:

:You'll do fine.:

We move to the back of the cave and see that they've piled some rocks on Kyel's body. Someone, maybe Ree, made a K on top of the pile with several white shells.

:He'd want me to keep this short,: Thom says, :so I will. Kyel was one of the toughest, bravest guys I've ever known. In a fight, he'd always have my back. I'm going to miss you, K-man. I hope someone's got your back, wherever you are now.:

:Can I say something?: Bria asks.

:You bet.: Thom nods to her encouragingly.

:I'm alive right now because of Kyel. I can't replace him, but I will do my best to be a useful member of this group. I . . . I'm never going to forget him.:

Penn looks up from the pile of rocks, a muscle ticking in his cheek. :I gotta say something, too. I know I screwed up, and Kyel's dead because of me. I realize you guys may want to toss me out because of what I did, and I won't blame you.:

Penn looks at Thom. :I'm sorry. I didn't think any of us would die when I mined that boat. I . . . I just wanted to make them pay for what they did to Sara.:

:That's right, you didn't think,: Thom says angrily, and he starts across the cave toward Penn.

Tobin and Ree grab Thom's shoulders. He lets them hold him back from Penn—for the moment, anyway.

:We'll vote tonight on whether or not Penn gets to stay with us,: I say, hoping I sound more confident than I feel. :But the only way this group is going to survive is if we can depend on one another. If we vote to let Penn stay, you *all* are going to have to forgive him for what he did.:

I look straight at Penn. :And you need to think about whether you can live by our decisions. Kyel was strong enough to do that. He gave up on attacking the Marine Guard vessel when we voted against that plan.:

I want to add, *And you didn't, and now Kyel's gone, and they're stuck with me trying to lead them.*

I suck in a deep breath. :All right, it's time we headed out.:

I look at Kyel's rough grave a final time. I wonder how many more of us we may leave behind in lonely sea caves like this one.

Wish me luck, I think to Kyel. *I'm just beginning to understand what a hard job you had.*

As we leave the cave and start swimming in our travel formation, I look back at the people who follow me. I think I know what Kyel would say. I have to take this job one day at a time. My goal for now is to keep everyone alive until nightfall.

chapter Thirty-one

WE TRAVEL STEADILY for three hours, and then the dolphins sense a Marine Guard vessel approaching. We have enough warning to hide under a rock overhang until the ship passes. Before the sun starts to set, Dai and Ton discover the wreck of a tugboat that's in good enough shape to protect us from predators.

After Tobin checks Penn's and Ree's wounds, we eat on the deck of the old tug. Kalli gathered some wakame, which actually tastes pretty decent combined with the lobsters we caught scuttling around down in the bilge. Still, I'm too worried about Penn to have much of an appetite.

:All right,: I say tiredly when we finish eating. :Let's get this meeting over with. I guess we need to vote on whether or not Penn should stay in this group.:

I glance at Penn. He's trying to look like he doesn't care what we decide, but I sense that he's scared to death. He's had all afternoon to think about trying to survive on his own. I consider everything I've learned so far about Penn, and I know how I'll vote.

When no one says anything, I realize that my companions

are waiting for me to begin. I sit up straighter and hope I can find the right words. :I think Penn made a mistake, but I vote to let him stay with us. He held his own in our fight this morning, and we all saw how hard he fought to keep Sara alive.:

I look at Penn. :I believe that you are brave and loyal. If you can be loyal to us, I know you'll be a valuable member of this team.:

We go around the circle, and each person votes. Bria, Robry, and Kalli vote in favor of letting Penn remain with us. Then it's Ree's turn. :You put us all in danger, and Kyel died because of you. I vote no,: she says stonily.

Thom is next. :No,: he says, his gaze smoldering as he stares at Penn.

Lena gives Penn a long look. :I know you loved Sara, but you shouldn't have risked our lives. I vote yes, but if you go against the group again, I'll say no next time.:

:I agree with Lena,: Tobin says. :I saw how hard you fought to save Sara. I vote yes for now.:

:You're too much of a hothead. You'll put us in danger again. I vote no,: Dai says flatly.

I let go the breath I'd been holding, and Penn relaxes as well. :That's six votes to three,: I tell him. :Which means you can stay with us. Think about what we said tonight; and those of you who voted no need to remember that most of us want him to stay.:

I pause and make an effort to lighten my tone. :There's one more change I think you're going to like. We won't take turns keeping watch all night long anymore. The pod will stay near us. Dolphins sleep with one half of their brains awake, and I know they'll give us plenty of warning if they sense a big predator nearby. We're going to be traveling hard for the next several weeks, and we need all the rest we can get.:

Kalli grins at me. :That's an *outstanding* change. Now I know why I voted to make you boss.:

:Right.: I smile back at her, feeling awkward. :Well, this meeting is over. Let's get some sleep. We'll leave right after sunrise tomorrow.:

I stop Thom with a private send as the others leave. :Can you deal with the way this turned out?:

Thom turns to face me. :I'm never going to like Penn, but I won't cause trouble, if that's what you're asking.:

:Thank you, and I'm so sorry about Kyel.:

:So am I. He was my best friend since I can remember,: Thom says, a bleak look in his eyes, and then he swims away.

I see Lena, Kalli, and Ree go off together, and Robry and Bria. Suddenly I feel like I'm Freak Girl back in school. Sighing, I go to say good night to the dolphins. Their happiness at seeing me cheers me up a little.

When Tobin approaches us, Kona, Ricca, Mali, Halia,

and Sokya dart in circles around him, and Mariah looks on tolerantly.

:I noticed that Kona had a cut on her tail,: Tobin says. :Do you want me to look at it?:

:That'd be great. I've been worrying that maybe it needs stitches.:

I call Kona. Tobin puts his hands gently about her tail, his expression thoughtful as he looks at her wound. I can see why the dolphins like him. There's something very comforting about being around Tobin.

:I don't think it's deep enough to need stitches,: Tobin says. :I saw that you put some ointment on it earlier.:

:It's an antiseptic cream my mother created that seems to help dolphins heal faster. For now, I guess we'll just keep an eye on her.:

Tobin's dolphin partner, Mali, crowds in close, thrusting her head under his arm.

:She's jealous. I think she's got a crush on you,: I tease him. :In fact, all the girls in the pod seem to really like you.:

Tobin laughs at that, but he blushes, too. :It's nice to know I have some fans. I think they're pretty amazing, too.:

:How's Bria holding up?:

Tobin turns away from the dolphins. :She's much happier since we met up with you. Some tough things have happened, but she really likes you and Robry, and she loves the dolphins.:

:She has a real gift for working with them.:

:She's not the only one with gifts. Nere, I hope you know that you did fine today.: Tobin's gaze is warm as he looks at me. :I'm happy you helped convince everyone to keep Penn.:

:Thanks,: I reply. Gazing back at Tobin, I wish he'd put his arms around me. I ache inside over Kyel and sweet Pani, and I need a hug.

:I'd be happy to give you a hug,: Dai says, breaking in on my thoughts. :If you wait for him to make a move, you're going to have gray hair.:

:Stay out of my head!: I twist around to find Dai hovering nearby, that familiar mocking expression on his face. Tobin looks from Dai to me, and the warmth in his eyes fades.

:Guess I'll go find my hammock now,: he says quietly, and moments later, he's slipped away.

:Look, there are some basic rules to being a telepath,: I hurl at Dai, :and I'm tired of you breaking them all the time!:

:Who said there are rules?:

:My mother taught me that you only read thoughts sent to you. You've got to stop reading my surface mind. It's rude.:

:My father didn't teach me any such thing. He taught me that telepathy is a weapon, and I have every right to use it when I want to win a fight.:

:But there's no fight here.:

Dai moves closer, his mocking expression vanished. Instead, there's this serious look in his dark eyes that makes my heart thud.

:Nere, you don't really get it, do you? He likes you, and I like you, but you don't know yet who you like. That's our fight and I'm going to make sure I win it.:

How arrogant can he get? I cross my arms. :I don't know what you're talking about.:

:Keep telling yourself that, if it makes you feel better.: His ironic smile is back. :Tobin's right, you know. You're doing fine as a leader, even though I think it's a mistake to keep Penn around.:

A chill steals over me when I remember Dai asking Kyel if he should execute Penn.

:Would you have killed him if Kyel had ordered you to?:

Dai searches my face. :I don't need to read your mind to know you'd be more comfortable around me if I said no, but I want to give you the truth. I would have done it. He could have gotten us all killed, and therefore his life was ours to take. That's how it works in the world I come from.:

There it is again, the strange, flat note I hear in his tone when he talks about his past.

:Can you tell me more about that world?:

:Maybe, but not tonight. You're almost asleep floating there. It's time for our new leader to get some rest.:

He places both hands on my shoulders. I think he's about to turn me around to send me back to the tug and my hammock, but first he dips his head. Before I can push him away, he kisses me. I find myself leaning in to the kiss even while my mind is screaming, *This is a big mistake!*

Just when I'm about to shove him away, Dai raises his head.

I glance at the tugboat. I *really* hope no one inside just saw what Dai did. :Don't do that again,: I tell him fiercely.

:I can't promise you that, but I can promise I won't do it again tonight. I just wanted to make sure you dream about me.: His words are smug, but his eyes are wistful.

I wish I could think up some crushing comment, but I'm too shaken. Instead, I whirl away from him and head for the tugboat. After checking to make sure that everyone but Dai is settled for the night, I pull my hammock from my seapack and find a spot to tie it near the rest of the girls, who are already sleeping.

As I stare up at the dark ceiling of the wreck, I find myself touching my lips. I wish I could just fall asleep, but Dai made that impossible. Every bit of me seems wide awake and tingling. I can't help thinking of my first and only kiss with Cam, and how different it was than Dai's. Cam never made me feel confused and furious all at once.

I remember what Ree told me, that I should just have fun with Dai. I'm not sure I can do that. Dai may drive me crazy, but already I care about him.

chapter Thirty-Two

WE HEAD OFF AT FIRST LIGHT. I ask Mariah to have two dolphins scout ahead of us. Every time I give the group an order, I feel like I'm pretending to be Kyel. Dai sends me amused looks, which doesn't help matters any. As we swim along, instead of watching out for trouble, I find myself thinking about his kiss and what he said to me last night.

Was he right when he said Tobin likes me? I feel so comfortable and happy when I'm around him. Was Dai telling the truth about his own feelings? I feel anything but comfortable or secure around Dai. He's amazing looking, but I don't really care about that. I think it's his aloneness that gets to me. I know all about being lonely. Plus, I still miss Cam so much, but I know I'll probably never see him again. I try to push all thoughts of Tobin and Dai—and Cam—out of my mind, but it isn't easy.

Midday, we eat and rest in a big kelp forest. There we help Kalli harvest some kelp we'll eat later. We spread out while we cut the fronds. I cut my share and tie them to my seapack. Then I let myself relax and drift with the current through the towering stems. I admire a big red, black, and white sheepshead fish I spot feeding on sea urchins.

Suddenly, I hear Lena give a mental scream.

:Lena, what is it? Where are you?: I shout, but she doesn't reply.

:I think she's just east of me,: Robry tells us quickly. :I'll go check on her.:

:Be careful!: I frantically push my way through the kelp to reach them both. Could Lena have come face-to-face with a shark?

:It's okay, Nere,: Robry tells me. :I found her, and she's all right.:

A long minute later, I find Lena and Robry floating together in the kelp. Lena's face is paper white, and I'm pretty sure she's been crying. Dai arrives right after me, his expression fierce and his speargun raised and ready for trouble.

:Are you all right?: I ask Lena.

:I . . . I saw something big and brown with dark eyes, and it charged right toward me,: Lena tells me with a quaver in her mental voice. :Then there were three of them, darting and swimming all around me.:

Dai lowers his speargun and looks disgusted. :You just ran into some curious sea lions.:

:They startled me.:

:You'd have to hit a sea lion on the head before it would be a danger to you.:

:I didn't know that,: Lena says angrily, but I can tell she's crying again.

:Well, you should have. I'm getting sick and tired of looking after a bunch of sea newbies who don't know a shark from a sea lion.:

:Then maybe you should just leave!: Lena yells at him.

:Hey, both of you, cool it,: I say before Lena can say anything else. I know Dai's frustrated with our group, and we can't afford to lose him.

:Lena, Dai just raced here willing to take on a shark to save you.:

:Thank you,: she says sulkily.

I turn to Dai. :And you should be easier on her. We're all scared and on edge down here. You've lived in the sea for a long time, but it's new to most of us. Even sea lions can be terrifying if they startle you.:

:Then you should have been better prepared for this,: Dai says.

:I *totally* agree with you,: I say, feeling furious all over again at my own parents, :but some of us weren't, and it's not our fault.:

:Well, don't scream like that if you see a sea lion again,: he says abruptly to Lena, :or I might shoot you myself.: With that, he flips around and vanishes into the kelp.

:God, he may be gorgeous,: Lena says, rubbing her arms, :but I don't know whether or not to take him seriously when he says stuff like that.:

:I think Dai just has a weird sense of humor. Are you okay?:

:Yeah, I'm fine. I guess the sea lions freaked me out.: She starts to give me the sullen look I know so well, and then her face crumples.

:No, I'm not okay,: she admits with a sob. :I hate it down here. I'm scared every minute that some Marine Guard diver is going to shoot me, or that a shark is going to tear me apart.:

She's crying so hard, I sling my speargun and put an arm around her. I expect her to shove me away, but instead she leans her head on my shoulder and cries even harder. :I just want to go home.:

:Um, Robry, could you tell everyone that we're going to rest here a little longer?: I ask him.

:Sure,: he says, looking very relieved to get away from a crying girl.

I rub Lena's shoulder awkwardly. :I'm sorry my parents did this to you. I'm sorry they did this to me.:

:I know it's not your fault,: Lena raises her head and says with a sniff. :It's just been easier to be angry at you and your mother than at my own parents.:

As I look into her face, I find myself blurting out, :Why did you stop being my friend?:

Lena sighs. :When I turned ten, I found out what your parents did to me. You know I've always *hated* having weak eyes and weak lungs, and being so different from everyone else.:

:And then you learned that my family was the reason why you were so different,: I say, starting to understand.

:I couldn't stand to be around the sea after that. I tried to get you to spend time with me in town, but you always wanted to go off in a boat with Cam or to help your mom train the dolphins. I missed you, but I knew I only had a few years left on land. After a while, I got tired of missing you. It was easier to be mad instead.:

:I probably would've felt the same way.: My throat tightens.

:So, after that, I decided to do everything I could to fit in at school,: Lena continues. :I never got very far with those stuck-up town girls.:

:But in the end, you made the boys like you.:

:I did.: Lena nods with satisfaction. :And I'm going to make Tobin like me.:

:But I think Thom likes you. You should see the way he looks at you sometimes.:

:He's just a big clumsy idiot.:

:He's not an idiot. He's very brave and very sweet.:

:If he's so great, you go for him.:

:I don't want to go for anyone.:

:Well, I do. I like Tobin, and don't forget it. Now, oh great leader, I think we have to find some more of these disgusting kelp fronds you ordered us to cut.:

Lena turns her back on me. Gritting my teeth, I swim

away from her. It's *so* unfair that she's giving me a tough time about being the leader when she wanted me to do the job in the first place. But nothing with Lena is fair anymore.

I wonder if we'll ever truly be friends again.

chapter Thirty-Three

WE MAKE GOOD TIME over the next several days. I worry, though, because we still don't really trust one another. No one talks much to Dai, except Bria, Robry, and me. Thom hasn't caused trouble with Penn, but he barely speaks to him, and Ree ignores him completely.

Penn is quick to follow any orders I give him, but I think he feels that everyone still blames him for Kyel's death. To make matters worse, whenever Tobin and I talk, Lena watches me resentfully. I try to ignore her because Tobin's a good listener, and he's one of the few people I feel like I can talk to at the end of a long, lonely day of trying to keep us all alive.

Late in the eighth day after Kyel's death, we run into a new danger.

:Stop, everyone!: I tell the rest. :Sokya says there is a big jellyfish swarm ahead of us.:

This isn't good news. Ever since fishermen fished tuna, swordfish, and sharks, and netted sea turtles to the edge of extinction, jellyfish populations have exploded. Our seasuits will give us some protection from their stings, but in a dense swarm they could sting our hands and faces, and make us really sick.

To make matters worse, we've been fighting a strong current that is carrying those jellyfish toward us. I have to make a decision, and I have to make it quickly.

:We either have to head west, out to sea, or farther east, toward land, to avoid the swarm,: I tell the rest, trying to look calmer than I feel.

:We're near the edge of the continental shelf here,: Dai warns me.

:I know, but every time we head closer to shore we encounter more boat traffic,: I reply.

:I *really* don't want to run into any more Marine Guard ships,: Lena declares.

:Not being chased by divers has been nice for a change,: Kalli adds.

I look at Dai. We both know predators like squid and the bigger sharks roam the area beyond the continental break, the place where the continental shelf ends. Beyond the break, the ocean floor slopes down to the abyssal plain, the deep, dark bottom of the ocean. But big predators are rare, unlike boats along the coast.

:We'll head out to sea,: I decide, :and hope we can get around this swarm pretty quickly. If we head west, though, I'm warning you guys, we may be swimming after dark for a while.:

:That's cool,: Ree says with a shrug, and the others seem to agree with her.

Soon we start to lose the light. When the mass of jellyfish gets too close, I call the dolphins to come and give us tows. With their help, we're soon speeding farther out to sea and staying clear of the leading edge of the swarm.

I look uneasily into the black waters beneath us.

:Mariah, how deep is it now?:

:the bottom is farther than I can sense.:

I swallow hard. That means we are probably past the continental break and swimming over the continental slope. I tell her I don't want to turn north until we are sure we are past all of the stragglers along the edges of the swarm. Jellyfish are so translucent, they are hard for us to see at night.

:it is safe to go north now,: Mariah says at last.

Finally. :Let's turn, and let me know when we can head inland again.:

The dolphins continue to tow us because we're tired, and I want to get us settled safely for the evening as soon as possible. We've only been heading north for a few minutes when the dolphins slow their pace and start clicking and sawing frantically.

:What's wrong?: I ask Mariah, cold shivers going down my back.

:something big is coming up beneath us. it comes quickly!:

I clench my speargun tighter and try to guess what could be under us. Maybe it's just a whale.

:squid, squid, squid!: Sokya cries.

I struggle to control my panic. :Dai, everyone, the dolphins say a giant squid is coming up beneath us.:

We've talked about this possibility before. Giant squid are fierce predators, and they are incredibly fast.

:Spread out! We want to make it harder for it to grab more than one of us at once,: I call to everyone. I stare down into the black water. My heart is pounding hard against my ribs. Where is the thing? Maybe it won't be a really big one.

:Remember, the dolphins can't help us outrun it, and they will be little help fighting it,: Dai tells us coolly. :Our only chance is to kill it with our spearguns before it can grab us and tear us with its beak.:

Suddenly, a dark, roiling mass shoots up through the water beneath me. Fighting the urge to flee, I raise my speargun. I get a glimpse of wildly waving orange tentacles and arms. Then the monster reaches out. It grabs Thom!

Thom shouts in pain as one of the squid's tentacles wraps around his body. The sharp sucker cups on that tentacle must be slicing into his skin. I shudder when I catch a glimpse of an eye the size of a dinner plate and the squid's diamond-shaped mantle. The creature is huge. Its head and mantle together are six feet long and its tentacles seem to stretch forever.

:Aim for the eyes!: Dai and I yell. I watch for a shot. The squid's arms are waving so wildly, they block any chance I have of piercing the creature's eyes. Our group has spread out around it. Robry, Kalli, Lena, and Bria fire at the squid, but their darts only hit its many arms. Ree and Tobin try to move in closer, but the squid knocks them away.

Thom yells and stabs at the squid as it pulls him toward its beak.

Suddenly Penn is there, right beside Thom! He fires his speargun at point-blank range into the squid's eye. The water around the squid fills with an inky, dark substance that makes it even harder for me to see what's going on. Penn gets knocked away, but Dai swims in close and fires at the wounded monster. I blink when I see a small flash of light and hear a muffled bang. Does Dai have some sort of explosive spear dart? The squid shoots away from us, Thom still clenched in its tentacles.

Dai motions to Ton, who races to give him a tow. I call Densil. I think he'll be brave enough to help me go after the squid.

:Everyone, stay together here,: I order. I won't risk their lives when Thom may already be dead. :Check Penn and make sure he's all right. Mariah, please ask the rest of the pod to stay here and keep everyone safe.:

Then I call Densil. :We have to follow the squid. Can you sense it?:

:it is not far.:

:Will you take me to it?:

:yes,: he says. I can feel his fear. Almost every species in the ocean steers clear of giant squid, for good reason.

We race downward after Dai and Ton and the squid. As we approach, I see that the squid is still shooting out spurts of ink, but its arms are flailing about more slowly.

:the squid is dying,: Densil tells me. :the tall boy shot something that made a hole in its head.:

So Dai did use some sort of explosive dart on it. But the squid still has a tentacle completely wrapped around Thom. Densil pulls me near the squid as it quivers a final time. Then the dead monster begins to sink slowly toward the bottom, taking Thom with it. I watch Thom carefully, hoping for some sign of movement, but his body is as still as the squid's.

:Dai, we've got to get him loose.:

:I know, but those sucker rings are incredibly sharp. We're going to have to pull that tentacle away from him carefully, or we'll slice Thom into hamburger.:

I force myself to swim closer. Blue-colored blood trickles from the remnants of the eye that Penn and Dai destroyed with their speargun shots. I see a half dozen other cuts on the squid's mantle. I slip between two of the squid's arms and study Thom. His eyes are closed and his features are clenched in pain, but his chest is still rising and falling. My eyes burn with tears when I realize how much I've come to depend on kind, cheerful Thom. We can't lose him!

:Thom, a-are you still with us?:

:I'm still here,: he moans. :But every time I move, I feel like I'm wrapped up in barbed wire.:

:We're going to get you free.:

:Good,: is all he says.

:Steady him, will you?: Dai asks. I get a good grip on Thom's big shoulders. Gently, Dai begins to pull at the tentacle that is wrapped completely around Thom's body.

Thom groans as Dai pries the tentacle loose. :Hang in there, tough guy.: Dai shakes his head. Then to me he says, :Somehow he got his dive knife out and stabbed this monster just about every place he could reach. Sea newbie or no, he put up an incredible fight.:

:I think we should have squid for break— Argh!: Thom cries out as Dai tugs the last portion of the tentacle loose, and then Thom is free. Dai takes him in a lifeguard hold and starts kicking swiftly toward the surface.

I realize from the pressure on my ears that the sinking squid has probably pulled us down at least a few hundred feet. I don't know how much pressure my genetically altered body can take, but I don't want to find out tonight. I follow Dai and Thom, and shudder when I catch one last glimpse of the mammoth creature sinking toward the ocean floor. Scavenger fish and three sharks have already appeared out of the darkness to feast on dead squid.

I catch up with Dai and bite my lip when I see the small

round cuts all over Thom's torso. The squid's sharp-edged suckers shredded his protective seasuit. It's like the creature pressed a hundred razor-sharp bottle caps into his skin, and each of those cuts is bleeding now. With a shiver, I realize that pretty soon we're going to be driving off sharks that want to feast on Thom, too.

chapter Thirty-Four

DAI CALLS TON, and the big dolphin gives both Dai and Thom a tow. I call Densil, who darts down from the surface, where he just went up to breathe, and he pulls me along beside Thom.

:What's happening, Nere? Are you guys all right?: Tobin contacts me worriedly.

:We're heading your way. The squid is dead, but Thom is pretty cut up. We're going to have to find a safe place where you can treat him. How's Penn?:

:He's a little bruised but otherwise fine.:

When we reach the rest, they all crowd around while Tobin quickly examines him. Penn is hanging back, but Thom's gaze finds him.

:Hey, man, I owe you one,: he says. :That was some good shooting.:

Penn ducks his head, but I can tell he's pleased.

Thom looks for Dai next. :You, too, dude. I don't know what you shot into that sucker, but I think you blew up its brain.:

:You would have killed the squid on your own eventually,: Dai tells him with a genuine smile. :You were doing a pretty good job of carving it into calamari with your dive knife.:

Thom tries to smile at that, but his smile quickly turns into a grimace of pain.

:What do you think?: I ask Tobin, fighting to stay calm.

:I can wind two wide bandages around his body. That might help slow the bleeding, but I need to treat each of those cuts, and he probably has a hundred of them. That's going to take some time.:

:Okay, wrap him up as best you can for now. We need to get out of here.:

Tobin gives Thom a sedative. Soon he has bandages wound around Thom's chest, back, and stomach.

We head out right away, Penn and Tobin carrying Thom while the dolphins take turns towing them. The rest of the pod swims in a protective circle around us as we head north, still trying to get past the last of the massive jellyfish swarm. My heart jumps when the first small blue shark appears. Densil chases it away, but the hungry shark returns and patiently follows us. Soon, other sharks appear, and the dolphins keep busy chasing off the smaller ones. Occasionally, Robry, Dai, or I have to shoot a larger shark, which triggers a feeding frenzy among the rest.

:the water is clear now toward land,: Mariah finally says. With a relieved sigh, I tell everyone we can head toward the coast. We swim as fast as we can, but we're all exhausted.

:How is Thom doing?: I ask Tobin.

:His pulse is strong but fast, and he's still bleeding. I need to get those cuts cleaned out. Is there any chance that squid put some toxins into him?:

:The beak of the giant squid is poisonous. We'll have to see if it managed to slice him with that, and there's a chance some of those cuts could get infected.:

Tobin must have heard the worry in my tone. :Thom's a strong guy. If anyone can pull through something like this, he can.:

:If only I'd had the sense to take us inland,: I say bitterly. :This is all my fault.:

:We all wanted to head out to sea rather than risk running into the Marine Guard.:

:Dai didn't, and I should have known better.:

:Well, now you do,: Tobin says in a matter-of-fact way that makes me realize I made a mistake, but all I can do now is deal with the situation.

Around midnight, Ton finds us a good-sized sea cave with an entrance so narrow that just one of us will be able to stand guard and hold off any sharks that come prowling in the night. We pile into the cave. I thank the dolphins for their help and send them off to feed and rest.

We each volunteer to help Tobin treat Thom, but in the end he chooses Lena, saying she has the most gentle hands. I'm surprised that Lena volunteered, but then I guess that she probably wants to spend more time with Tobin. I assign myself to help, too, which earns me an irritated look from her. But Thom was hurt because I decided to take us beyond the continental break, and I won't be able to rest until Tobin finishes caring for him.

I tell everyone else to string their hammocks and get some sleep. I also assign sentry shifts throughout the night. Then I turn to help Tobin and Lena, who are gently pulling off Thom's tattered seasuit. Tobin has given Thom another sedative shot, so now Thom is barely conscious and acting drunk.

When Tobin starts cleaning Thom's cuts, one by one, with that stinging antiseptic I remember only too well, Thom reaches out and grips Lena's hand, and she lets him. Occasionally she even strokes his hair and forehead, which makes Thom smile blissfully despite his pain.

While Tobin works on Thom, I glance around the sea cave. Dai seems restless. He keeps twisting around in his hammock. At last he sits up and puts on his fins and grabs his seapack and speargun.

He meets my gaze across the sea cave. :I'll make sure sharks don't get too close,: he promises, and then he's gone.

I frown as I look after him. He must need to get some rest.

:He never sleeps through an entire night,: Tobin tells

me as he continues to methodically treat Thom's cuts.

:Are you sure about that?:

:I've noticed him coming and going. He seems to only need three or four hours of sleep each night. The rest of the time he goes off prowling on his own.:

:Why didn't you tell me this before?:

Tobin shrugs. :I figured it was pretty much his business.:

:It's our business if he gets himself killed.:

:I think Dai can look after himself.:

There's nothing I can say to that, because it's so obviously true. Still, there must be dangers in this sea too great for even Dai to handle on his own.

:Be careful out there.: I reach out to Dai.

:I always am.: At first he sounds annoyed, but then he adds, :I like that you're worrying about me again.:

:I can't seem to help it. You were right. We shouldn't have gone beyond the continental break. What did you fire at the squid, anyway?:

:It was an explosive spear dart.:

:That's a handy thing to have.:

:I only have three left, but this seemed like the right time to use one.:

:Thom and I agree with you there.: I decide to push my luck. I'm getting tired of the mystery surrounding him. :Dai, why don't you need as much sleep as the rest of us?:

He doesn't respond to my question for so long that I

begin to wonder if he's swum out of my mental range. :I guess someone spliced too many restless genes into me,: he replies at last with a bitterness I don't understand. :I'll be back in time to take my watch at four o'clock,: he adds, breaking off the contact.

By three in the morning, Tobin has finished treating Thom. The moment Tobin tells him he's done, Thom sags back in his hammock and falls into a deep sleep. Lena volunteers to watch over him for a few hours more and keep small fish from nibbling at his cuts.

:Do you think he'll be all right?: I ask Tobin wearily.

:It just depends on whether or not those cuts get infected and how strong his immune system is,: Tobin says as he packs away his first-aid gear. :He's lucky the squid didn't slice him more times with its beak. I only found one shallow cut on his chest.:

:Dai says Thom was so busy stabbing it with his dive knife, the squid probably didn't have a chance to attack the way it usually would.:

:That squid definitely grabbed the wrong guy.:

But what would have happened if the squid had grabbed Bria or Robry instead? One of them might be dead right now. Tobin must guess what I'm thinking, because he puts an arm around my shoulder. I feel so tired and frightened for Thom, I can't help leaning in to him—even though I'm very aware that Lena is watching us both.

:Hey, at the time, heading out to sea seemed like the best idea,: Tobin tells me. :And it's what most of us wanted to do. This is your first mistake, and you're just going to have to learn from it. Sometimes you'll even go against what the rest of us want to do, but I trust your judgment down here. Everyone else does, too. That's why we voted to make you leader.:

:You don't think I should resign after this?:

:No way. You're the only one who can keep us together and get us to your dad's colony in one piece.:

:I hope I start doing a better job, then,: I say, rubbing my eyes.

:You'll only be able to do that if you get some rest right now. By the way, we probably need to hole up here a day or two until Thom is stronger.:

:That's not such a bad idea anyway. I think everyone was getting worn out. Lena's got those nasty blisters on her heels, and Bria's hamstring is sore.:

:See, that's part of why you make a good leader. You are aware of each of us in a way that Kyel never was.:

:Thanks,: I say, and I mean it. Talking with Tobin always makes me feel better. Reluctantly, I ease away from him because I know he needs to rest as much as I do.

Lying in my hammock waiting for sleep to come, I keep seeing our fight against the giant squid in my mind. Finally I force myself to picture the summer constellations instead, and recite them one after the other.

As I drift off to sleep, I feel the vast weight of the ocean pressing down on me, and the weight of the job I still don't know if I can do.

chapter thirty-five

THE NEXT MORNING, Thom is running a fever. Tobin gives him an antibiotic and some meds, and the rest of us lounge around and rest. Kalli, Ree, Tobin, and Bria, who all know how to sew, take turns mending and patching the many tears in Thom's tattered seasuit.

Kalli has put herself in charge of our supplies and equipment. She comes to me at noon to discuss an issue that's been troubling us both. :Nere, our spear-dart supply is running seriously low.:

:I know,: I admit. :And I'm not sure how we're going to get more.:

Our spear darts are long, straight rods made from a light and strong titanium composite. We've been careful to shoot the fish we eat for food with spear darts attached to lines, which means we usually get them back. But we couldn't use lines when we had to fight off big sharks or Marine Guard divers, and those conflicts cost us dozens of spear darts.

:Maybe we can buy some from a scrounger,: Kalli suggests. :We'll be traveling past San Francisco soon, and there must be hundreds of sea scroungers working those waters. If they're willing to risk free diving inside old buildings and sifting through floating garbage, they shouldn't be afraid to sell spear darts to some kids.:

:I've met a few scroungers who worked the area around San Diego Bay,: I tell her. :They'll do anything if the price is right. The problem is, I think some of them would turn us over to the Western Collective in a heartbeat.:

:Maybe we can come up with another solution, but we need to find it soon, or the next time we're in a big fight, we'll have to throw rocks.:

That afternoon we all take sand baths wearing just our swimsuits. Dai showed us this trick back at the *Alicante*. We don't sweat anymore, but it still feels good to rub our skin down from time to time with clean sand.

The dolphins, who are curious about everything we do, come down to watch, and before I know it, Mali snatches a rag that Tobin was using to rub sand on himself. Then Ricca steals it from her, and Robry steals it from Ricca.

Soon we're teaming up with our dolphins to play a wild game of keep-away. We spread out across the rocky bottom outside our cave, skimming over ledges and ducking behind rock pinnacles. Even Ton and Dai, who at first seemed puzzled by our play, join in this time. Dai makes a big show of letting a giggling Bria steal the rag from him when I know he could have caught her easily.

I call a halt when a small anemone stings Robry. Reluctantly, we finish our sand baths and climb back into our seasuits, but the game was good for morale.

Late in the afternoon, Thom's fever has broken and he sleeps more peacefully. By midmorning of the next day, he is so tired of lying in his hammock that he insists we let him get up for a while. That's when I call a group meeting to determine how close we're willing to travel to San Francisco, and whether or not we want to risk buying spear darts from a scrounger.

:We'll be better off staying as far from San Francisco as we can,: Dai says flatly. :The continental shelf is wide there, which means we can travel forty miles off the coast without crossing the continental break. This time of year, there will be a huge dead zone by the bay, thanks to all the fertilizer your idiotic government keeps putting on its farm fields.:

:It's not my government anymore,: Penn points out quickly.

:Well, thanks to someone's government, so much phytoplankton will have bloomed and died near the city, there will be little oxygen left in the water. Dead zones are bad news. On the edge of one you can breathe fine one moment, and the next you're suffocating.:

:Then we'll make sure we give the entrance to the bay plenty of sea room,: I say. :But I still think we should consider contacting a scrounger. We've got to get hold of more spear darts somehow.:

:Then we can all have fun when that scrounger hands us over to the Western Collective,: Dai declares.

:So, what's your brilliant suggestion for replacing our spear darts?: Ree turns on him.

:Don't lose any more,: Dai replies.

:You want us to pull the darts out of every shark you shoot?: Lena says sarcastically.

:If we have to, yeah. That's safer than dealing with scroungers. Most of them are slime who would trade away their own kids for a profit.:

:I knew some scroungers back in LA,: Ree says with a shrug. :They weren't so bad.:

:So, we'll stay well off the coast as we pass the bay,: I say, concluding our meeting. :And we'll watch out for a good, safe chance to trade with a scrounger. In the mean-time, we've got to be careful to retrieve the spear darts we have left.:

:I think Penn should go back and dig out those two spear darts he put into that mongo squid that tried to eat me,: Thom says with a straight face, and everyone cracks up.

As they leave the cave, I notice Ree and Tobin patting Penn on the shoulder. Clearly the group is giving Penn the credit for killing the squid, when Dai's explosive spear dart really finished the monster.

:What troubles you now, oh fearless leader?: Dai asks me with an ironic look. :C'mon, don't I get points for being polite and asking for a change, instead of reading your mind?:

I decide to tell him the truth because I want to reward his good behavior, and because I have a hunch he'll probably be able to tell if I lie to him. :I'm happy that everyone seems to have finally forgiven Penn for Kyel's death, but I'm sorry that you aren't getting more credit for killing the squid.:

Dai shrugs. :You're worrying about me again. Face it, they're never going to accept me as one of them.:

:Robry and Bria like you fine. I can't see why the others don't trust you more.:

:I'm just too different, and I don't know the right things to say or how to make jokes like Thom,: he says moodily, looking away from me.

The bitterness I hear in his tone makes me want to reach out and touch him. But I keep my mental shields up and force myself to concentrate on our conversation. :It helped that you joined in the game yesterday.:

Dai smiles wistfully. :I liked that game. I hope we play it again soon.:

:Knowing Mali, Sokya, and Laki, they'll probably get another game going this afternoon,: I say, even as I wonder if Dai ever had much chance to play, growing up with a research scientist who dragged his son around the oceans of the world.

In the afternoon, Sokya does come to us wanting to start up some kind of competition. Robry suggests we try a form of capture the flag, so we divide into two teams, and each team hides their own flag deep in their own territory. Then the dolphins and their human partners have to find each team's flag and steal it; but only a human/dolphin pair working together can actually move the flag.

The game is such a hit that we end up playing several rounds. Even Thom and Densil participate, but we just let them guard their team's flag. Bria and Robry are by far the best players, clinging like limpet fish to their dolphins while Nika and Ricca dart and zigzag through the water. Dai and Ton could make a team of their own, but as they go charging fiercely after their opponents, we have to remind Dai several times that it is only a game.

I call a halt after a few hours so we can rest up and eat dinner. People are smiling and joking with one another as the two teams come back to the cave. I even overhear Ree telling Dai that he played a good game.

Lena and Penn go out to find food, and return with a large yellowtail. As we eat, Penn tells everyone how Lena bagged the big fish.

:This sucker must have dragged her for a quarter mile before she managed to kill it, but she was *not* gonna let go of her line.:

:Whooee, big fishies, you better watch out, or Deadeye Lena's gonna spear you,: Thom teases her.

Lena blushes, but I can tell she is proud that she's caught our dinner.

In the morning, Tobin declares Thom strong enough to travel, and we head north at first light.

chapter Thirty-six

WE TRAVEL STEADILY, but for Thom's sake, not too quickly. We take a longer break than usual at lunch, and I insist on the dolphins giving him some tows in the afternoon. He looks pale and tired, but he never once complains.

Late in the day, I start noticing a difference in the taste of the water in my mouth. It's becoming bitter and oily.

:That's what the water around LA tasted like,: Ree tells me. :And I think it's going to get worse before it gets better.:

We spend the night in an old wreck, and none of us sleeps well. My head aches and my eyes burn when I wake up in the morning. I lead us farther from land, and yet the pollution in the water only gets worse. We also start encountering more boat traffic as we approach San Francisco. Big sailing vessels and solar-powered skiffs ferry cargo up and down the coast of the Western Collective, and diesel-powered Marine Guard vessels are more frequent here.

Every time we hear a boat we split up and travel in pairs. If a boat comes too close, we scramble to find hiding places.

Around midday, Kalli and Penn, who are traveling closest to shore, contact me in a panic. :We think we're in one of those dead zones Dai was talking about! We can hardly breathe here!:

:Stay calm and head straight west if you can. I'm sending the dolphins to tow you out of there.:

The dolphins quickly find Kalli and Penn and tow them farther out to sea, where the water is better.

:That dead zone really was bad news,: Kalli reports in a shaken voice. :One moment we could breathe just fine, and the next, there was no oxygen left in the water. We were gasping like stranded fish.:

We head even farther away from the coast after that, hoping to avoid more dead zones. By midafternoon, we start encountering big rafts of floating garbage—mounds of trash bags, plastic fencing, gallon jugs, bits of furniture, and pieces of junk all twined together.

:we do not like the water here,: Mariah tells me uneasily. :it makes our skin itch.:

:We don't like it, either. We'll get past this area as fast as we can.:

Late in the afternoon, we manage to reach the northern end of the bay. As the dolphins search for a safe place for us to spend the night, Densil contacts me. :you asked us to watch for small boats. there are many tied near here just off a point.:

:Okay. We'll check them out after we get settled.:

Once we find a good cave to spend the night, we eat a

quick supper. I ask for a volunteer to come with me to see if the boats nearby are part of a scrounger community. Ree's hand shoots up before Robry's and Tobin's, and I nod to her. I'm glad she wants to come because she seems to know more about scroungers than the rest of us. Dai doesn't volunteer, but I'm not surprised when he and Ton end up coming along anyway.

As we start off into the black sea, I'm glad for Dai's company even though it's clear he disapproves of our mission. Soon we start seeing dark masses beneath us. I shudder when I realize we're swimming over drowned piers and buildings, the lowest portions of old San Francisco that were claimed by the sea a hundred years ago.

Densil leads us straight to the circle of boats. We surface thirty yards out and study it. The circle is made up of a colorful assortment of rafts, houseboats, and small wooden sailing craft. Many of them look like they've been cobbled together from old oil barrels and other sorts of trash. There are men, women, and children walking back and forth among the various vessels. Several are lit by solar floodlights, and the smell of food cooking makes my mouth water.

:They're scroungers all right,: Ree says. :They often make floating villages like this.:

:I'm surprised the government lets them live out here.:

:I'd guess they don't cause the government any problems.: Ree shrugs. :And local agents of the Collective probably collect some sort of tax by taking the best stuff they scrounge.:

:I think we should try to trade with them,: I decide. Seeing women and children has reassured me a little.

:They're going to think it's pretty strange if I just swim up and ask to buy thirty spear darts. We need a boat of some kind,: Ree says.

In the morning, we divide into patrols to find a boat or raft we can commandeer for Ree. By noon, all patrols report back to me that each raft and boat they've found is securely chained or locked.

:Why don't we just make a raft for Ree?: Kalli suggests. :It sounds like some of those scrounger rafts you saw are just piles of garbage roped together.:

:Kalli, you're brilliant!: I say.

I call in all the patrols, and after we eat, the dolphins lead us to the nearest garbage raft. After I send the dolphins out to watch for boat traffic, we start cutting pieces of garbage loose that we can use to build our own raft.

Penn—who turns out to be very clever with his hands—and Kalli quickly take charge of the project, but everyone pitches in. By late in the afternoon we've managed to build a long, narrow raft from plastic jugs, an old truck tire, and sea floats. Penn and Robry finish making two paddles just as the sun starts to set. I think we would have enjoyed the project if the water around the garbage didn't taste so horrible.

Kalli christens our homely raft the S.S. *Neptune*. The excited dolphins help us tow it back toward the scrounger colony and the sea cave where we slept last night.

We figure out that the raft can actually support the weight of three people. In the end, I choose Penn and myself to go along with Ree. I wish that Thom could come, too, since he's the better fighter. But he's still recovering from his cuts and is probably too heavy for the raft anyway.

:Is it really necessary for you to go?: Tobin challenges me, his eyes worried. :This group needs you.:

:I'm our strongest telepath,: I reply, avoiding Dai's gaze. We both know he's actually the strongest telepath in our group. :I want to go along so I can get a reading on what the scroungers are thinking, and give Ree some warning if there's going to be trouble.:

After dark, the dolphins help us tow the riderless raft as close to the colony as we dare. My pulse is racing as Penn, Ree, and I climb aboard and take turns paddling it toward the circle of boats. The rest of the group follows along beneath us in the water with their spearguns loaded, ready to help if there's trouble.

chapter thirty-seven

REE, PENN, AND I paddle as quickly as we can, because we know we only have a half hour or so before we start getting light-headed. As we approach the colony, I concentrate on any stray thoughts I can pick up. Our arrival causes curiosity but no real excitement.

A wiry old man catches the rope Ree tosses him and helps us tie up next to his own sailboat. It's actually a trim-looking wooden vessel that reminds me of James's *Kestrel*.

After looking us over carefully, the old man introduces himself as Crab. He's clean-shaven, his skin is wrinkled and tanned dark by the sun, and his long white hair is caught back in a ponytail. Smiling, he raises his left hand. I try not to wince when I realize it's frozen in a twisted claw. When Ree asks him where we can buy some spear darts, he says he's actually a trader and invites us to sit on his foredeck. Ree and I climb up onto his boat while Penn stays with our raft. Crab hustles into his tiny cabin and returns shortly with a basket of bread.

Finally I get to eat something that isn't fish or kelp! But I'm surprised that the bread feels so dry and strange in my mouth. The longer I chew, the more the bread nauseates me.

I stare at the rest in my hand. I want to tear it to pieces and fling it into the sea. I glance over and see that Ree has only taken one bite of her bread, too.

"Just how many spear darts would yeh be wanting?" the old man asks us.

"Thirty that are three feet long and five-sixteenths of an inch in caliber," Ree says bluntly. "If you can get ahold of that many. And they need to be made from a titanium composite or stuff that's even lighter."

I sense Crab's surprise as he studies us out of his shrewd brown eyes. I wonder if we would have been smarter to contact more scroungers.

"My friends and I make good money from spear fishing up the coast from here," Ree adds with a shrug. "But we lose our rigs sometimes when we go after the bigger fish."

Crab has strong natural shields that keep me from hearing his specific thoughts, but I can sense his eagerness to make a good sale.

"I'd like to know yeh can pay. It'll take me some time to gather up that many darts for yeh."

Ree pulls a small round discn of real gold from her pocket. Each of us has two of these sewn into our seapacks. Shielding it with her hand, she passes it to Crab. He takes it, bites it, and then gives it back quickly with a nod.

"Aye, I'll take six of those for thirty spear darts."

"That's robbery, you old bandit. You can have just one

gold discn and count yourself lucky to be making such a good trade."

I stare at Ree. :Are you crazy?: I ask her telepathically.

:He expects us to bargain. We'd make him suspicious if we didn't,: she replies quickly.

"It will take me all day tomorrow to come up with such a stash of spear darts, and it will cost me, too. I'll take five discn, and no less, yeh young gouger."

Trading insults, the two bargain back and forth until my chest aches from the effort I'm making not to pant.

:Ree, you better finish this up. I'm getting a little dizzy here. He's bound to notice there's something strange about us if we start gasping like fish.:

Reluctantly, Ree agrees to pay him three gold discn for thirty spear darts, and the two shake hands. Crab invites us to stay for supper, but Ree turns him down politely.

"Well then, come back this way tomorrow night."

"We will, and thanks for the bread," Ree tells him as we climb back aboard our raft and he casts us off.

As soon as we have our backs to him, I drop the rest of the bread I hid in my palm into the sea. I finally allow myself to start panting as I struggle to get more air.

"Hang in there, Nere," Penn whispers behind me. "We'll be back in the water before you know it."

As soon as we're beyond the reach of the solar flood-lights, I slip into the sea and submerge, letting the seawater flow into my dry, hot lungs. Penn and Ree do the same. Once we've caught our breath, we start back to the cave.

After we make it safely there, we use a rope from Penn's seapack to anchor the S.S. *Neptune* to an old truck lying on the sea floor nearby.

~ ~ ~

The next morning Dai insists that I call a meeting.

:Any number of things could go wrong when Ree heads back to that scrounger town,: he tells me curtly. :You should have a plan in place in case Crab decides to tip off the Collective about you. There's a large Marine Guard base in San Francisco Bay. Ten boats could be after us in ten minutes.:

Even though I liked Crab, I can see the sense in what Dai is saying. I call everyone together, and we spend most of the morning talking about what we should do if we run into trouble.

In the end, we adopt a plan made up of ideas contributed mostly by Dai and Robry. Our current sea cave is an ideal hiding place because its mouth is so small and hard to see. If the Marine Guard comes after us, the main group will head straight back for the cave, but two teams of our fastest swimmers—Dai, Kalli, Robry, and me—will try to lay a false trail by heading south. We hope to give our slowest swimmers a better chance of reaching safety, and we may fool the Marine Guard into thinking we aren't traveling north. Midday, we will go out and find two smaller caves, where our decoy "foxes" will go to ground.

:Hopefully after we hide, their ships will range on ahead of us. Then we should be able to slip back to the main cave, and we'll head on north together,: Robry concludes.

:One final thing—I don't think Nere should go in with Ree and Penn this time,: Dai proposes.

:Agreed,: Tobin says quickly.

I start to protest, but Robry, of all people, cuts me off. :Nere, think about it. Ree and Penn function better out of water, and you can still use your telepathy to get a reading on Crab if you're in the water beside the raft. There's no reason to risk any more lives than we absolutely have to.:

I can tell from their expressions that everyone agrees with Robry, so I give in.

I feel the tension rising in our group as the sun sets. We force ourselves to eat a light dinner and then head for the scrounger colony with our spearguns loaded. As Penn and Ree paddle the raft in, the rest of us swim along in a tight formation right beneath it. I'm so anxious, I'm afraid I'm going to throw up the five bites of halibut I managed to choke down an hour ago.

Now I can see a dozen different ways our plan could go wrong. Maybe Dai was right all along about trading with scroungers.

:I can see the old guy. He's definitely on the lookout for

us,: Ree reports as she and Penn approach Crab's boat. I risk popping my head out of the water on the seaward side of the raft, where Crab can't see me. I focus my senses and try to read his surface mind.

:Can you get anything from him, Nere?: Ree asks me.

:The old guy's got some naturally tight mental shields. All I can tell you is that he's very tense right now and excited. Maybe this is a really good deal for him.:

I close my eyes and let my mind range outward. I do sense that the scroungers near us are on edge. :Everyone seems too nervous,: I tell the others. :Let's make this deal fast and get out of here.:

The moment Ree steps onto his boat, Crab asks her and Penn to sit and eat dinner with him.

"Thanks, but we need to get going. Do you have the darts?"

"Are yeh sure yeh don't want to be staying? I made a pot of fish chowder, and no one makes fish chowder better than old Crab."

"I bet your chowder is great, but we need to go," Ree says impatiently.

"Well, then, here are your spear darts. Thirty, just as yeh wanted," Crab says slowly.

:He's stalling!: Penn says.

I see Ree quickly hand him the three discn. Then she looks down at the three heavy bundles of darts he just handed her.

:*Dios mio!* He's wrapped a flyer around the darts, and it has our pictures all over it!:

Just then, I pick up an image in Crab's mind of four rough-looking smugglers coming to his boat, and his feeling of sharp regret.

:Ree, get out of there!: I yell at her. :It's a trap!:

Moments later, two burly men burst out of Crab's cabin. Before they can grab Ree, she jumps into the water, holding the spear darts. A second later, Penn dives off the raft.

:Help!: Ree cries as she sinks past us toward the bottom. :These suckers are heavy.:

:Give one bundle to Thom and one to Tobin,: I say, :and let's get out of here!:

I hear the bass thrum of powerful boat engines in the distance as Tobin and Thom flash down to the bottom and take two bundles of spear darts from Ree. Bria helps Ree scramble into her fins, and Lena helps Penn with his.

:two boats come from around the point,: Densil warns me.

They must have been waiting to ambush us.

We sprint as fast as we can away from the scrounger colony. As soon as we're beyond the lights I call the dolphins, and they tow us out to sea.

:Main group, head back to the cave NOW,: I order. The four of us who are going to lead a false trail head south, swimming right at the surface so we're easy to spot.

I wait for a long thirty seconds while Sokya tows me

through the water, and then I contact Mariah. :Which way are those boats heading?:

:they follow you fast,: she says, sounding very worried.

:They've taken the bait,: I tell everyone. :Main group, stay in that cave until we can get back to you. Foxes, let's dive now and get to our holes as quickly as we can.:

The dolphins take a final breath at the surface and then they pull us down under the waves. The sound of engines grows louder much faster than I expected. My heart lurches when I realize these smugglers have sent small, fast speed-boats to track us.

In no time, the two boats catch up to us. Dai swears when both boats slow down, right over our heads. Someone's definitely tracking us on sonar.

I swear to myself, but I try not to broadcast my worry to the others. Our whole plan was based on getting a good head start on big, lumbering Marine Guard vessels, not small smuggler speedboats.

:Let's split up and see if we can lose them,: I say, trying to sound more positive than I feel.

:two big boats come fast from the south,: Mariah warns me, and I tell the others.

:We're in deep trouble now,: Dai says, :and we have no mines left.:

Our small group's spear-dart supply is dangerously low, too. We may be fighting hand-to-hand with more divers in a few minutes, but I only have two spear darts left in my quiver. Some commander I make. I just sent our new supply back to the main cave!

Suddenly, Sokya begins clicking and sawing. I bite my lip. The last thing we need right now is to run into a shark or a squid.

:friends come!: she tells me excitedly.

Moments later, the water around us fills with a large school of wild bottlenose dolphins. Over fifty of them swim and swoop around us.

:It's the cavalry!: Robry shouts in elation.

:Mariah, I love you!: I yell as I realize what my clever friend has done. Somehow she has coaxed a wild school of dolphins to swim with us, which may give us just enough time to reach our hiding spots.

:Let those landlivers try to figure this one out on their sonar scopes,: Dai says with relish.

We sprint for our caves while the big school of dolphins splits into swirls and eddies, darting every which way and confusing our sonar signature. Suddenly, the smaller boat that was tracking Robry and me races off to the west, chasing a group of four wild dolphins.

Two minutes later, Robry and I reach our small cave. We duck inside, gasping and panting. Sokya and Nika rush off to play with the wild dolphins.

:Kalli, Dai, are you safe?: I call to our other pair of decoys.

:Yeah, we just made it to our cave,: Kalli reports in. :And the boat that was following us headed south a minute ago. Those wild dolphins really saved our butts.:

I reach out my senses farther and contact Mariah. :How did you get them to swim with us?:

:are you safe?: she asks me first, sounding remarkably like my mother.

:We're tucked away in a nice little cave where their sonar will never find us.:

:good. the wild ones were curious about why we were swimming with so many humans. I made them understand that the boats were hunting you, and they could help by swimming with you.:

:They probably just saved our lives.:

:I am glad. the wild ones are leaving. they do not like the feel of the water here.:

:I can't blame them. Now that we're safe, please take your own family to cleaner waters. I will call you when we start traveling north again. Good hunting.:

:rest well,: Mariah says, and then she breaks off the contact.

:Did Mariah send that wild school to help us?: Dai asks me curiously.

:It was her idea, start to finish.:

:I can't believe she showed so much initiative. She's a remarkable animal,: Dai says. I know he means to be complimentary, but his tone is still annoying. The dolphins will always be more than "animals" to me.

:Mariah's my hero.: Robry grins.

I reach out and tell everyone in the main cave what happened. We stay in our caves and doze on and off until two a.m. Then Robry and I slip outside and listen carefully. When we decide there are no boats nearby, we sprint back to the main cave. Kalli and Dai arrive right behind us.

We find Tobin on sentry duty. His face relaxes when he spots me. He starts in my direction, and I think he wants to give me a hug, but then he realizes Robry, Dai, and Kalli are right behind me and he stops short.

:Welcome back,: he says, a smile lighting his green eyes. :Sounds like you guys had a close call there.:

:Mariah really saved the day,: I tell him.

:I'm glad you're all okay,: Tobin says to everyone, but his gaze is focused on me. :Mariah is amazing. The more I talk to her, the more she seems like a real person to me.:

:She is amazing, and smarter than many humans I know,: I say with a pointed glance at Dai. I'm tempted to stick my tongue out at him, but that doesn't seem like a very leader-like thing to do.

:Can I see that flyer Crab slipped to us along with the spear darts?: I ask Tobin instead.

His smile fades. :Yeah. Lena left it under a rock for you, next to the pile of our seapacks.:

I swim into the cave and find the laminated flyer just where Tobin said it would be. A cold dread creeps across my skin as I pick up the flyer and study it. I realize I'm looking at a wanted poster with pictures of every one of us except Dai. The Western Collective is offering a thousand dollarns for each of us, or any information leading to our capture.

chapter Thirty-eight

EVEN THOUGH I ACHE all over from swimming
hard, it takes me a long time to fall asleep. The Western
Collective must want us badly to offer that kind of money.
No wonder the smugglers wanted to catch us. If Mariah
hadn't called those wild dolphins, some of us might be dead
or prisoners right now.

At last my tired body wins out over my racing brain.
When I wake up the next morning, everyone except Dai is
sacked out in their hammocks. Since it's not a travel day, I
let people rest. After we're all up and we've eaten, I call a
meeting to discuss the flyer Crab managed to slip to us along
with the spear darts.

:This is like the posters they used to send around when
they wanted to catch Kyel's dad and his fighters,: Thom
says, looking much more somber than usual. :Only this one
claims we're all members of a dangerous mutant gang
dedicated to bringing down the Western Collective.:

:I like the part where it claims we're terrorists and
a danger to law and public order.: Kalli shakes her head.
:Robry and Bria sure look like dangerous terrorists
to me.:

Bria grins at Kalli, but then her big eyes grow serious. :I don't think I've ever broken a law. I did shoot that diver in the leg, but that's because he shot Kyel. It isn't very nice of them to tell everyone that we're bad people.:

:We're not bad people.: Tobin slips an arm around her shoulders. :It's our government that isn't very nice or truthful.:

:I wonder why that old man gave this to us,: Robry muses.

:I think he was trying to warn me,: Ree says as she studies the flyer.

:I do too. I felt his regret as he handed you those spear darts,: I tell her. :Maybe one of the other scroungers ratted us out, or the smugglers threatened him.:

:Whether or not that old scrounger sold us out doesn't matter anyway,: Dai says with a scowl. :What does matter is that we now know that every smuggler, scrounger, and black-market fisherman between here and Vancouver Island is going to be on the lookout for us.:

:Actually, they're going to be on the lookout for *us*, not you. I think it's interesting that your mug shot isn't on here with the rest of ours,: Lena points out sharply.

:Since Dai hasn't lived on land since he was ten, I don't think that's much of a surprise. He may not even be in the Western Collective's databases,: I say quickly, trying to head off a fight. :What I want to know is why are they making such a huge effort to catch us?:

:They could want to use us. I know the Collective sometimes interrogates prisoners with telepaths,: Thom offers. :They're pretty quiet about it, since telepaths aren't supposed to exist in the first place.:

:Yeah, maybe they seized a computer that belonged to a Neptune Project scientist, and they found out that we're all telepaths,: Robry suggests.

:It might be about control, too,: Penn says bitterly. :The Western Collective may be threatened by the idea that a new force could grow in the ocean that might turn against them someday.:

:There are so many pictures here of kids we don't even know. Maybe we'll meet up with them along the way,: Bria says as she pores over the poster.

:I'm afraid some of them may already be dead,: Kalli tells her gently. :There's a picture of my cousin Ter.:

I wince when I see her point to the picture of a handsome smiling boy who looks just like her. :He never even made it out of Oxnay Harbor,: she says, grief coloring her tone.

:These are just the kids from the south,: Bria says hopefully. :There could be a bunch more heading for Dr. Hanson's colony from the northern sector.:

I smile at Bria. :You're right. There is some good news in this flyer, and I'm going to concentrate on that.:

Our meeting breaks up, and the next morning, as soon as the sea starts to lighten, we head north again.

~ ~ ~

After we leave San Francisco, the dolphins give us plenty of warning when we need to change course to avoid smuggler, Marine Guard, or fishing vessels. As our group grows fitter, we often make thirty miles a day.

After ten travel days, we leave the southern sector behind. The northern sector coastline is more craggy and rocky. Boat traffic actually increases because the Western Collective has been moving its population north as temperatures soar in the south.

I'm glad to see that our group seems to be getting along better. Everyone teases Robry and Penn about their huge appetites. Thom and Kalli crack us up with their jokes. People even appear more comfortable around Dai, who's always trying to get us to eat more kinds of seafood. We liked the eel, scallops, and oysters he coaxed us into sampling, but his sea cucumber and sea urchins didn't go over so well.

I grin when I remember Kalli's reaction to his sea cucumber. :Dai, I know you mean well, but why would I want to eat something that looks like a giant orange caterpillar, eats sludge all day, and can vomit up its own intestines?:

After that description, Lena looked like she was ready to

vomit up her own intestines while Dai ate his sea cucumber with enthusiasm.

Dai gives me good advice about our course each day, which makes me wonder just how many times he's traveled these waters. Tobin always seems to know how people in the group are feeling and what their problems are. Kalli is good at nagging us to eat plenty of sea plants along with the fish we spear.

Thom is the first to volunteer for any chore, including the nastiest ones. We start calling Penn "The Fixer" because he's so great at fixing broken spearguns and fins. Lena and Ree keep our seasuits patched up and become two of our most successful hunters. Because Robry's always thinking about the big picture, I often talk to him about our long-term problems. The dolphins love Bria, and more and more I trust them to relay their scouting reports through her.

As the days and weeks wear on and we have no further fights with the Marine Guard or run-ins with nets and giant squid, I begin to relax a little. I think we all are becoming more comfortable in our new world. Farther north, the sea is cooler and healthier. We see more seals, bigger game fish, and thicker kelp forests.

One afternoon, we even come across a pod of rare humpback whales.

:Please-oh-please-oh-please, Nere, can we swim near them for a while?: Bria begs me.

:As long as we don't get too close. They're usually gentle, but they could crush us when they breach.:

We swim a little nearer, and with the dolphins' help, we keep pace with the whales as they head north, their massive tails driving them through the water.

:Man, these suckers are huge.: Thom shakes his head.

:The big one is bigger than two of our houses back home,: Bria says, her eyes wide.

:Check out all the barnacles they have growing on their skin!: Robry exclaims.

:Are those smaller ones babies?: Lena asks as she points to the two calves.

:Yeah,: I reply. :They were probably born four months ago down in the warm waters off the western coast of the Southern Republic.:

:Those are some big babies,: Ree says.

The calves are shy at first and peek at us from behind their mothers, but after a while their curiosity wins out and they swim closer and closer to our group.

:Um, Mariah, is this really a good idea?: I ask as one of the whale calves swims so close that I can almost touch it. :I don't want those big mama whales getting angry with us.:

:the old ones know you mean their little ones no harm,: Mariah reassures me.

Soon our dolphins are towing us over and around the

playful whale calves. All the while, the grown whales study us as curiously out of their wise eyes as we study them. I do my best to describe to the others the unearthly whale songs I heard when my parents took me south to visit the humpbacks' breeding grounds years ago.

:Mariah, can you tell me what the whales sing about?:

She takes a moment to consider my question. :it's hard to put into human words, but I feel their meaning. the old ones sing of caring about their youngsters and one another. most of all they sing of their love for the ocean and everything that lives in it. every year their song changes, but all the male whales in the same sea know to sing the same song.:

Her words give me goose bumps and make me happy at the same time. The biggest whales, the blues and the finbacks, are extinct now, but I'm so grateful the humpbacks have managed to survive. We're all sorry when the humpbacks eventually head farther out to sea. At dinner that night, we are a quiet group, but everyone is smiling.

As we travel, I never forget Crab's flyer and how careful we must be to avoid landlivers and airbreathers, as Dai calls them. I know the group gets irritated when I make us swim a mile out of our way to avoid sonar contact with some boat, but I'd rather take longer and get us all to my father's colony alive.

One afternoon, Kalli, who has been acting very mysteriously, along with Bria, asks me to halt for the night when we reach a beautiful rock canyon.

I stop swimming long enough to admire the walls of the canyon. They're alive with small fish, fuzzy pink strawberry anemones, giant rock scallops, spiny red sea urchins, and some bright yellow sponges. I even spot some lavender hydrocorals, which have become rare in the warmer seas farther south.

:Ton's found a perfect cave for us near here, and there's that big kelp forest we can use as an escape route if we need it,: Dai adds with unusual enthusiasm.

:But we still could make four or five more miles today,: I say, even though I'm torn. I'm tired from constant travel, and sick of being responsible for everyone's safety.

:Nere, we have to stop now, because we have an important mission to fulfill this afternoon,: Bria says, trying to look very serious.

:Exactly what mission would that be?: I ask, starting to realize that something's up.

:This is our mission. Today is your birthing day, and we have to celebrate it properly,: Kalli adds, her eyes dancing.

:Robry, you are such a little snitch!: I turn on him.

:Actually, Lena remembered it first,: he says quickly.

I look at Lena. She shrugs and says, :Hey, you know I'm always looking for a good excuse to take a break.: But then she sends me a real smile.

:It was almost time for a rest day anyway,: Tobin adds. :We're all tired, and I think it's a good idea if we take it early.:

:If that's what our chief medical officer orders,: I say helplessly. I feel myself blushing as they all grin at me. I hate to be the center of anything, much less an undersea birthing-day party. Kalli must sense how uncomfortable I am, and she quickly takes control of the situation.

:First off, the birthing-day queen has to take off her seapack and settle herself on this nice, relatively barnacle-free rock here. Now, we all know no birthing day is complete without presents, and the dolphins are in charge of your shopping.:

I smile because this is an old game with us. The dolphins scatter and soon come back with an odd assortment of treasures they've found for me. I make a big show of exclaiming over the shells, bits of rock, and even a small octopus that proud Tisi drops in my lap, which promptly spurts a cloud of ink at me before it shoots away, and makes everyone laugh.

Then Thom, who has been busy with his dive knife while the dolphins were giving me presents, serves us some very handsome flower-shaped yellowfin wrapped in wakame.

:These would do your grandma proud,: I say, even as I wonder how his big hands managed to make such deli-cate blossoms out of fish meat. Kalli comes around with a contribution of her own, a kind of sweet mash made from wakame, which we all like much better than the green seaweeds and kelp we usually eat.

After we finish with our meal, Tobin waves to get our attention. :Of course, no party would be complete without music,: he declares with a bow and a flourish. :May I present the coolest sound in undersea entertainment today—The Reef Raiders!:

He pulls two aluminum medical canisters from his pack and begins hitting them together in an infectious rhythm. Thom joins in, making a deeper sound from beating the barrels of two spearguns together, and Penn shakes a small metal box full of pebbles and shells.

In a flash, Ree and Kalli are up and dancing to the beat. Lena grabs Bria and Robry, and Dai comes to find me. Suddenly, we're all dancing in the middle of the beautiful, sunlit canyon. The dolphins swim in crazy circles around us, excited by the strange noises the boys are making. After a time, we go from dancing to a wild game of limbo in which we all try to dance under a speargun held by Dai. Poor Thom is out almost at once, which makes everyone laugh. Bria, who can bend her flexible little body into knots, wins easily in the end, and then we all float around trying to catch our breath.

:Nere, now it's time for your very best present,: Ree declares. :We're giving you a chance *not* to worry about us, because we know that's pretty much what you do all day. Dai's offered to be your escort and bodyguard, and we want the two of you to go someplace and relax and have *fun*.: She finishes with such an arch look that my cheeks burn again.

:We promise to stay right here and not get eaten or stung or hurt while you two are gone,: Bria says solemnly.

I can't help smiling at sweet Bria's promise, even while my stomach lurches. I know Ree means well, but I'm not sure their present is a good idea. I've been trying to avoid being alone with Dai over the past few weeks, and mostly I've been successful. Now I have to go with him or disappoint everyone.

Dai must sense my dismay, but his only response is an unsympathetic grin. He takes my hand and pulls me firmly after him. As I leave the others, I can't help looking back at Tobin. For one moment, our gazes meet, and I see the hurt in his eyes before he looks away.

:Tobin, I . . . .: I start to apologize on a private send, even though I'm not sure what I'm apologizing for.

:It's all right, Nere. Ree's right. You do deserve some fun,: he says shortly, and then he breaks off the contact.

Dai tugs on my hand impatiently. When I look at him, he isn't smiling anymore.

:I told you he likes you, but he has good mental shields. He also has some stupid principles about not wanting to weigh you down with caring about him when you have so much on your mind. I, on the other hand, have no such principles.:

Then Dai smiles that reckless smile of his, and I realize I absolutely want to go with him.

chapter Thirty-nine

DAI IS SMART ENOUGH to not say anything right after that. :Just float,: he says quietly, :and let me do all the work.:

It's wonderful after days of hard swimming to be towed slowly up and down the canyon walls. He points out species of sea creatures I've only read about before, his expression unguarded in his enthusiasm. He tows me deeper, out of the sunlit zone into darker waters, to show me beautiful billowing white cloud sponges and the juvenile rockfish that hide in their folds and tubes. We see decorator crabs walking across the sponges on long delicate legs, and funny little red fur crabs that wedge themselves into impossible spots when we approach. This Dai—the Dai who sincerely loves the sea as much as I do—slips right past the walls I've been trying to build against him.

Then we swim back up into brighter, shallower waters, and he pulls me deep inside the kelp forest. There, he turns and puts his arms around me. Suddenly I'm not feeling relaxed and lazy anymore.

:That was one smooth move.: I laugh to hide my nervousness. :Just how many girls have you lured into a kelp forest before?:

:Maybe a few, but I never felt this way about any of them. I didn't know I could,: Dai says, and then he lowers his head and kisses me. I decide to go for it. I wrap my arms around his neck and kiss him back.

I forget about being nervous, I forget that I am Freak Girl, and I forget that somehow I'm supposed to get ten people and twelve dolphins safely to my father's colony. There's just Dai, and he's really good at this kissing business.

But then he holds me tighter and tighter against him until I realize it hurts where his hands grip my shoulders.

:Dai, you're hurting me,: I say.

His eyes darken. For a moment that seems to stretch into forever I'm afraid he won't let go. A tremor goes through him and then he flings himself away. He floats with his back to me, breathing hard.

I can't help massaging my shoulders. They ache. I'd forgotten just how strong he is. Now I remember how easily he gutted those big sharks when we tried to save Sara. He sliced through their thick, tough hides as though sharkskin were butter. He glances at me once, and his face tightens when he sees I'm rubbing my shoulders. Quickly, I drop my hands.

:It's all right. You didn't really hurt me.:

:But I could have.: The self-loathing I hear in his voice makes me shiver.

:Dai, I'm fine.: I start toward him, but he retreats from me.

:Go back to the rest of them. Go back to Tobin. Go back where it's safe.:

:Y-you're not going to leave us, are you?:

:No.: He sighs. :I can't.: He swims swiftly away. :I'll be back by tomorrow morning. Nere, I'm sorry if I ruined your birthing day.:

:You didn't,: I call after him firmly, even though we both know he has.

I stay by myself for a long time in the kelp forest. Densil comes to find me there. Patiently, he lets me hug him. Then together we watch the late afternoon sunlight filter down through the dense fronds.

~ ~ ~

I go back only when I'm fairly sure I can hide what happened from the rest.

:Thanks for the nice vacation,: I tell everyone with the best smile I can manage. :I'm happy to see no one got eaten while we were gone.:

:Where's Dai?: Bria asks in surprise.

:He and Ton offered to scout on ahead of us,: I say lightly. :He'll be back by tomorrow morning.:

Ree and Tobin frown and send me searching looks, but I'm relieved when they don't question my explanation. We eat a quick dinner, and while I do my usual nighttime dolphin check, Tobin appears beside me. I can feel he's watching my face carefully, but I can't make myself meet his gaze.

:Are you all right?: he asks at last.

:I'm fine,: I say tightly, even though I'd love to tell him what just happened with Dai. But after the way I hurt him this afternoon, I don't deserve his sympathy.

:I'm glad,: he says after an awkward moment. His tone is so kind and forgiving that I almost lose it right there.

:Bria and me, we have a little birthing-day present for you.:

He hands me a delicate carving of a mermaid swimming beside a graceful dolphin. I realize that the carving is actually a small pendant hanging on a black cord.

:This belonged to our mother. She always loved dolphins and the sea. Bria and I talked about it, and we both decided that we wanted you to have it. Bria thinks the mermaid looks just like you.:

:I can't take something that belonged to your mother,: I protest.

:We have other special things to remember her by. Please, we'd like you to have this. I think she'd be grateful that you are trying so hard to make a new family for us.:

:Thank you,: I manage to say without crying.

I try to put on the pendant, but my braids get in the way.

:Here, let me help,: he says. I pick up my braids and he deftly fastens the cord for me.

The pendant rests right at the base of my throat. :During the day, I promise I'll keep it tucked inside my seasuit to make sure it doesn't get lost.:

:It looks good on you,: Tobin says, his palms resting lightly on my bruised shoulders. His gaze goes to my face. I look back at him, wishing he could make my bruised heart feel better. His eyes are such an amazing green, and I love the warm cedar color of his hair and eyelashes.

:Nere, I'm sorry if he hurt you,: he says as if the words are torn from him. :I promised myself that I wasn't going to do this until we reached your father's colony.:

He bends his head and kisses me. Gently, he gathers me closer. I like being in his arms. Tobin is so safe and comfortable. But even as I kiss him back, I think of Dai, and I worry about where he is and what he's doing right now.

If only Tobin had kissed me first.

Suddenly, I realize I'm not being fair to him, and Tobin deserves my honesty. I stop kissing him and press my hands against his chest. He raises his head and studies me for a long moment, his eyes filled with pain.

:Dai's already won, hasn't he?:

I stare back at him, struggling to find the right words. :Tobin, I—:

:It's all right. You can't help how you feel. Whatever happens, I just want you to know I'll always be here for you. Happy birthing day, Nere,: he says quickly. Head down, he swims away from me.

:Thank you. Thank you for everything,: I call after him, desperately hoping that he'll still be my friend in the morning.

Going to find my hammock, I wonder at my luck. Two different guys just kissed me, and this still turned into one of the worst birthing days ever.

~ ~ ~

When Dai returns to us in the morning, he's his old withdrawn, sarcastic self. He's so rude to anyone who talks to him directly that we leave him alone. At sunset I go to the surface to check our latitude and longitude. With surprise, I realize we are only four days now from my father's colony. I return to the group and tell them the good news.

Everyone smiles and grins except for Dai. His face tightens, and he slips away from our meeting without a word. The next day he's more distant than ever. When Bria bumps into him by accident while we're traveling, he jumps and speaks to her so sharply that her face crumples. After that, she swims right next to Tobin and stays far away from Dai.

:There's no excuse for your being mean to Bria,: I tell him at lunch.

:It would have been even more inexcusable if I'd shot her.:

:She really likes you, you know, and she's a sweetheart.:

:I know,: he surprises me by saying. :She is a sweet kid, and I'm sorry I got mad.: He tugs at the end of one of his braids. :I just have a lot on my mind right now.:

:You want to talk about it?:

:No.:

:How about what happened in the kelp forest?:

:I definitely don't want to talk about that.:

:You didn't hurt me. You just startled me there for a moment. I know you wouldn't do it again.:

:Nere, you don't know that. You don't know anything about me.:

As I search his bitter face, I realize he is retreating further and further from us.

:If that's true, whose fault is that?: I ask, then turn away. He makes no move to stop me or to talk with me alone again.

~ ~ ~

The next afternoon, Sokya arrows up to me, whistling and squeaking in excitement. :there's a large group of humans like you ahead,: she says.

:Sokya, that's wonderful news!:

Quickly, I relay what she told me, and we all start grinning at one another. I can sense the excitement rising in my companions. For so long we've been hoping to find other

Neptune kids. I pick up the pace, and the rest follow me as quickly as they can.

:Nere, you don't want to let our group get all spread out like this.: Dai swims up next to me, his face set. :Not everyone you meet in the sea is as friendly as you are.:

:But Sokya said they're like us.:

Dai doesn't answer, but he looks so tense and his mind is so tightly shielded that I feel uneasy. I slow my pace and wait for our group to resume our normal travel formation.

:Um, everyone, make sure your spearguns are loaded and ready.:

:Are you crazy?: I can hear the disbelief in Lena's tone.

:Just do it,: I tell her.

I keep peering ahead into the deep blue-green water, and suddenly I see them. There's a group of a dozen or so kids like us spread out across the rocky canyon we've been following to the north. It looks like they're blocking our path, but I try to push that thought from my mind. Dai is making me paranoid.

Sokya and Laki, who are excited and pleased to meet more humans, range ahead of us and swim right up to the other group.

:aeeeee!: Sokya whistles in shock and fear. :they shot a spear dart at us!: Seconds later, she's swimming back to us as fast as she can, Laki at her side.

:Mariah,: I say sharply, :tell the pod to stay behind us!:

I reach out with my senses, and I don't like what I pick up. The group ahead of us is radiating excitement and hatred.

:Who are you, and why did you shoot at our dolphins?: I ask them, unable to hide the anger in my tone.

:We were hungry, and they looked like a good lunch to us,: a cool female voice answers.

As we draw closer, I realize I'm staring at some of the strangest kids I've ever seen. They look like members of an undersea street gang. They all have bizarre haircuts and strange, swirling tattoos on their faces. They wear seasuits, but theirs are gray and black, covered with odd embroidery and insignia. I blink when I realize that one of the boys has two extra sets of arms.

I tell my companions to halt. Every kid in the new group has a powerful-looking speargun, and those spearguns are trained on us.

:Who are you?: I ask again. We're facing three girls and eight boys, and the girls look just as savage and wild as the boys.

:Names aren't important, but what I'm about to tell you is.: A striking, thin girl in the center of the group raises her speargun until it's pointing directly at me. She has short black hair, catlike amber eyes, and high cheekbones. I swallow hard. I think we're out of range of their spear darts, but I'm not absolutely sure.

:*You* are invading *our* turf,: she declares.

:I'm sorry, I didn't realize anyone had 'turf' around here. It's a big ocean.:

:Well, now you know. Run along back to where you came from, and we might let you live.:

I can't believe she's threatening us! I tighten my grip on my speargun and take a deep breath. :We don't want to bother anyone, but we aren't running anywhere. We're heading north to join my father's colony.:

The girl's eyes narrow, and I wonder if I've made a big mistake by telling her where we're going.

:Isn't that sweet? She wants to go home to her daddy.: The girl mocks me, and the others grin at her words. :Well, little girl, we're not going to let you go anywhere now.:

Ree and Thom move up beside me. :We can take them if we have to,: Ree says, directing her thoughts only to our group. Her expression is fierce.

:There're eleven of them and only ten of us,: I counter. :And something tells me they know how to use those spearguns.:

chapter forty

:BUT WE HAVE THE DOLPHINS,: Thom says. :They're like an army in themselves.: He looks calm and ready to get into a full-scale battle with these strange kids, but the idea terrifies me. I just want to get us all safely to my father's colony.

:There's no reason to get into a fight here if I can talk us out of one,: I think at my group quickly. :Let me try that first.:

I look the black-haired girl straight in the eye. :If we fight you, a lot of people are going to get hurt. Some may even die.:

:We're not afraid of dying.:

:Good for you,: I say, trying to keep my mental tone even. :Me, I am afraid of dying, at least over something as stupid as 'turf,' as you call it. I'd rather live, and I bet a bunch of your friends probably would, too.: I can tell my words are surprising them. :So, why don't you tell us the boundaries of this turf of yours, and we'll just go around it.:

:Maybe we don't want to let you go around us,: she says. The eager look in her eyes makes my heart fall. For some reason this girl *wants* to fight us.

:Our group can shoot.: Dai speaks up for the first time. :She's right.: He gestures to me. :A lot of us are going to get hurt if you push this to a fight.:

Dai and the strange girl stare at each other for a long moment, and I wonder if they are talking on a private send.

:All right.: She addresses me again, and her yellow eyes still smolder. :If you cowardly bunch of sea slugs head west for five miles, we'll leave you alone. But the toll for your passage is one of your dolphins. I meant it when I said we were hungry.:

:Why would you want to eat dolphin when we can give you fresh tuna?: Dai says smoothly. Moments later, Ton appears, a big albacore struggling in his jaws. He drops the large fish in the no-man's-land between our groups, and one of the boys shoots the crippled tuna through the heart so quickly that I flinch. Now I'm convinced that we don't want to get into a shooting fight with these guys.

:Come on, Wasp, albacore beats dolphin any day,: one of the boys speaks up.

This earns him a furious look from the girl, but clearly the rest seem to agree with him. Two even break ranks and eagerly fetch the dead fish.

:All right, you can go, and we'll leave you alone. For now,: she says with a disgusted look at the boys.

Without another word to her, I quickly lead us seaward, up and over the western edge of the undersea canyon we had been following. We keep a close eye on the group behind us until the rock ridge hides them from view.

:What was that all about?: Kalli asks in disbelief.

:Let's talk about what just happened while we keep swimming,: I say. I realize I'm trembling. :We need to get some distance between us and that group. Dai, you and Thom are our rear guard.:

Then I reach out to Mariah. :Tell the rest of the pod to stay close, and let us know if you sense them coming after us. I think they meant it when they said they eat dolphin.:

I can feel Mariah's fear and revulsion. :we will watch. there was something very wrong about them.:

:Dai, do you know anything about that group?: I ask as I head west.

:I've run into them before, and you don't want anything to do with them. Their leader who spoke to you is called Wasp, and she deserves her name. She wears gloves because her fingers are covered with the same venomous tentacles as the sea wasp.:

I feel the hair rise on the back of my neck. The sea wasp is the most lethal species of jellyfish in the sea, killing many more people every year than sharks do. :How can she possibly have sea-wasp venom on her fingertips?:

:Maybe she's a really messed-up Neptune kid,: Kalli suggests.

:Or maybe someone else has been doing some gene

splicing besides the scientists who created us,: Robry speaks up.

:You mean, someone else got the bright idea of breeding fish-kids?: Lena asks.

:Yeah, that's exactly what I mean,: Robry replies grimly. :I was watching the guy with the extra arms while Nere was talking, and the skin on his face actually changed colors when Ton brought the albacore. I know it sounds crazy, but I think someone spliced some octopus genes into him.:

:Is that possible?: Tobin asks skeptically.

:Is it possible that we're all here with altered eyes that can see in the nighttime ocean and lungs that can breathe seawater?: Robry counters.

:Good point,: Penn says.

I go back to trying to dig more information out of Dai. :Can you tell us anything else about them?:

:Just that you did the right thing to avoid a fight with them.:

:But where do they live? Do they have a base around here?:

:I'm not really sure. I only know I've run across them in these waters before,: he says with his mind so tightly shielded, I'm sure he knows more than he's telling me. But it's clear I'm not going to get anything else out of him for now.

~~~

I'm determined to reach the safety of my father's colony before that mutant gang decides to challenge us again. We swim well into the night until we find a cave. I assign four of us guard shifts throughout the evening. We start off before the sea lightens, and other than a brief encounter with a big sixgill shark that Densil runs off for us, it's a tense but uneventful day.

At sunset, when I figure our position, I realize we should be able to make my father's colony by late tonight if we push hard. Heading down to the rock overhang where we're eating dinner, I frown when I see Dai swimming toward me. I refuse to speak to him first. Over the past few days he's been so short and sarcastic that I don't want to give him a chance to be horrible to me again.

He stops right in front of me, blocking my way to the others. :So, are you happy that you're about to see your dad?: he asks.

:I'm . . . not sure,: I admit, surprised by Dai's abrupt question. :I haven't seen him for two years. He and my mother staged an accident that made my brother and me think he was dead. I cried for months after we lost him. And I can't forget he's part of the reason I'm breathing water right now.:

:Can you forgive him?:

Of course Dai barges straight to the painful heart of the matter.

:I don't know,: I say, glad that I don't have to speak past the sudden lump in my throat.

:If he could hurt you that much, you must love him a lot, which means eventually, you'll end up forgiving him.:

:If you say so.: I shrug.

Dai sends me a crooked smile. :Nere, you're not very good at acting callous. You're all about loving and forgiving. I'm banking on that—that you'll have to forgive me, too, in the end.:

I frown as I try to sort through his words. :You make me sound like some kind of mushy-minded sea cucumber.:

:Just the opposite. I don't know how you can care so much.:

:That's the job they gave me,: I say quickly, hating the fact my cheeks are starting to heat. Why do I always end up blushing around Dai? :I'm supposed to look out for everyone.:

:Nere, they gave you the job because you were already doing it.: Dai sighs and shakes his head. :We could argue about this all night. Instead, I want to ask you a quick favor.:

I look at him suspiciously. :What is it?:

He smiles at me, a real smile with no mockery or anger in it, and my heart begins to thaw.

:Just close your eyes for one minute.:

:All right,: I agree doubtfully, and I make myself close my eyes.

I feel from the currents in the water that he's moved up right in front of me, but I can't tell what he's doing. After half a minute, I can't bear the suspense any longer. I cheat and peek. He's just floating there, staring at my face.

The sadness in his eyes keeps me from teasing him.

:You could just kiss me, you know,: I blurt, and then I can't believe I just said that.

:But I might hurt you again.:

:You didn't really hurt me before.:

:All right. I know I'll be mad at myself later if I don't.: Without touching me anyplace else, he presses one long sweet kiss on my lips, and heads back to the group with a flick of his fins. After barely speaking to me for days, he goes and does this. Being with Dai is like being tossed and spun inside a killer wave.

I take a second to pull myself together and then swim down to the others. As I speak, I try not to look at Dai. :I know we're all worn out, but I think we should keep going. I *really* don't want to run into that Wasp girl and her gang again. We're closer to my father's colony than I realized, and there's a chance we can reach Safety Harbor tonight if we swim hard.:

:I don't want to run into those kids again, either,: Lena says with a shudder, and the rest agree with her.

As I lead off, Dai's kiss tingles on my lips. Swimming through the black ocean, I can't help thinking about Wasp and the strange, angry boys and girls who were with her. They seemed to know we were coming. I wonder if they've stopped and fought other Neptune kids, and why they hated us so much.

James's final words to me, that our father's colony had come under attack, start to make sense. Maybe Wasp and her gang are somehow part of his problems.

Suddenly, Mariah startles me with a frantic call.

:the strange ones are all around us!:

chapter forty-one

I GRAB FOR MY SPEARGUN AS I desperately try to figure out what's happening.

:Nere, those freaky kids are back!: Ree yells.

:Everyone, load your spearguns!: I shout. Chaos erupts as kids with tattooed faces charge at us from every direction. Our brave dolphins rush to protect us. Pulses of searing white light, like intense camera flashes, blind and confuse me. Ree is wrestling furiously with a boy who is trying to wrench her speargun out of her hands. Thom is slugging it out with the big boy with six arms. I take aim at Ree's assailant, but Kona gets in my way.

Through the tumult, I hear Dai shout, :NO! Don't take the little girl!:

I whirl around just in time to see Dai charge right at a tall skinny boy who is holding Bria. The skinny boy lights up brighter than a flare torch, sending out a pulse of light so intense that I have to shut my eyes. When I open them, I see that another boy, one with a tattoo of a lightning bolt on his cheek, is sneaking up behind Dai.

:Watch out, Dai!: I yell. I'd shoot, but I'm afraid I'll hit him. The boy reaches out his hand and places it on Dai's back. I swear I see a bright spark travel from his hand to Dai's body.

Dai convulses violently for several seconds, and his body goes slack. He's unconscious now, or worse—it's like Cam on the beach all over again. I force down my pain and panic and take aim at the boy with the lightning bolt on his cheek. Then a harsh female voice invades my mind.

:Everyone, stop where you are, or I'll kill her!:

I look at Bria and shiver. Wasp has hold of her now. Her ungloved hand is at Bria's neck.

:Mariah, tell the pod to stop attacking,: I order, fear for Bria rising inside me in a choking wave.

:Do you know what I have on my fingertips?: Wasp's amber gaze meets mine.

:I've heard that you have sea-wasp stingers,: I say, fighting to keep my mental voice steady. I swim to Dai's side. I'm relieved to see his eyes flutter open, but he looks dazed.

:That's right. If I sting her on her neck and face, her airway will constrict, and she'll be dead in less than a minute.:

Bria's face is paper white and her hazel eyes are as round as sand dollars as she stares at me beseechingly. She stays absolutely still. I glance at Tobin. His face is even paler than Bria's.

:Should I shoot her?: Robry asks me on a private send.

Robry is hovering a little above me, his expression cool and focused, his speargun already aimed right at Wasp.

:No, her hand is too close to Bria's neck. If you shoot at her and miss, she might kill Bria out of spite.: There's something so angry and twisted in Wasp's eyes, I don't want to push her.

:You show some signs of intelligence, for a Neptune idiot. Even if he did hit me, I'd definitely make sure she died, too.: Wasp sends me a cold smile.

I blink when I realize Wasp just overheard the thoughts I directed only at Robry. She must have a strong inherited telepathic ability like Dai and me.

:Wasp, don't do this. Let the little girl go,: Dai says to her, his mental tone pleading.

:Then stop being so stupid and come home.:

I look from Dai to Wasp and back to Dai again, completely confused. :You know her?:

:Of course he knows me. He's one of us,: Wasp says impatiently. :Now, are you coming, or do I have to hurt her?:

:I'll come,: Dai says with so much anger and bitterness leaking through his mental shields that I wince. Then he looks at me. :I'm sorry, Nere.:

He leaves my side without another word and swims over to the other kids. All I can do is stare after him in disbelief. As soon as he joins their group, Wasp shoves Bria away from her with her gloved hand. Bria darts back to us fast as a frightened minnow, and Tobin catches her in a reassuring hug.

:Dai?: I call out to him, but he won't look at me. His face is more closed than I've ever seen it.

:I'd love to see you again in our own backyard,: Wasp declares with a triumphant glance at me. :Ask your daddy where to find us, and you can come visit Dai whenever you want.:

She backs out into the center of the canyon, her gang gathered around her and Dai, their arsenal of spearguns pointed at us. Moving in a tight formation, the group swims away to the west. I notice that Ton follows them, keeping his distance.

Our frantic dolphins dart back and forth. My human companions cluster around me, talking and arguing about Dai. I feel their confusion. They call him spy and traitor, their angry words pounding at my mind.

:Is everyone okay?: I have to shout mentally to get their attention.

:Penn has a spear-dart cut on his arm, and Kalli has a graze across her ribs,: Tobin reports.

:That mutate with the six arms shot some kind of ink at my face,: Thom says furiously. :My eyes are burning.:

:Mariah, are any of the pod hurt?:

:Mali and Ricca have cuts.:

:All right. Ree and Lena, I want you to help Tobin treat our wounded people. Robry, you keep watch while I look after the dolphins.:

:But what about Dai?: Ree asks.

I turn away from Ree because the last thing I want to do is talk about Dai. :I guess he wasn't who we thought he was,: I reply tightly. :We need to patch everyone up and push on. I think Wasp and her crew got what they wanted.: I can't keep the bitterness from my tone. :But I don't want to risk running into them again.:

After Tobin finishes sewing up Penn and Kalli, he turns to the nasty cut across Ricca's back. I help steady and calm Ricca as he works. The moment he's finished treating her, she flashes away into the dark sea.

:I know I hurt her with those stitches.: Tobin sighs as he packs away his first-aid gear. :I hope she's not going to hold that against me.:

:Mariah made her understand that you were helping her.:

Tobin gives me a steady look. :Nere, I'm sorry about Dai.:

:I can't believe he lied to me,: I burst out. :He lied to all of us.:

:I don't know why he did it, but for what it's worth, I think he really cared about you.:

:That's pretty hard for me to believe right now,: I reply.

I wish Tobin would hug me the way he hugged Bria, but there's been a distance between us ever since my birthing day, and I don't know how to cross it.

Swiftly, we gather everyone together. Swimming with our spearguns loaded, we head out for Safety Harbor.

chapter forty-two

WE HAVE TO TRAVEL SLOWER than usual because we're all exhausted and because of Kalli's and Penn's injuries. Thom's eyes are almost swollen shut, but to my surprise, Lena stays right beside him and acts as his personal guide.

I can't help thinking about Dai as we kick tiredly through the sea. He hinted, more than a few times, that he came from a tough world. But could he really have been part of Wasp's gang? Was he working for them all this time? Why did he find our group and travel with us for so long? Who is Dai, really? And where did those kids come from? I hope my father will have some answers for us.

Midmorning, I ask Kalli, Thom, and Penn if they need to stop and rest for the remainder of the day, but Kalli replies promptly. :We want to keep going. We don't want to run into that gang of mutates again.: Thom and Penn nod firmly to show they're in agreement, and so we continue on.

A few hours later, Sokya rushes back toward me with three dolphins swimming beside her. The strange dolphins circle us curiously.

:more humans like you ahead, and they have dolphins!:

My blood begins to pound in my ears. :Are they like us or like that other group?:

:they feel more like you,: Sokya says confidently, but she always sounds confident.

I alert the rest, fighting to hide my growing fear, and we raise our spearguns just in case. Anxiously, we watch the water ahead. Out of the blue-green sea, six swimmers appear, wearing seasuits and carrying spearguns like ours. Six more dolphins keep pace in a tight formation around them.

A strong, stocky girl is swimming point. She stops just out of speargun range, and so do we. I can tell she's studying us all carefully, including Kalli and Penn and their bandages. The six dolphins surge forward and, moments later, the two pods mix joyfully and swim in dizzying patterns all around us.

:Our dolphins seem very happy to meet yours,: the girl says in a guarded tone, :but I still have to ask you to identify yourselves.:

:My name is Nere Hanson. These are my friends. We're looking for my father, Dr. Mark Hanson.:

The stocky girl lowers her speargun and grins. :The doc's going to be glad to hear this news. We've been on the lookout for you for days now. Welcome to Safety Harbor!:

:Thanks,: I manage to say, surprised by the large lump in my throat. I look at Thom, Penn, Robry, Kalli, Lena, Tobin, Bria, and Ree. We did it. We've finally reached my father's colony.

~ ~ ~

:The doc is topside doing some research in his boat. We can take you to him right now if you'd like,: the girl is saying.

:That'd be great,: I manage to reply.

As we swim, the friendly girl says her name is Janni, and then she introduces her companions. Most of their names just wash over me; I'm too busy thinking about my father. I'm so glad he's alive, but does he know about Gillian? What am I going to say to him after he lied to me about his death and changed my whole life? My stomach has started to twist and churn.

I'm vaguely aware that Lena has moved up beside me, and I'm grateful that she is introducing our group.

We surface near the bow of a small wooden boat. I look up and see my dad. He's busy working on a computer pad. My eyes prickle with tears. He's thinner than I remember, and his brown hair is long and shaggy.

"Hey, Doc, we brought you a present," Janni tells him cheerfully.

My father turns toward us. His brown eyes light up at the sight of me. He stands and jumps right off the bow of his little boat, landing with an awkward splash that makes Janni and her companions laugh.

Moments later he engulfs me in a long, soggy hug. He smells like my dad, and he feels like my dad, and I hug him back as hard as I can.

"Nere, I'm so happy you made it. I'm so glad you're okay," he says over and over again. We start sinking, and suddenly

I remember he can't breathe water. I back away from him a little so he can use his arms to stay afloat.

The next moment, the dolphins are on us, Mariah leading the charge. They crowd closely around my father. He is not telepathic, but Mariah and her family have always loved him.

Our gazes meet across the backs of a dozen happy dolphins. "You know about Gillian?" I ask him, my eyes filling with tears.

A shadow crosses his face. "I do know. A trader got word to me."

"I'm so sorry," I say.

"I'm sorry, too," he says, his voice gone rough. "She'd be so proud of you."

As a daughter or as an experiment? I'm sure my mother the scientist would be proud of what I've done. I love my father, but I know he helped her to change me. Dad puts one arm around my shoulder and another across Mariah's back.

I sigh and lean in to him. For now, I'm just so, so glad to be here.

"You all must be tired," Dad says, and smiles at my companions. "Come see your new home. I'm sure you have lots of adventures to tell us."

His words remind me that I can't relax yet. I slip out from under his arm and turn to face him. "We ran into some bad trouble," I say and explain what happened to us.

His face tightens as I speak, but it's clear he's not surprised by our news.

"Do you know where Dai went with Wasp and her gang?" I ask him.

"I do know," my father replies, his expression grave. "Wasp and her companions were created by a renegade geneticist named Ran Kuron, who left the Neptune Project years ago. He has his own twisted vision for human existence in the sea and can't seem to leave us alone to pursue our own vision. He—" He stops short and shakes his head. "But that's a conversation for another time. Some of you are hurt, and you look exhausted. Follow me, and I'll take you inside Safety Harbor."

He swims around to the stern of his little boat and nimbly climbs aboard. He powers up its electric motor and leads us east. Soon we come to what looks like a wall of bubbles, extending up from the sea floor to the surface. The wall stretches for as far as I can see in either direction, blocking the mouth to an inlet off the strait.

:This is our security system. The bubble wall frightens off sharks and scavenger fish, but trained dolphins have no problems crossing it,: Janni explains.

:It's so simple, it's brilliant,: Robry says as he gazes at the perimeter.

We follow Janni's lead through the bubble wall. For a moment, all I can see is a thousand small bubbles right in front of me. They tickle my nose and chin as they flow past my face. Then I'm through the wall, and I pause to take in Safety Harbor.

The community is spread out across a series of steep rock walls dotted with dark cave openings. The walls are covered with red and pink soft corals, yellow sponges, and feathery white plumose anemones. I blink when I realize that dozens of young people wearing fins are darting back and forth among the caves. Dolphins come and go freely.

Suddenly, we're surrounded by grinning kids, some as young as Bria and Robry, and others who look a little older than Penn and Thom.

:Wow, they seem so happy to see us,: Kalli says.

:We're always glad when more Neptune kids arrive here safely. We all had our own adventures getting here, but we know you came the farthest,: Janni says to me, and I hear the respect in her tone.

Then she turns to the group gathering around us. :Don't mob them, you guys,: she calls out. :You know we'll have a proper welcome dinner and hear their story tonight.:

The kids give a big cheer, and gradually the crowd surrounding us disperses.

Mariah pokes me gently in the stomach to get my attention. :now you are safe, we go to meet the other dolphins.:

:We are safe, thanks to you,: I tell her, and try to project all the love I feel toward her and the pod. She and the rest flash away.

:Are you ready to explore Safety Harbor?: Janni asks us.

:In just a sec.: I swim to the surface to find my father watching for me from his boat. He smiles, but then his gaze grows serious as he studies my face. "I'm glad you're finally here, but I think my little girl has grown up a great deal in the past two years." I hear both pride and a hint of sadness in his voice.

"Are you coming to show us around?"

"I'll be along in a bit, but I need scuba gear to go the places Janni wants to take you."

As I watch him head toward shore in his little boat, I realize with a pang that my father and I truly live in separate worlds now. When I duck under the water, I see that our two groups are starting to mingle. Ree is talking with Janni, and Robry is clowning around with a younger boy from Janni's patrol. I hang back for a moment, taking in all the kids streaming between the caves.

:It does seem like a lot of people after being on our own for so long.: Tobin sends me an understanding glance.

:Are you ready to see your new home?: Janni calls to me.

:I'm more than ready,: I say, and I realize I'm telling the truth. I smile at her and swim forward to join the others.

acknowledgments

WHEN A WRITER with only a BA degree in history decides to tackle a subject as wonderful and complicated as the sea, she needs LOTS of help. I'm grateful to the many people who gave generously of their time, ideas, and knowledge to help me depict the fascinating underwater world of *The Neptune Project*. First of all, I would like to thank Sue Manion, Fishery Biologist (NOAA), for answering my countless questions about fish and the sea; and her husband, Captain John Manion (NOAA), who made sure I got most of the boat parts right. Ron Dotson, Fishery Biologist (NOAA), graciously helped to explain what would and wouldn't grow on the borders of the sunlit zone in the Channel Islands.

I'm likewise grateful to my science consultants, Cindy and Jamie Gay, who patiently taught me genetics, starting with mitosis and meiosis, and had great ideas about Neptune nutrition. Kristin Gonzalez cheerfully answered a dozen phone calls and e-mails on a crazy variety of science topics, and she helped to dream up c-plankton. Her son Ian Straehley gave me some excellent ideas as to how telepathy would really work. Bill Burton was a brilliant help hypothesizing how lasers would react with water. Thanks to Joe Champ for being my lifetime dive buddy and for gamely sampling with me a daunting range of raw seafood, from eel to sea urchin. Josephie Jackson, thank you for your enthusiasm for the whole Neptune premise; and Dr. David Jackson, thanks for the virus-shot vector and so many good suggestions about Neptune biology. Corinne McCarthy, I so appreciate your making sure I got all the medical stuff right. Sharon Trent, thank you for being such a wonderful listener.

To my readers Lou Ann Bode, Jane Champ, Nolan Crosson, Corinne McCarthy, Bobby and Toby Wright, Sue, John, and Kevin Manion; Alyson, Katie, and Jake McFarland; Pacia Wojcik, Ned Ryan, and Hema Penmetsa— your feedback and enthusiasm kept me going during the nerve-racking wait before the book was acquired. Of course I need to thank the most supportive ole critique group south of the Red River: Robert Eilers, Pam McWilliams, Hillary Ralles, and Joe Chicoskie—your insights made this a much, much better book. Here's a special shout-out to Brenda Quinn, freelance editor extraordinaire, who keeps trying to teach me to use em dashes properly and has hugely improved every story she's edited for me. And thank you, Maria Isabell Cruz, for all your help with Spanish translations.

I'm indebted to the wonderful staff at the Channel Islands National Marine Sanctuary. Robert Schwemmer, Cultural Resources Coordinator, was terrific about sharing his incredible dive photographs and knowledge; and Laura

Francis, Education Coordinator, thank you for answering my questions about the marine life that grows on and in wrecks. Thank you both for the great work you do to protect such a unique natural gem.

I'm grateful to the following women for answering my many questions about dolphin behavior: Mary Stella, Director of Media and Marketing at the Dolphin Research Center; and Julie Richardson and Holli Byerly at Dolphins Plus.

To Cyrus Ghaznavi, emergency software consultant—thank you for being there when I needed you!

I'm grateful to Seth Fishman for his excellent taste in literature, and even more so to my fabulous and kind agent, Doug Stewart. He made my dream of writing for kids come true and manages my energy and enthusiasm with great diplomacy. I'm indebted to Lisa Yoskowitz, my brilliant editor, who probably now knows more about dolphins and giant squid than she ever really wanted to know.

And to the members of my tolerant and loving family, who understand that my cooking gets even worse when I'm writing: you guys are the best!